Gavin watched a
Silve

The morning sunshine highlighted her hair, and he thought of angels. The imagery struck him as ironic, especially considering the fact that Claudia Parrish was as likely a suspect as anyone in the ongoing corruption within the Homicide Unit. After all, the evidence tampering hadn't ended when her partner's life had. And the most recent involved one of Claudia's own cases.

Gavin hadn't been surprised to learn of Judge Warner's dismissal of the Brown case. Reports of the missing gun were in the file his lieutenant had handed him weeks ago—a thick file that made Claudia Internal Affair's prime suspect.

After five years on IAD, he prided himself on his ability to read people. Claudia Parrish, however, wasn't easy to read. Either her defensiveness was an honest response, or there was more behind the sharp tone she'd adopted with him earlier.

He definitely had to be careful. He couldn't afford to alienate Claudia. Not when he needed to get close to her—close enough to find out the truth.

FALLING FOR HIM
Morgan Hayes

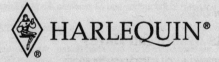

TORONTO • NEW YORK • LONDON
AMSTERDAM • PARIS • SYDNEY • HAMBURG
STOCKHOLM • ATHENS • TOKYO • MILAN • MADRID
PRAGUE • WARSAW • BUDAPEST • AUCKLAND

ISBN 0-373-70886-6

FALLING FOR HIM

Visit us at www.romance.net

Printed in U.S.A.

For Lynette.

Also...

To The Hutch—I'd be lost without you gals!

To Jackie Navin and the rest of my stunning critique group.

And with very heartfelt thanks to Sgt. Steve Lehmann
of BPD Homicide—a *real* hero.
And to the rest of the guys on the Unit:
Mike, Cliff, Bill, Homer, Wayne, Joe and too many others
to mention. You know I love you guys!

PROLOGUE

CLAUDIA KNEW HE WAS DEAD even before she'd brought her car to a skidding stop along that cold, dark street. She knew the second she heard the Federal Hill address crackle over the police radio. Her mind refused to grasp the idea, but in her heart, through her entire body, she felt it, as surely as if a part of herself had died.

The ambulance, the half-dozen squad cars with their revolving lights, and then the crime-scene van parked outside the two-story row house confirmed her fears.

Frank was dead.

Claudia leaped from the car, hardly registering the sharp pellets of icy rain slapping her face as she made her way through an already gathering crowd and ducked under the yellow crime-scene tape.

"Detective Claudia Parrish," she said, giving the officer barely a second to acknowledge the silver shield she flashed, before mounting the front steps two at a time.

The stairwell seemed tighter than usual, hot, with a cloying mustiness that she didn't recall in all the times she'd been up here. She was out of breath before she reached the top-floor apartment, but it wasn't the two flights that had winded her. It was shock. It closed around her chest like a fist, clenching steadily until she thought each gasp might be her last.

Frank.

Even the entrance of the apartment didn't seem right—it felt cramped and narrow. The splintered door, half-off its hinges, displayed the force that had been used to gain entrance.

The world tilted briefly, and she lifted her hand, about to catch herself against the ruined doorjamb. But she stopped. This was a crime scene. Instead, she buried her hands deep in the pockets of her trench coat. Not that it mattered—they would find her prints all over the apartment anyway.

"Detective Parrish," she heard one officer say. Surprise lifted his tone as she stepped past him and several other uniformed officers.

"Come on, guys. Clear out." She recognized Sergeant Gunning's growling voice from farther back in the apartment. "It's getting crowded in here. Everyone out except the techs, all right? Now."

She moved through the apartment, each stride shakier than the last, until she drew near the open bedroom door. Frank's bedroom.

He was dead. But she still expected to hear *his* voice above the others, analyzing the scene—after all, he was the squad's best.

There was the bright flare of a camera's bulb, the high-pitched whine of its recharge, and then another flash. Sergeant Gunning's hulking figure filled the doorway, his head bowed and shaking in disbelief.

I shouldn't have left you last night, Frank. The

thought tumbled through her mind, over and over. *I should have been listening instead of arguing. Instead of accusing. I should have believed you. Should have trusted you.*

She stopped in the doorway, her gaze involuntarily drawn past the crime-scene technicians to the corner beside the bed. She caught a glimpse of his white leather sneakers, and the first wave of nausea churned in her stomach.

She must have gasped, because Sergeant Gunning turned to face her.

"Oh, damn. Claudia. What are you doing here?"

"I heard…on the radio…"

Her sergeant's exclamation alerted the others of her presence. They parted. And then Claudia saw him.

She took one unsteady step forward. Sergeant Gunning's hand settled on her shoulder for a brief moment, as if intending to hold her back. But he didn't.

"Frank." His name didn't echo only in her thoughts. Claudia heard her own voice, thin and wavering, fill the sudden silence. Her breath shortened, and her heart raced as she took in the scene.

Nothing, not ten years in uniform and another two in Homicide, could have prepared Claudia for seeing her own partner sprawled across the carpeted floor.

Even as she stood over his body, she expected him to move. It couldn't be Frank's lifeless body lying there, dressed in blue jeans and a T-shirt…the Baltimore Ravens T-shirt she'd bought him just last month. But it was. Claudia choked back a sob and struggled against another rush of queasiness. She tried to focus, process this like any other crime scene.

Detach. Put your emotions aside. Think like a detective, Frank would have advised her.

Claudia scanned the room. There was no indication of a struggle. The bed was made with Frank's suit laid on it for work. His pager and cell phone were on the dresser, and his shoulder holster hung over the back of the chair next to it. Empty. The 9mm police-issue Glock was in Frank's hand instead.

"No signs of forced entry," Claudia heard Gunning say behind her. "The boys had to use the ram to get in when no one answered. Neighbors reported the gunfire. Claudia? You gonna be all right?"

Her knees threatened to buckle as a numbness crept over her. She lowered herself to kneel next to Frank.

"No one was seen entering or leaving the apartment," Sergeant Gunning went on. "Couple people heard the shot less than an hour ago and called it in. We're going to conduct a thorough canvass, but…it doesn't look like…"

Sarge's voice faded from her awareness. As did the rest of the room and the people around her. She *couldn't* detach. It wasn't possible. This wasn't just another victim.

This was Frank. Her partner of two years, her best friend…

The edges of her vision blurred until there was only Frank. Her hands shook when she reached for him. Part of her knew she shouldn't touch him, but no one in that room would dare to stop her.

The sob Claudia had fought so hard to contain escaped at last. His hand was still warm as though there was life. She caressed it, turning it over and sweeping her fingers across his broad palm, feeling its softness. Strong hands, yet lovingly gentle, she thought, remembering how they had felt on her body, how they'd touched her and held her in a way no other man ever had.

She lifted his hand to her face and pressed it against her cheek. There was the faint trace of after-shave—the same smell she'd woken to this morning, lingering on her sheets from the day before...before their argument.

I'm sorry, Frank. I'm sorry I didn't listen. Sorry I didn't believe you. I should have been here.

She squeezed his hand, half-expecting a response. His hair was mussed, and she had to force herself not to brush her fingers through it. It was getting long again, she thought. He needed a cut.

She was about to touch his face when someone grasped her shoulders.

"I'm sorry, Claudia. You can't."

She started to resist the person pulling her away, until she looked up. She recognized Lori Tobin from the crime lab.

"We're not finished," she told Claudia with an apologetic expression. "I'm really sorry." Her whisper was sincere, and Claudia only vaguely noticed the woman's sympathetic touch as she guided her to one side. For Claudia, there was only Frank.

She wanted to cry. No, she wanted to scream. She

wanted to touch him, to hold him, to feel him with her once again—alive.

The fist around her chest clenched tighter, and Claudia swallowed hard against the bitterness that crept up her throat. She straightened her shoulders. She had to pull herself together. Frank would want that, she thought. He'd want her to be strong. To be professional, and to keep up appearances.

"This isn't what it looks like," she managed to say, fighting the tremble in her voice.

"There's nothing to make us think otherwise," Gunning argued. "The door was locked from the inside. There's no sign of a struggle."

"This is not what it looks like," she repeated, trying to convince herself against what was so painfully obvious.

"We've got a single shot, with a contact wound to his right temple." Gunning placed one broad hand on her shoulder, but it did nothing to calm her whirling emotions as suspicion prickled along her neck. "I'm sorry, Claudia. I know you don't want to believe Frank could have done this. No one does."

"He didn't kill himself, Sarge."

"Claudia—"

"I know Frank."

"His own gun's in his hand, Claudia. Don't do this."

"Don't do *what?*" She stepped away from him. "Frank did *not* kill himself. There's something not right here. Something…I don't know what, but this just doesn't *feel* right."

She shook her head and then madly scanned the

room once more. This *wasn't* right. When her gaze found Frank's body again, there was the hot sting of tears. She clenched her jaw to dam them.

"He wouldn't do this. It's not his way. I know him, Sarge. I *know* Frank." Better than any of them did. Better than any of them even realized. He was more than just her partner. More than her best friend. Frank was her lover, the one person she cherished more than life. And now...

What am I supposed to do, Frank? Tell me what I'm supposed to do? This time, when Claudia tried to lower herself to Frank, needing to feel his warmth once more before it was gone from his body forever, Sergeant Gunning held her back. And this time, nothing could stop the tears.

CHAPTER ONE

IT WAS HER LAST SHIFT of a week on midnights. Claudia glanced up from the file on her desk and out the windows of the sixth-floor Homicide offices. At five o'clock the city hall dome was taking on the first rosy reflections of the morning sun. Her optimism grew. The squad might just make it through the night without a call. One more hour and the next shift would be in to relieve them. Then she could go home to a long-awaited and well-deserved bath, and finally to bed.

Claudia stretched. She'd been up twenty hours straight, and every muscle was stiff with fatigue. From the main office around the corner where the rest of her squad had spent the night in front of the TV, she heard the early-morning news. Again she prayed for the phone not to ring.

If memory served her, she actually had the weekend off. And she planned to make it two glorious sleep-filled days. Turning back to her desk, Claudia confirmed her schedule on the wall calendar. Had she not looked, she probably wouldn't have taken note of the day. October 16, the anniversary of their first kiss.

It hardly seemed an entire year ago. She could still

recall the scent of Frank's aftershave. Throughout their two-year partnership in Homicide she'd smelled it on him, but on that particular night, his very ordinary aftershave had suddenly become intensely arousing. She remembered the feel of his hand and the taste of his kiss, with the subtle hint of red wine. But then, it wasn't a kiss easily forgotten, Claudia decided as images of that initial encounter whispered through her memory. And definitely not a night easily forgotten—filled with tenderness and passion, deep love and mutual respect. And the two brief months that followed had been the best in her life.

Claudia cast her gaze to the desk abutting hers. Frank's desk—clean, neat…empty. After ten months, it continued to be unassigned, in part because of budgetary constraints, but primarily because it remained a silent memorial. Sarge had cleared out any necessary papers, but the rest went untouched. Even the calendar blotter was still there, left at last December, as though time had stopped after Frank's death.

But hadn't it? Hadn't time stopped for Claudia since that night?

She glanced at the stack of open case files on her desk. Her work had certainly gone on, even if her life hadn't. There had been no easy answers, no real way to deal with the loss. She'd spent weeks after Frank's death arguing with herself and with others in the unit that he wasn't capable of suicide, that Frank Owens wasn't a quitter. It wouldn't have mattered how intensely Internal Affairs had hounded him with their false allegations of evidence tampering, Claudia had contended. Frank had withstood the pressure and could have continued doing so. He would have pulled through IAD's investigation, untainted, proved innocent and, most of all, alive.

Yet, as the months slipped by and the inquiry into his death had come to a conclusion, even Claudia had begun to wonder if Frank *had* been a quitter. She'd wanted to believe he'd been murdered, but in the end, she'd only been wasting time and energy searching for a nonexistent killer. The final reports hadn't lied; the facts were there in black and white— *suicide.*

With no evidence proving otherwise, Claudia had found herself reevaluating the superb detective she'd known, the strong man she'd loved.

Claudia looked to his desk again, the empty chair, his folded reading glasses and an unopened box of Cracker Jacks that no one would even think about touching. In a way, she blamed herself; she should have listened to Frank that last time she'd seen him, when they'd argued about IAD's unrelenting pressure. Maybe then she would have seen the signs.

But she couldn't hold herself entirely responsible for Frank's suicide, Claudia thought, leaning back in her chair and closing her eyes. Internal Affairs was as much to blame—especially whoever had suspected Frank in the first place. If they'd done their job properly, the allegations would have been cleared up quickly, and the *real* person behind the evidence tampering would have been caught.

Instead, the department, the entire force, had let Frank take the fall. His suicide had sealed a guilty verdict in the minds of his co-workers and allowed the true perpetrator to go free.

Yes, IAD had pulled that trigger as surely as Frank had, Claudia decided long ago. And if there had been any way for her to find out exactly *who* had headed the inquiry into the corruption, she would have.

She'd tried early on. But from the start the IAD probe had been hush-hush. It had taken weeks of rumors before anyone even knew what it was IAD was looking into, and no one could identify the lead investigator. Not that it was general practice to publicize that kind of information. But usually with a few well placed questions to someone who knew someone else, an answer could be had. In this instance, however, Claudia had been met with nothing but closed doors and tight lips.

"Are you still alive back here?"

"Not really," she said, her eyes shut. "You wanna call Homicide or should I?"

Tony Santoro laughed softly. Claudia heard the hard-soled click of his shoes as he crossed the room. And when she opened her eyes, she watched a playful smile brighten his usually careworn expression. After six years with the unit, there was no denying the job had taken its toll on Tony's otherwise handsome face. Dark circles under his eyes and deepening creases along his forehead were telltale signs of the long shifts and too much overtime.

Frank had begun to take on that appearance, Claudia recalled. And when she glanced in a mirror she'd be greeted with similar features. It was definitely a hazard of the job.

Tony perched on the corner of her desk. "You *do* look sorta dead, Parrish. Why don't I call it in?" he joked. "Any suspects?"

"Sure. You can start with the State's Attorney Office."

"Oh yeah, you had the Brown arraignment yesterday."

Claudia nodded. "Not that it made any difference. Brown's out on the streets right now, probably shooting someone else."

"I heard they dismissed it. I'm sorry."

She straightened in her chair and closed the Brown file, wondering why she'd even bothered to look at it again. Just another drug-related shooting.

"Oh well," she said. "I guess that's what happens when you can't manage something as simple as maintaining a murder weapon. Without it, the State's Attorney Office had no case."

"It's not your fault."

"No? It was my investigation. The evidence was *my* responsibility."

Tony moved behind her and lowered his hands to her shoulders, gently massaging out the knots of tension for her. He seemed to recognize that no words were necessary. It had been ongoing and completely random—missing or tampered-with evidence. And, according to IAD, the source wasn't Evidence Control. Claudia wasn't the only detective in Homicide who had fallen victim to it. Even Frank, with all his careful work, had had three cases thrown out at the arraignment stage because of lost evidence. No doubt, this had been the reason IAD had targeted Frank.

Still, for Claudia, losing a case because of "misplaced" evidence was not something she ever figured would happen to her.

Obviously aware of the topic's sensitivity, Tony changed it. "By the way, since you've been holed up back here working on your files all night, I bet you didn't know the new guy was in."

"New guy?"

"Yeah. Monaghan."

"I thought he was with the other shift."

"He was until today. He switched over. Been in Sarge's office for about three hours. Swapping war stories. Sounds like he's got some heavy-duty experience under his belt."

"Oh, please. Are we talking about the same guy? Just finished a stint driving the commissioner's car?"

"Yeah, for a year. But who can blame him for taking a cushy job after eight years with DEA, and several before that with Homicide in D.C. That's pretty heavy-duty, if you ask me."

Claudia nodded. Obviously she'd been too buried in her own work these past few weeks to catch enough of the rumors circulating the unit.

"So I guess this means Sarge is counting on Monaghan's vast experience to boost our clearance rates, hmm?"

"Oh, no, Detective Parrish," Tony said with comedic flourish as he reclaimed his position on the corner of her desk. "We've got *you* to do that for us."

Claudia gave him a sarcastic smile and started putting her files away.

"So what do you think?" Tony asked, stretching his arms over his head. "Ready to pack it in? Other squad should be here soon. Guess we're not going to get a call now."

His words still hung on the last shred of silence in the office before it was shattered by the warbling ring of the phone.

"Kiss of death, Tony. You do it every time," Claudia muttered as she reached for the receiver. "Homicide. Detective Parrish."

Sure enough, it was a call. Over the phone, Central Dispatching gave Claudia the details, and by the time she had jotted down the address, she glanced up to see Sergeant Gunning enter the room.

"All right. We're on our way." Hanging up, she wheeled back her chair and stood. "Five hundred block of Boston Street," she told her sergeant. "White male. Looks to be a shooting."

"Do you want me to take it, Sarge?" Tony asked. "I think Claudia here is running on empty."

Under normal circumstances, Claudia would already have been out the door, but today "running on empty" hardly began to describe her exhaustion.

"No," Gunning responded at last, scratching at what had to be two-days' worth of stubble. "I want Claudia on this one."

She kept her groan to herself. Then again, it wasn't as if she couldn't use the extra work to keep her mind off other things.

"I'm on it, Sarge." She took her gun from her

desk drawer and holstered it, shoved a fresh notepad into her jacket pocket and started for the door. "I'll just get my coat and—"

"And take Monaghan with you," he added.

Claudia stopped dead. "Pardon me?"

"You heard me. You're partnering up."

"Sarge, I haven't partnered on a case since—"

"I know. That's why I want you to take Monaghan."

"Uh, Sarge," Tony interrupted, obviously hoping to rescue Claudia. "Look, why don't I go with Claudia on this one. We'll get it wrapped up before breakfast and be done with it."

Gunning shook his head. "This isn't Claudia's case. It's Monaghan's. I want you to back him up, Claudia."

"You're assigning *Monaghan* as the primary detective?" She tried to curb the disbelief in her voice. "Come on, Sarge, he's only just started with the squad. You can't honestly tell me that he's ready to lead his own investigation."

And then, as if on cue, a man stepped around the corner. He cleared his throat quietly, and Claudia felt the immediate flush of embarrassment warm her cheeks.

There was no doubt in her mind regarding the man's identity. In fact, he even *looked* the part of the commissioner's driver, so clean-cut and crisp that she could easily imagine him in some chauffeur's monkey suit. Immediately Claudia found herself hoping Tony was right about Monaghan's experience, because the man bore little resemblance to a seasoned detective who'd reputedly been run ragged by Drug Enforcement and Homicide.

With his jet-black hair clipped short, the angular lines of his face seemed even more pronounced—regal, almost. They accentuated a strong jaw and square chin.

He towered over Claudia, and as he looked down at her, his mouth curved into a charismatic smile. But it was Monaghan's eyes that riveted Claudia. They were absolutely penetrating, and every bit as dark as the brows that arched over them in an almost expectant expression. It was obvious he'd heard her last remark.

"Claudia, Gavin Monaghan," Gunning introduced. "Gavin, this is our illustrious Detective Parrish. You can just ignore the foot in her mouth. And don't let her give you any grief. If she does, I don't wanna hear about it."

Monaghan extended his hand in greeting. "It's good to meet you, Claudia."

She should have anticipated his smooth voice. It matched his looks, rich and seductive. The kind of voice that probably swept most women off their feet at the mere sound, Claudia decided, returning his firm handshake with one she hoped would make him flinch. He didn't.

"Sergeant Gunning's told me a lot about you."

"Well, maybe you'll get to hear my side of the story sometime," she said quickly, wishing she could break her gaze from his. "But right now, I have…I mean, *we* have a homicide."

"I'll get our coats," he offered, turning on the heel

of one perfectly polished black wing-tip oxford. His stride was assured as he walked down the corridor. She watched him, unable to resist admiring the impressive outline of his body, his broad shoulders and tapered waist. The expensive suit looked good on him, she decided. Probably better than any monkey suit. Then again, with a body like that, Gavin Monaghan probably looked good in just about anything.

"He needs to get his feet wet," Sarge said, as Claudia saw Gavin veer into the main office out of sight. "He's put in his time with Homicide in D.C. In fact, I'm sure he could even teach *you* a few tricks, but I still want you to show him the ropes around here."

As though foreseeing the impending argument, Tony mumbled something and made a hasty exit.

"Sarge—"

"No, Claudia." He held up one thick hand. "No arguments. I've catered to your wishes long enough. You know this unit works on the premise of partnerships. I can't exclude you from that any longer. It's time. You gotta put the past behind you. You're working with Monaghan."

In his hard, gray-eyed stare, Claudia recognized that protest would get her nowhere. She took a deep breath and adjusted her suit jacket. "Fine. I'll show Monaghan the ropes."

Sergeant Gunning gave her a solemn nod. "I'm expecting you to make this partnership work," he told her over his shoulder as he left for his office.

Optimism, Claudia thought as she watched Gavin Monaghan step into the corridor again. She'd give him the benefit of the doubt, and with any luck he'd prove to her that all his experience counted for something.

He held her trench coat in one hand and clipped his holster with the other as he joined her. "I've got the keys," he said, heading for the elevators. "I'll drive."

AT FIVE IN THE MORNING, with minimal city traffic, it took only fifteen minutes to drive from Central to the Eastern District. Still those minutes seemed like an hour for Claudia. She wondered if she should apologize to Monaghan. He'd been silent during the entire drive, and no doubt he'd stay that way unless she spoke first.

She snatched another quick glance at him, as she had throughout the drive, then cleared her throat. "Listen, Gavin, about what I said back in the office... I should probably explain."

"Hey, you don't owe me an explanation." He flashed her a look of apparent understanding. "I've been around long enough. I know no one likes being saddled with the new guy until he's proved himself."

Claudia felt another twinge of regret. "Actually, that's not the real reason I objected. Honestly. I know you're not a rookie. It's just—"

"No, but you probably think I'm burned-out. Driving the commissioner's car around for the past year doesn't exactly give people a lot of confidence in my abilities."

Studying his chiseled profile in the soft shadows of morning, Claudia had to admit she appreciated his candor.

Gavin slowed the white unmarked Lumina at a red light, double-checked for traffic and accelerated through the intersection. "Look, if it makes you feel better," he said, "I promise you won't be stuck picking up after me on this investigation. But there's something else, right?"

He caught her quick glance this time.

"You can't escape the rumors," he continued. "I'm aware that you've refused to work with anyone else on the squad since your partner died."

"You mean since my partner shot himself, don't you?"

"I was trying to be tactful."

"Well, if we're going to be partners, you don't need tact. Besides, I've dealt with it."

She directed her gaze out the windshield and saw the sign for Boston Street zip past them. "You missed the street," she said, and Gavin braked. "I guess the Commissioner never had much need to come out to this armpit of the city, hmm?"

She caught the enticing amusement in his glance before he turned the Lumina around. "All I'm saying is I respect the fact that you prefer working alone. It seems to me Gunning is determined to partner us up, but if you're going to have a problem working with me, perhaps we should speak to him together. I can certainly handle a homicide on my own."

"Oh right, and you actually believe you'll get out of working with me that easily? I don't think so. If you screw up, it'll be *me* taking the grief from Sarge." She wasn't sure why she said it; she should have welcomed Gavin's offer to work on his own, to relieve her of playing his shadow on every move in this investigation. Perhaps it was that honesty and candor of his, but for the first time in months, the idea of working with a partner—particularly Gavin Monaghan—was beginning to have appeal. Besides which, as Sarge said, it was time. And what *better* time to put Frank behind her than on the day of their anniversary. Not to mention the fact that maybe she *could* learn a thing or two from Gavin.

The north side of the five-hundred block of Boston Street was lined with aging row houses, some boarded up, others literally crumbling to the sidewalk. The south side of the seemingly deserted street was dominated by the old Marmack Bed & Mattress Company, a weather-beaten red-brick warehouse that had been converted, apparently unsuccessfully, into a series of offices. Parked outside the building's main entrance were a couple of police cruisers, and Claudia realized that in the time it had taken her to argue with Sarge about Gavin, the crime-scene unit had got the jump on them.

Gavin pulled to the curb, and Claudia was out the door before he'd taken the key from the ignition. In moments he was at her side, his long stride keeping easy pace with hers as they headed down the sidewalk to the main doors. She directed another glance at him, half-expecting to find Frank at her side. It felt odd, she thought, responding to a scene with someone else.

And she wasn't the only one who seemed to think so. The uniformed officer who greeted them at the door—a young rookie she recognized from previous scenes—gave her a quizzical look, obviously surprised to see her with someone.

"Detective Parrish." His greeting had a questioning lilt.

"Hey, Marty. How's it going?"

"Good." He touched the brim of his cap and then eyed Gavin.

"This is Detective Monaghan. He's in charge."

"Oh."

"Can you tell us what we've got? Or is it a surprise today?"

"Nah. No surprises. Looks like a shooting," he said. "Maybe a burglary gone wrong. Who knows? That's *your* job, Detective."

"Do we have a name on our victim?"

"Early-morning cleaning staff found him. They verify it's James Silver. Runs a PI business." He pointed to the Silver Investigations sign in the only lit window on the first floor.

Claudia nodded slowly, muttering a thank-you, and started for the doors. *James Silver.* A numbness came over her. She struggled to cover the reaction, but it didn't work.

Gavin put a hand on her arm, stopping her in the foyer. "What is it, Claudia? You okay?"

She straightened her shoulders. "Yeah. Of course. I'm fine."

"Do you know this guy? James Silver?"

She looked down the hall to the sign over the PI's door.

"Claudia?" he prompted her again.

"Yeah," she said at last, and headed toward the open doorway. "Yeah, I know him."

CHAPTER TWO

"CLAUDIA, WAIT." Gavin put his hand on her shoulder and spun her around to face him.

Almost immediately he regretted doing so. The second she lifted her gaze to meet his, Gavin felt as though the corridor had suddenly become too narrow. She stood close enough that he caught the residual traces of her perfume. He'd smelled it in the car, as well—something seductively intimate, with the slightest hint of jasmine. But at least while driving, he hadn't been challenged by the added allure of staring directly into those captivating gray-green eyes.

Those same eyes had caught him by surprise when she'd first looked at him, back at headquarters. Sure, he'd studied the photo in her file: he'd stared at it for the past five weeks—a newspaper clipping taken from the *Baltimore Sun* two years ago when she'd been presented with the Maryland Officer of the Year award.

The faded black-and-white photo hadn't done justice to the vibrant golden highlights in her hair or the glow of her perfect skin. But in the picture, Claudia had been smiling, and in the weeks he had studied her file, Gavin had imagined seeing that lush smile in person. Instead, there was concern on her face; it furrowed lines across her forehead and tightened her mouth as she gazed up at him.

"What is it?" she asked.

"This guy Silver. You *know* him?"

"I told you, yes."

"Well, maybe you shouldn't be here then."

"If it's a conflict of interest you're worried about, Gavin, forget it. I met the man a couple of times, but haven't seen him since January. He was an acquaintance at best."

Gavin wondered if the subtle twitch at the corner of her right eye indicated a lie. "You're sure about this?"

"I'm sure. Now are you coming in or do I have to conduct your investigation?"

She slipped her arm from his grasp, and her trench coat whirled in the air behind her as she turned once more. Gavin watched her and wondered how it was that someone who stood barely five foot five in heels could command such presence.

It shouldn't have surprised him though, he thought. After all, her file was chock-full of commendations and an endless stream of laudatory reviews from her sergeants, past and present. And besides the award, there had been the bronze star four years ago. Gavin had been impressed from the moment his lieutenant had handed him her file back in the Internal Affairs offices.

"Okay, guys, what have we got?" Claudia's voice interrupted his thoughts.

He watched her pull a notepad and pen from her pocket and then just as quickly shove them back in, obviously remembering her role as the secondary detective on the scene.

"This is Detective Monaghan." She gestured an introduction. "He's the primary, so any details you've got go to him."

She wasn't liking this one bit, Gavin decided. It wasn't her case, she wasn't in control, and she hated that fact. Frustration appeared to stiffen her stance.

But when she stood over the victim, Claudia's expression softened. In his years on patrol, then in Narcotics and finally Internal Affairs, Gavin had seen his share of violent deaths. It struck him now, however, that he'd never worked one with a woman. As Claudia studied the body of James Silver, a look of compassion seemed to wash over her face. It was a look rarely seen on the faces of seasoned detectives, and Gavin couldn't help wondering if there was, in fact, more to her relationship with Silver than she'd admitted.

She hadn't clarified the context in which she knew the private investigator. And then, as Gavin scanned the PI's office, he saw the Baltimore Police cap on one bookshelf and the framed academy diploma on the wall.

He joined her, lowering his voice to a whisper. "Tell me how you know this guy."

"This isn't the time, Gavin." Her response was barely audible, her focus never leaving the body crumpled in the corner amid a scattering of files.

"He was a cop. Did you work with him?"

She didn't respond.

"Because if you worked with him, you know Sarge will have to take you off—"

She turned on him, a flare of impatience in her eyes as her whisper sharpened. "I *told* you, I hardly knew him. Now, are you going to take charge here, or do I have to?"

"Fine." He withdrew his own notebook from his pocket, flipped to a fresh page and clicked his pen. "I want you to start by getting the report from the responding officer, and then arrange for an initial canvass of the area. After that, I need you to interview the custodial staff. Talk to whoever found him, see what they know about his hours, if they saw or heard anything. Do you think you can handle that, Detective Parrish?"

It was clear Claudia hadn't expected him to take such swift authority. She stared at him for a moment, and Gavin wondered if it was a smile that tugged at the corner of her lips instead of the indignation he'd expected.

Then she gave him a subtle nod. "That's more like it, Detective Monaghan."

THE MEDICAL EXAMINER HAD removed Silver's body at six o'clock, and by seven the crime-scene technicians appeared to have breakfast in mind as they hurried to wrap up their work. She and Gavin had been on the scene for close to two hours now, and throughout Claudia had watched him. She couldn't deny that she was impressed.

Gavin's command of the scene had been almost immediate. As Claudia had spoken to the responding officer and waited for him to write up his report, Gavin had stood over Silver's body for the longest time, both hands buried deep in the pockets of his trench coat. At first, Claudia had wondered if perhaps he'd forgotten his past work. Then she'd seen how carefully his gaze scrutinized the area, locking on details, assessing the surroundings, studying the position and condition of the body, until he'd finally moved on to talk to the ME at length.

Obviously a one-year stint chauffeuring the brass around had not robbed him of his experience. The investigation was in capable hands. And yet, if there had been any way for *her* to take the case, Claudia would have jumped at the opportunity.

From the moment she'd heard James Silver's name, she'd wanted this one. She hadn't lied to Gavin about knowing James Silver, about meeting him. It *had* been only twice, but Silver had been more than the ''acquaintance'' she'd told Gavin he was. He'd been a good friend of Frank's, and his partner on patrol years ago in the Eastern District. It had been a decade since Silver had worn a uniform, yet his friendship with Frank had remained loyal.

She knew enough about James Silver to know he'd been a good man, a good cop, and a good friend to Frank. So good, that he was the one person who may never have been convinced by the evidence indicating Frank's suicide. She hadn't spoken with Silver since three weeks after Frank's death. It had been a brief phone call, and they'd done nothing but argue: Claudia explaining the evidence, and Silver determined to dispute it.

Seeing Silver now—shot dead in his own office, lying behind his desk, his chair toppled, and his files and drawers rifled through as though his death was only an inconsequential result of a burglary gone awry—Claudia regretted that last contact with the PI.

Maybe she should have listened to his theories. But at the time, she'd been attempting to resign herself to the truth and come to terms with her loss of Frank. Silver's disbelief had been more than she'd been able to bear. Now she would always wonder what theories Silver had concerning Frank's death. And she would wonder if he'd ever given up.

"How's the canvass going?" Gavin came to her side, flipping his notebook closed and lifting a hand to loosen his tie a notch.

"Nothing yet. Half the row homes across the street are vacant. And with the few that aren't, it's not looking as if anyone heard anything. We've got officers still knocking on doors, but I wouldn't hold your breath."

He nodded to where Silver's body had lain. "So what do you think?"

"I'm sorry, Detective, that's not how this works. You're the primary. What do *you* think?"

He contemplated the scene again before speaking. "Well, I'd have to say that he was most likely seated at his desk when his attacker arrived. Perpetrator came through the door, probably already had his gun out, and fired as soon as Silver looked up. One bullet caught him in the left shoulder, and the second took him in the chest as he started to stand. Considering Silver's background as a cop, he either knew his as-

sailant and was surprised, or the shots were fired rapidly, giving him no time to take cover or return fire.
His own weapon is still in his desk drawer.

"As for the disarray of the office," Gavin went
on, "it has the appearance of a random burglary, but
my gut feeling is that our perpetrator was looking for
something specific. Then again, until I find out what
kind of stickler Silver was for organization, I can't
rule out the fact that some of this might be the usual
state of his office. It doesn't help that he didn't have
a secretary. Even if something *was* missing, we're
not likely to know about it."

"You got a real whodunit here, Detective Monaghan," Claudia told him, scanning the office again,
hoping she'd missed some obscure yet crucial clue.
"Hardly the kind of case you'd want to start with,
I'd say."

"What are you suggesting? That I can't handle it?
That I should give this case over to you and wait for
the next one?"

Claudia shrugged casually. If she appeared too eager to take over his investigation, he was *sure* to
balk. "All I'm saying is that for your first homicide
in this city—your first case on the board—you're better off with one that's going to go down. This...I
don't know. It could be a tough one. You've got a
dead PI. A former cop. He probably has a list of
enemies longer than your arm, not to mention the
fact that you've got zero witnesses so far."

She dared to glance up then. Was it amusement
she saw sparkle in those dark eyes?

"You really want this case, don't you?"

"Not necessarily," she lied. "It's just probably not the ideal case to get your feet wet."

His smile broadened. "Well, why don't you let *me* worry about my own feet, okay?"

"Claudia." Lori Tobin called to her, and Claudia was grateful for the interruption. She wasn't sure how long she would have been able to hold Gavin's penetrating stare.

She turned as Lori crossed the office to join them. The younger woman snapped off a pair of latex gloves and wadded them into one hand. She tucked a stray wisp from her dark ponytail behind one ear.

"How are you doing, Claudia?" As usual with Lori, the question was more than simple courtesy. Her sincerity and concern was punctuated with a hand on Claudia's arm. The gesture reminded Claudia of that night ten months ago.

Lori had guided Claudia from Frank's bedroom to the living room and then consoled her. She had even phoned a couple of times to check on her afterward. In fact, Claudia had almost admitted the truth about her relationship with Frank to Lori. In the end, though, she'd remained silent.

"Looks like you've got an interesting one here," Lori said. "So far we're not coming up with anything useful. We'll probably need another hour, but I didn't know if you wanted us to box up all the files and paperwork, as well."

"No, we'll take a look at everything here before—"

Gavin cleared his throat behind her.

"Actually," Claudia corrected, "since this is Detective Monaghan's investigation, you should ask him. I doubt you two have met. Lori Tobin, Gavin Monaghan.''

Claudia watched the technician's face brighten somewhat as she gazed past Claudia's shoulder and up at Gavin.

''So you've finally got yourself a partner.''

''It would appear that way,'' Claudia answered.

''Good to meet you,'' Gavin offered in his smooth voice as he shook the technician's hand. ''And I think Detective Parrish's suggestion is fine. We'll look through the files here and submit the relevant material ourselves.''

''Very good.'' Lori nodded, and Claudia couldn't help noticing how the woman's gaze lingered on Gavin for a moment before she turned back to her work.

''So what now?'' Gavin asked.

''Now? Now I suggest we head down to Jimmy's for coffee and a bite to eat. We're only going to be in the way here, and I don't know about you, but I'm not willing to wade through any of this paperwork until I've had a good kick of caffeine. The techs will seal the office when they're done, and then we can go through this mess and figure out just who might have wanted James Silver dead.''

JIMMY'S WAS CROWDED as usual. To Claudia, there seemed no rhyme nor reason behind the high demand for tables at the greasy spoon down on the waterfront in Fells Point, but without fail, seating was scarce. It

had to be the coffee, she thought as she took another sip. It certainly couldn't be the food.

Across the table of the window booth they shared, Gavin was finishing his own breakfast. Claudia watched him spear another piece of omelette and fought back the urge to reach across with her fork to sample some. She'd have done exactly that, a year ago, when it would've been Frank sitting with her. And, while she did that, he would have been stealing her last slice of bacon.

As usual, she tried to clamp down on the nostalgia.

"So you met James Silver only a couple times?" Gavin had asked the question already once after she'd explained Frank's connection to the dead PI. Even so, a glimmer of suspicion wavered in his voice as he studied her over the rim of his juice glass.

"That's right," she assured him again. "What? You think I'd lie about something like that? Why would I?"

"Maybe so you could stay on the case?"

"Please. Give me a little credit for professionalism. I understand what conflict of interest is. If I had actually been friends with Silver, I'd remove myself from the case, all right?"

"All right." The defensiveness in his voice attested to the bite she'd heard in her own, and immediately Claudia regretted her harshness.

"I'm sorry. I don't mean to snap. It's just…I've had a long twenty-four hours, you know?"

"Sure."

Gavin reached across the table and snagged her last piece of bacon on the end of his fork. Speechless, she watched him take one bite and then pop the rest into his mouth. For ten months, she'd been returning to Jimmy's for breakfast, and for ten months, she'd always left that last slice of bacon. Until this morning no one had touched it.

He must have seen her surprise because he said, "Oh, I'm sorry. Were you saving that?"

"Not at all."

He nodded, finishing the bacon. "Look, you're right. It's been a long twenty-four hours for you. Maybe you should just call it a day. I can look through Silver's files myself and—"

"No way." She took another swig of coffee. "You're not getting rid of me that easy. I'm still among the living. Another cup of coffee and I'm good to go. We'll head back and check out Silver's office, see if we can figure out what cases he'd been working on these past few days, who he's been talking to, and who he may have ticked off."

"Honestly, Claudia, I can handle it."

"It'll take us half the time working together. Besides, I have the next couple days off. After this, I've got a twelve-hour power nap scheduled, followed by a full-night's sleep." She flagged down the waitress for one more refill and the check. "Besides, I could use some work to help me forget yesterday."

Gavin nodded. "I heard about the Brown case."

Of course he had heard. By now the entire unit would know about her case being thrown out of court.

"Yeah. Lamont Brown." Closing her eyes briefly, Claudia massaged the bridge of her nose. She *was* tired, and if it wasn't for her personal interest in Silver's murder, she would take Gavin up on his offer and go home right now.

"I heard the judge dismissed for lack of evidence."

Claudia nodded. "I shouldn't let it bother me. It was just another drug-related shooting, you know? So what if Brown walks on this one? He's a punk. In no time he'll be back, clogging up the system, arrested on some other charge. He'll do his time eventually."

"You'd just hoped it would be your charge that put him away, right? Hey, you don't have to explain to me. I understand."

When she looked across to Gavin, she met his reassuring smile. It was the kind of don't-let-the-bad-guys-get-you-down expression Frank would have given her, and at that moment, Claudia hated that Gavin reminded her of him, that their working relationship—so new—had already begun to take on nuances of what she'd had with Frank as a partner.

She blinked. Again forcing back the unwanted memories.

"Of course it would've been nice if my charge had been the one to put Brown away," she said, trying to stay focused on the conversation. "I put a lot of time into that case, piecing it together, interviewing dozens of witnesses, preparing the reports. Only to have it all thrown out because the murder weapon went missing. That gun was on the scene. I pointed it out to the techs. Heck, I even saw them bag it, and then I saw it down at Evidence Control myself. But somewhere between me and the lab, that gun must have grown legs and walked off on its own, because it was never seen again. I had Lori turn the place upside down trying to find it.''

''And they hadn't run any tests on it before it disappeared?''

''No ballistics. No fingerprints. Nothing. They hadn't gotten a chance before it went missing. And now it's as if that gun never existed except in the crime-scene photos. It's my own fault.''

''How is it *your* fault?''

Claudia shrugged. ''I should have walked the gun down to the lab myself. I should have watched them run the tests I needed.''

''That's not your job, Claudia.''

''No, but it's my job to see that the investigation is run properly, that witnesses and suspects…and especially *evidence* is handled correctly. And in this case, it wasn't. So, instead of a smoking gun with the suspect's prints all over it, we got zilch. It falls on me. Doesn't make me look too good. Not to mention the fact that the state's attorney is all over me with accusations.''

''Accusations?''

She'd said more than she should have. Even to Tony—with whom she'd worked for three years— Claudia hadn't revealed as much about the Brown case, nor had she mentioned the state's attorney's threats.

But for some reason, with Gavin Monaghan, Claudia felt more willing to discuss yesterday's proceedings at the courthouse. Maybe she *was* tired, she thought as she stared at him across the Formica-topped table. Or maybe it was Gavin's eyes. Something about him made her want to trust, even though trusting had never come naturally to her.

"It's probably nothing," she said, trying to minimize its importance.

"Come on, Claudia, accusations from the State's Attorney Office aren't generally 'nothing.'"

"It was just a warning really. After the judge dismissed it, the state's attorney pulled me aside and basically implied that if it weren't for my otherwise flawless record, the office would suspect me of getting rid of the gun for a bribe, and they'd be looking to accuse me of evidence tampering."

Gavin seemed to consider her revelation for a moment before responding. "Well, I wouldn't let it get to you. It happens to the best of us," he offered, calmly wiping his mouth and tossing his napkin onto his empty plate.

"It doesn't happen to me. I mean, maybe that sounds arrogant, but as much work and precision as I put into the Brown case—*all* my cases—well, that gun going missing…it shouldn't have happened. It's a sign of sloppy police work. Bottom line."

"So is that how you explain what happened to your partner then? Seems he had a similar problem with evidence 'growing legs.' Are you saying that was sloppy detective work?"

Maybe ten months of grieving had drained most of the fight out of her. Maybe, after finally believing that Frank had taken his own life, Claudia no longer felt as strong an impulse to jump to his defense. Or maybe it was just something about Gavin. Because instead of the usual surge of resentment that a comment like his would have normally spurred within her, Claudia found herself able to bite her tongue and respond calmly.

"Frank was never sloppy."

"Fine. But he did have more than one case thrown out when evidence went missing, correct?"

Claudia studied Gavin. Was he attacking Frank's reputation or simply using it as an argument to defend hers?

"You seem to know a lot about a unit you've only just joined, Detective," she said.

"I hear rumors."

"Oh yeah? What kinds of rumors?"

"Both sides," he explained as he leaned back from the table. "For instance, you've got some who say your partner folded under the pressure of that whole IAD investigation. And then you've got others—fewer, mind you—who still think maybe he knew too much and was silenced because of it."

"And which theory do you favor?"

She watched Gavin take his wallet from his back pocket and toss two fives onto the table.

"I don't know," he said, meeting her gaze. "I worked Homicide in D.C. I know it's tough—the responsibility, the pressure, the expectations from your fellow detectives, your sergeant, the State's Attorney Office. Not to mention the kinds of cases and suspects you deal with on a daily basis. But still, by the time a cop makes his...or *her* way to the level of Homicide, you figure that most of the weak ones have been weeded out. Face it, the burn-out rate in this job is high, but for the guys in Homicide? I think it takes more than an IAD probe to push someone over the edge once they've achieved those ranks.''

Claudia scrutinized Gavin, wishing the twitch of suspicion would leave her. It was breakfast conversation, she tried to reason; two detectives having coffee, new partners getting to know each other, that was all.

Why then did she get the feeling Gavin was on a fishing expedition?

"So based on that assessment," she asked at last, "you're suggesting it's more likely someone killed Frank?"

"I'm not suggesting anything. After all, why should *I* have an opinion? I never met the man. You're the one who was closest to him, being his partner. What do *you* think happened?"

But Claudia was already pulling money from her wallet. This was not a conversation she intended to pursue with Gavin Monaghan, or anyone else for that matter. Especially today.

"I think either way it's history," she replied briskly, hearing the sharp tone of defensiveness in her own voice as she tossed down her five and picked up one of his. She handed him the bill and reached for her coat. "And right now, Detective, we've got a *fresh* homicide to develop our own theories on.''

CHAPTER THREE

THE PATROL CARS WERE GONE from the front of the former Marmack Bed & Mattress Company when Claudia parked the Lumina along the curb. The yellow crime-scene tape had been stripped, as well, except for one broad band fixed over the suite door. James Silver's office was clear of technicians and officers; the only remaining pieces of evidence that a crime had occurred were the black powder smudges and the dark stain on the floor behind the desk.

They spent an hour going through the PI's file cabinets and drawers, sifting through endless paperwork on the remote chance they might uncover some lead. They listened to the incoming messages on Silver's answering machine, but there were no obvious links to the man's brutal slaying. Even so, Claudia confiscated the machine and its tape, boxing them up with several other items of possible relevance.

"Looks like you might have a next of kin here," Claudia said eventually, breaking the silence.

Gavin glanced from the files he'd been searching to where she sat at Silver's oak desk.

"Eileen Silver. Probably his mother." She handed him the address book she'd just thumbed through. "It's a Key West address. You might want to contact authorities down there to break the news to her, instead of telling her by phone. That's about it though. No other Silvers or anything else that appears to be family.''

It was the most she'd said to him since they'd left Jimmy's. From the moment he'd asked about Frank Owens, Claudia's reserve had grown. Her response to anything he'd asked had been clipped and to the point, leaving him to wonder if perhaps he'd made his move too soon.

In retrospect, he might have done better to not bring up the subject of her former partner during their very first encounter. On the other hand, the conversation over breakfast had taken a natural turn in that direction. It might have seemed even more obvious had he *not* asked for her opinion regarding her partner's death.

He watched her continued exploration of Silver's desk. As the morning sunshine slipped through the wooden slats of the blinds behind her and touched the highlights of her cropped hair, Gavin thought of angels. The imagery struck him as ironic, especially considering the fact that Claudia Parrish was as likely a suspect as anyone in the ongoing corruption within the Homicide unit. After all, the evidence tampering hadn't ended when Owens's life had. And the most recent involved one of Claudia's own cases.

Gavin hadn't been surprised to learn of Judge Warner's dismissal of the Brown case yesterday. Reports of the missing gun were in the file Gavin's lieutenant had handed him five weeks ago—a thick file compiled by the previous IAD agent who had failed in his attempt to expose the corruption. Failed like the two IAD investigators before him. And it was because of their failures that Lieutenant Randolph had at last caved in to Gavin's request to be reassigned to the case. Only this time, Gavin vowed, it would be different.

A year ago, Gavin had been appointed to oversee the first investigation into the corruption that seemed to surround Baltimore's Homicide unit. Back then, however, the direction of the investigation had been dictated by others. By the time he'd come on board to head the probe, Owens was already IAD's primary target.

From the start, Gavin had been uncomfortable with the case. He'd tried to turn it around, slow it down, anything to give him time to prove that Owens was truly guilty. He'd tried to reopen past investigations into Evidence Control and Violent Crimes, suspecting the problems might come from there instead, but the brass had only come down on Gavin for straying—Owens was their target. IAD had increased their pressure on the seasoned detective, stopping only once Frank Owens had killed himself. IAD didn't seem to care, but Gavin had never been able to rest easy. He'd spent the past ten months wondering…suspecting Owens's innocence and knowing that the man had died because of the investigation *he* had led.

He'd demanded to be taken off the assignment, and Lieutenant Randolph had complied. Since then, the probe had practically ground to a halt. Gavin had watched the blunders of the next three agents, until finally his conscience had forced him to step in. But he'd insisted they would now do things *his* way.

"I want to start from square one, Lieutenant," he'd told Randolph. "I want to look into everything, not just Homicide."

"Monaghan, you'd be wasting your time. We've done all that. The corruption stems from the Homicide unit. There's no doubt. Weapons and critical evidence in murder cases are going missing, and someone's taking a payoff. It *has* to be a detective, someone with connections to the street and the capacity to reach, and deal with, the suspects. No one in Evidence Control would have that kind of access."

"Fine. Then put me undercover. Let me work within the unit."

Lieutenant Randolph shook his head. "We don't operate that way, and you know it. Only for extreme—"

"This *is* extreme, Lieutenant. A man lost his life. A good detective."

"Let it go, Monaghan."

"I can't let it go. Frank Owens killed himself because of the allegations against him. And honestly, I don't know for certain they were valid allegations."

"Yeah, well, we also don't know that he *wasn't* guilty, do we?"

"No? Then how do you explain the fact that the evidence tampering hasn't stopped?"

Randolph handed Gavin a file.

"What's this?"

"Claudia Parrish. Owens's partner. The one person who was probably close enough to him to know about the corruption, and the one person who might be continuing his practices. Or, who knows, maybe she was in on it from the start? She was the secondary detective on all three of Owens's bad cases. It could have just as easily been her taking payoffs from the start. It could have been *her* implicating him.''

Gavin opened the file and fingered through the reports as Randolph continued.

''And just recently, Detective Parrish had a case of her own go bad. No doubt, it's going to be thrown out of court just like Owens's were.''

''So she's your target?''

''Definitely.'' Lieutenant Randolph nodded, and Gavin experienced déjà vu. This was the Frank Owens investigation all over again.

''I'm not going on another witch hunt, Lieutenant,'' he said, closing the file, prepared to hand it back if his superior disagreed. ''We do this my way, or I'm out. If Claudia Parrish is guilty, if she is the source, I'll flush her out for you. But I'm not starting any fires until I know for certain.''

Fortunately, Randolph had accepted his terms. And by the end of the afternoon, they'd compiled a cover story for Gavin, right down to the believable detail of his having been the commissioner's chauffeur. With a false background in place, coupled with the fact that IAD so rarely went undercover, Gavin felt confident he would raise few, if any, suspicions from the detectives he'd be working with. Most importantly, from Claudia Parrish.

Now, in Silver's office, knowing Claudia for barely five hours, Gavin wasn't sure what to make of her reaction to his bringing up the question of Owens's death. She'd defended the integrity of her dead partner, as Gavin would expect any respectable detective to do, and her voice had remained relatively calm throughout. But her expression had wavered, and in it Gavin sensed the emotion just beneath her calm exterior.

After five years with IAD, Gavin prided himself on his keen ability to read people. Claudia Parrish, however, seemed beyond his comprehension. Either her defensiveness was an honest response, or there was more behind the sharp tone she'd adopted seconds before she snatched up her coat and stalked out of Jimmy's.

Gavin hoped her edginess was only exhaustion. He definitely had to be careful. He couldn't afford to alienate Claudia.

She seemed calmer now, as she opened one of Silver's desk drawers and lifted out another stack of papers. She, as well, had surrendered to the stifling heat of the office; her suit jacket lay draped over the back of one chair. When she stood at last and stretched, Gavin let his eyes take an appreciative sweep over her small, trim figure. Her short-sleeved turtleneck puckered where the leather straps of her shoulder holster pulled at the delicate fabric. But from there, the formfitting top left little to the imagination, hugging every sensuous curve leading to her slim waist.

Keeping an eye on Detective Parrish was certainly

not going to be an unpleasant aspect of his assignment.

He watched her pace, admiring the lithe movement
of her body. Fine lines creased her forehead, and
Gavin wondered if she was thinking of Owens or
Silver, or quite possibly both; he wondered if she,
too, toyed with the theory that there may be some
relation between the two deaths.

She stood at the window for a long moment, staring at the traffic crawling down Boston Street. When
she turned suddenly, her gaze caught his, and Gavin
knew she'd been aware of his perusal. But she remained silent. She returned to the desk and set to
work once again.

A full twenty minutes passed before she spoke
again.

"I think we might have something here," she said
so quietly Gavin had to look up to be sure she'd
actually said something.

He crossed the office to stand next to her chair, as
she flipped through one of two hard-bound journals.

"Silver's date books?"

She nodded. "Obviously he didn't want them
found. They were jammed at the back of the drawer.
Look at this." She turned to the end of last year's
journal, traced one slender finger across the page and
stopped at a scrawled entry.

"This was last December. Silver met with Frank.
On the fifth. On the sixth. And here again on the
eighth." She pointed to one entry after the next,
working her way to the date of Owens's death.

"Of course he met with Owens," Gavin offered. "You said yourself they were friends."

Her hand trembled slightly as she continued through the pages, and he doubted it was from the four cups of coffee she'd had.

"But he documented the meetings. Made appointments. I doubt he'd do that if they were just social visits. And it appears they were discussing the allegations against Frank." Her finger stopped at the bottom of the page. There, in bold, block letters was written: IAD. With a blue ballpoint, Silver had gone over each letter several times so that they practically glared off the page.

"And take a look at this." Claudia opened the next journal. "After Frank's suicide there's nothing really. The entries are haphazard—scattered references to other cases he was working, people he met with, names, numbers, addresses. Nothing remarkable until last week."

Claudia drew Gavin's attention to the margin. Again in Silver's block letters: CC# 2L5915.

"What's that?" Gavin asked, even though he recognized the number immediately.

"It's the incident number from the investigation into Frank's suicide."

"So you're suggesting Silver was looking into Frank's death?"

She shrugged.

"Why now, after all these months?"

"I don't know. But maybe that's what got Silver killed."

They were definitely thinking along the same lines,

Gavin decided. He leaned closer, one hand on the back of her chair and the other planted firmly on the desk beside this year's journal. He was close enough to smell that subtly provocative perfume of hers again. And definitely close enough to feel the heat of her body as his hand brushed past her wrist to turn the page. He let out a silent breath, trying to ignore the way his body responded to that brief touch. He focused on the journal entries. Scanning each page, he noted names and numbers, none of which rang any bells. Until he reached the bottom of one page.

The date: October 13. Only three days ago. There was no missing it. The name was written out in bold red ink along with her home phone number and address: CLAUDIA PARRISH.

Gavin straightened abruptly. "I thought you said you hadn't seen Silver since January."

"I don't know what my name's doing in there."

Gavin pointed at the journal. "Well, my guess would be he intended to call you."

"That might be, but I didn't speak with him."

Did her voice carry a twinge of defensiveness? Gavin wondered.

"I didn't," she repeated, "I swear, I haven't talked to Silver recently."

He reached out and turned another page. October 14. Again, Claudia's name, but with this entry there was a location scrawled on the line below: JIMMY'S.

Gavin didn't have to say anything.

"I don't know why he wrote these entries in his

date book," she said. "Obviously he intended to call me, but he didn't."

"You didn't have breakfast with him two days ago?"

"No. I told you, until this morning I haven't seen Silver since just after Frank died." She must have noted the skepticism in his expression, because she added, "You don't believe me?"

He shrugged. "I just have to wonder. After all, you did hesitate when we first arrived on the scene this morning." *As though she knew what was waiting for them in the office,* Gavin thought but didn't dare say.

"And I admitted to you then that I knew Silver. Of course I hesitated when I found out he was our victim."

"So you don't know what Silver was working on? There's nothing you're not telling me?"

She pushed the chair away from the desk and stood. "There is *nothing* I'm not telling you." Her gaze locked with his. "What is this really about, Monaghan? Are you suspecting me of something? Because if you are, I'd appreciate if you'd just come right out and say it."

He didn't respond, but, instead, watched her, searching for something that might convince him she was telling the truth.

"You don't trust me, do you?" she challenged. "You think I have something to do with this? With Silver's murder?"

"Well, you can't deny that it does appear a little suspicious. Our victim's got your name, your num-

ber, even your address. And obviously he was intent
on calling you, judging by the exclamation mark beside your name." He picked up the journal. "Then
a couple days later he turns up dead."

He flipped a few more pages in the journal, but
there were no more references to Claudia or anyone
else in the last two days of Silver's life.

"You gotta admit," he said, "you'd be coming to
the same assumptions if the tables were turned."

"Assumptions? So what kinds of 'assumptions'
are you making then? That he contacted me, and over
a plate of greasy eggs we had a disagreement about
Frank? And because of that, I came over here last
night and shot him? Is that it? Well, I think you'll
find some flaws with your theory, Detective Monaghan. For one, I was on shift last night."

"I didn't ask for an alibi. But since you mention
it, the squad wasn't on until midnight."

She let out a sharp breath, a caustic smile pursing
her lips. "So just because my name's in his date
book you're going to view me as a suspect? Is that
it? Well—" she crossed the office and snatched the
journal from his grasp, snapping it shut and practically tossing it back at him "—you've really got
your work cut out for you then, Detective, because
there are a hell of a lot of names in there."

She turned from him, as if to storm from the office,
but Gavin caught her arm. When she tried to tug free,
he tightened his grip and pulled her around.

"Claudia, listen to me."

He waited for her gaze to meet his and was struck
by the quiet fury that darkened them.

"Look, I don't want to get off on the wrong foot here."

"Well, I'm not sure about the other units you've worked with, but accusations aren't generally the best foundation for a partnership."

"I wasn't accusing you of anything."

"No? It sounded like it to me."

"I'm sorry. It's my first case." He tried to adopt a tone of sincerity, hoping to convince her. He couldn't afford to lose her trust so soon, in spite of his own suspicions. "I just want to be sure I'm getting all the facts," he said calmly.

"Truly, Gavin." He was glad to hear her adopt a softer tone. "I have given you all the facts. I told you how I know Silver. I told you we had little contact in the past. And in spite of what his date book might imply, I never met with him two days ago. I'll even go one step further and admit that yes, I *was* at Jimmy's for breakfast that day. But I ate alone. I was going over my files to prepare for the arraignment hearing on the Brown case. I didn't meet anyone at Jimmy's. And I most certainly did not meet with James Silver."

"All right. I believe you."

Claudia looked exhausted, spent, even more than she had when he'd met her. She combed her fingers through her hair with obvious frustration as she closed her eyes and turned away from him. Releasing a long breath, she peered through the slats of the blinds and lifted a hand to her neck in an attempt to massage the stress that no doubt had settled there.

"Claudia, we're both tired. Why don't we call it

a day? Get some sleep. We can box this stuff up, take it in, and look at it when we're more awake. Less on edge.''

She nodded silently, her gaze fixed out the window.

Gavin tossed the two date books into the box, along with several other files he'd set aside, and folded the top closed. Claudia was still staring out the window when he came to her side and handed her her jacket.

''Thanks.'' Even her voice sounded weary as she slipped her jacket on and tugged the bottom over her holster. ''And I'm sorry for snapping. I need sleep.''

''No apology necessary.'' He liked the smile that struggled to her lips, giving her mouth a wry but sensual curve. It was only a smile, Gavin reasoned; yet he felt himself respond—a low, warm tug deep in his gut—when he imagined what those lips might feel like against his.

But imagining was all he'd be doing when it came to Claudia, Gavin resolved as he turned from her to the box on Silver's desk. Suspicions or no suspicions, she was definitely off-limits. He was hardly going to jeopardize his case, his entire career, for the sake of a woman. He'd never done it in the past, and he certainly wasn't about to start now, no matter how alluring Detective Claudia Parrish was.

AFTER SHE AND GAVIN HAD closed up Silver's office, Claudia drove them back to headquarters. Gavin's car had been parked in a lot along the way, and she'd dropped him off before hauling the box of Silver's files to Evidence Control. She hadn't bothered to go back to the office after that, but went directly to the garage to get her own vehicle. It was noon by the time she steered her weather-beaten Volvo onto Shakespeare Street.

She parked halfway up the block, outside a yellow-brick three-story Victorian row house. Shouldering her briefcase, she took the marble steps to the massive oak doors and shoved one open.

From the first-floor apartment, she could hear Mrs. Cuchetta playing the baby grand piano she used for lessons, but as Claudia staggered up the stairs, exhausted, the thick walls of the old, converted row home swallowed the classical melody. And when Claudia finally closed her door behind her and threw the dead bolt, there was nothing but silence. Gratifying silence.

She dropped her keys onto the front hall table and stepped into the small but cozy apartment she'd called home for the past three years.

Shedding her jacket and holster and kicking off her shoes, she put some water on for tea.

On the corner of the kitchen bar, next to a mounting stack of bills, the answering machine blinked. She tossed a tea towel over it, covering the demanding red light. It hardly mattered; even before she'd finished pouring her tea, the phone rang.

"Faith, I just got in," Claudia told her sister after being verbally censured for not returning her calls.

"Well, I wanted to be sure you were all right. October sixteenth and all."

Claudia stirred sugar into her tea. Leave it to her

little sister to remember anniversaries that weren't even her own. Faith remembered everything to do with family; not at all like Claudia. The only things she managed to remember these days were the details of her cases. It hadn't always been that way, of course. Before Frank's death, before she'd immersed herself so completely in her work that it seemed there was nothing else, things had been different.

Now, faced with Faith's concern, Claudia wondered if maybe she should never have told her sister. It might have been easier to let the secret die along with Frank, so that no one could remind her of the love she'd shared so briefly with him.

"Look," Faith was saying. "Greg mentioned just this morning that it's been a while since you've been out here. And you know it's only a forty-minute drive. You'd think it was a forty-minute *flight* given the number of times we've seen you in the past year. So what do you say to dinner tonight? I know it's short notice, but it wouldn't be if you actually listened to your messages."

Claudia didn't respond. She yanked the tea towel off the answering machine, the red light blinking as insistently as ever. *James Silver.* What if he *had* tried to call her? With preparations for the Brown arraignment, she hadn't checked her messages in days.

"Faith, I'll have to get back to you on that. Maybe tomorrow? I've been up since yesterday morning. I'm exhausted. But I'll call."

There was a pause before Faith finally complied. Making Claudia promise to call, and assuring herself that her big sister was really okay, Faith at last hung up.

Claudia's hand hovered over the answering machine for a moment before she at last pressed Play.

As predicted, three of the messages were from her sister. But there were five others—all hang-ups. Using her Caller ID, Claudia wrote down the number, and within a minute she'd confirmed her hunch. The Yellow Pages lay in her lap, open to the listings for private investigators.

James Silver had called her five times in the past three days. It didn't surprise her that he hadn't tried her at the office, not if her suspicions were correct. If Silver had been looking into Frank's death again, then the Homicide office was the last place Silver would have risked calling. But why hadn't he bothered to leave even one message? Maybe because he thought this too would be a risk?

Claudia stared at Silver's ad for a long time, her mind staggering over the countless alternate scenarios that might have played out had he actually been able to reach her. Would he be dead now? Would they have uncovered something new about Frank's death? Could she have intervened?

Switching off both the machine and the phone, Claudia moved to the living room couch and turned on the TV. But the aimless flicking through channels did nothing to divert her thoughts from Frank and Silver. If she knew one thing for certain, it was that Silver had been taking a second look at Frank's death. It was the only explanation behind his attempt to reach her.

But why? What had prompted him to relaunch his investigation into Frank's death?

Claudia set down the remote control and reached under the couch. She groped for the orange press-board binder that had been hidden there, unopened, for at least six months. Sliding it out, she brushed the thin layer of dust from its cover.

CC# 2L5915.

It was one thing to remove a case file, or any portion of it, from headquarters. The breach of security was done on occasion by detectives and overlooked by their supervisors. But to duplicate an entire file, from cover to cover—all the reports from officers and supervisors alike, from the Chief Medical Examiner's office and the various crime labs, interview transcripts, detective's personal notes, even crime-scene and evidence photos—was completely against department policy. Not to mention punishable by suspension, Claudia thought, as she eased the thick binder into her lap.

For Claudia, copying the file had been worth the risk. Ten months ago she had believed that Frank couldn't have killed himself, and that everything in the reports must have been a cover-up.

She probably should have destroyed the file once she'd submitted to the consensus that Frank *had* taken his own life.

Yet, now Claudia was grateful she had kept it. After all, maybe questions remained to be asked and answers to be found. Obviously Silver had believed so. But had there actually been new information? Or had he simply been grasping at the same old straws he'd had the last time they'd spoken?

Claudia opened the file, trying to avoid the pages of photos. She was unsuccessful. The four-by-six color images brought back that unforgettable night as though it had been only yesterday. She relived the disbelief and the horror. And then the utter emptiness she'd felt when she held Frank's hand for the last time.

She remembered crying, and then Lori trying to console her. It wasn't until Claudia had caught sight of the picture on Frank's mantel—a photo of the two of them receiving their bronze stars—that Claudia had finally pulled herself together that night. For Frank, she'd kept up appearances. For him, she'd never once let on that he'd been anything but a partner to her.

Claudia stared at the open binder in her lap. The crime-scene photos blurred with her tears. Frank couldn't have killed himself, she thought for the millionth time. The Frank she had known, the man she'd loved…he hadn't been a coward or a quitter. And yet, what else could she believe now that all the reports were in?

God, but she missed him.

She missed his voice and his laughter. She missed the excitement of working a case with him, having him by her side and knowing she was with the best detective on the force. And she missed the little things about Frank—the familiar gestures and wisecracks that could bring laughter to any gray day, his knowing smile when he'd look up from his desk to where she sat across from him, the light that would touch his eyes when she'd open her apartment door and find him standing on the landing, and the way his hand had felt in hers—rough, warm and secure. She missed the feel of his body against hers, and she missed the way he'd whisper his love for her and tell her they would always be together.

But in spite of her longing for him, Claudia wasn't certain she could ever forgive Frank for giving up. With the file open in her lap, she closed her eyes and settled her head against the top of the couch. Maybe that was the real reason she hadn't gotten rid of the case file—maybe she felt that by hanging on to it she still held a piece of Frank. And maybe she would never be able to let him go. He lived in her heart, along with her anger and her resentment. No one could ever come close to touching her the way Frank had.

Inexplicably, Gavin Monaghan entered Claudia's thoughts. She'd be lying if she said there wasn't a glimmer of attraction there. It was certainly the first time she'd felt anything like it since Frank. And she hadn't been the only one who'd toyed with such thoughts—she'd seen the way Gavin had looked at her when they were in Silver's office.

She remembered the effect his smile had had on her when she'd dropped him off at his car and apologized again for her behavior in Silver's office. He'd had every right to question her. If the roles had been reversed, she would have demanded the same from him. He'd accepted her apology and given her a smile. Her entire body had responded to that smile with a quick shiver of excitement.

Claudia closed her eyes. She had to push Gavin Monaghan from her thoughts. It was ridiculous to think she was attracted to a man she barely knew. She was, Claudia rationalized, only because he'd done a couple of little things that had reminded her of Frank. That was all.

Besides, how could she possibly have feelings for anyone when her heart still belonged to Frank?

CHAPTER FOUR

GAVIN BROUGHT HIS FIST against the upper panel of
the door at the top of the stairs. It had taken him a
good fifteen minutes to find the three-story row house
in Fells Point that corresponded with the home address he had for Claudia. And he would have thought
that those fifteen minutes should have cooled his
temper. He'd been wrong.

He raised his hand a second time, the resounding
thud echoing down the narrow stairwell. It was
enough to wake the dead. Certainly enough to cause
the tenant on the first floor to stop playing the piano
and listen.

Where the hell was she?

Gavin took a deep breath, hoping to quell his impatience, and was about to knock a third time when
he heard movement from inside. There was the slide
of a dead bolt and the scrape of a chain before Claudia opened the door.

She wore the same suit he'd seen on her earlier,
only now the pants and turtleneck were creased. Her
hair was a tousle of blond curls and she lifted a hand
in an attempt to arrange them.

"Did I wake you?"

She rolled her eyes, puffy with sleep. "What do

you think? I hardly slept in two nights." She rubbed a hand over her face. "What are you doing here anyway?"

"Can I come in?"

She held his stare, as though debating the wisdom of allowing work into her home. Finally she stepped aside.

The apartment had the same charm as the building's facade, Gavin noted as he brushed past her into the tiled foyer. With the day's light dying behind the half-drawn blinds, the living room beyond the arched portal lay in shadow. Even so, there was an immediate homey feel to it, a lived-in sense that evaded his own row house across the city. And there was an underlying scent that permeated the apartment, very similar to the one he'd smelled on Claudia earlier, one that was rapidly becoming enticing.

But he wasn't here to be enticed.

Claudia began switching on lights in the adjoining kitchen and the living room. He watched her scan the apartment as if checking that everything was in order.

"Sorry for the mess," she stated, even though there wasn't one—only her jacket and holster slung over the back of a chair, and a few newspapers strewn about the room. Even the kitchen was spotless in comparison to his own. A toppling stack of mail was the only sign of disarray.

"Why are you here, Gavin?"

"I tried to call." He curbed the impatience in his voice.

"I had the phone turned off."

"And your pager?"

"It's in my briefcase. I mustn't have heard it."

Again she lifted a hand to her mussed hair. "Can I get you something to drink?"

He'd definitely woken her from a sound sleep; her voice held that sleepy quality, deep and a little raspy.

And undeniably seductive, Gavin thought.

"No, I'm fine." He watched her move behind the breakfast bar to the fridge and take out a bottle of water.

"So what is this about?" she asked, twisting open the bottle and taking a long drink.

"I'm looking for the journals."

"The journals?" she repeated.

"You know, Silver's date books."

"Looking for them? Why? They're in Evidence Control. I told you I was going to submit the box after I dropped you off this morning."

"I thought maybe you'd brought them home instead," he offered, still struggling to contain impatience and anger, trying to give her the benefit of the doubt.

"Why would you think that?"

Confusion tightened her face then, and Gavin could only wonder if it was genuine. She set the bottle on the counter, the force sending a few droplets of water spraying onto the thin fabric of her shirt.

"Because they're not in Evidence Control, Claudia."

Her expression tightened another notch. "What do you mean they're not in Evidence Control?"

"Exactly that. I went down there, figuring I'd take

a closer look at the journals myself, and when I searched the box there was no sign of them.''

In his years with IAD, he'd done his share of staring corrupt cops in the eye. He'd watched them attempt to lie their way out of a variety of situations. But none of them could come close to Claudia's convincing performance. She stepped around the counter, the look of disbelief deepening, creasing fine lines at the corners of her eyes and furrowing a small series of ridges along her forehead.

When he'd rummaged through the box and discovered the journals missing, the flare of suspicion had been immediate. There had been no doubt then that Claudia had disposed of them in order to eliminate evidence of her connection with Silver, not to mention her possible motive for wanting him dead.

But now, seeing her standing before him, her eyes and voice heavy with sleep, and that soft femininity and allure accentuated by the warmth of her own surroundings...Gavin wished the surprise on her face was real.

"Where are they, Claudia?'' he asked, unable to drop the accusation in his tone.

She maintained a calmness he'd not expected.

"Look, Gavin, there's obviously been a mix-up. I don't know what you think I did with those journals, but I can assure you the last time I saw them they were in that box. And I submitted it.''

"So you don't think they might have...accidentally fallen out?''

"Fallen out? No. That's ridiculous. I didn't even open the box, so if they're not there, then maybe they got mixed up with some other evidence submitted at the same time. Or maybe Sarge took an interest in the case and went down to see for himself what we brought in. I don't know. Maybe you didn't even look in the right box.''

''It was the right one. I checked the inventory list.''

''And?''

''And there wasn't a single notation indicating anything resembling a journal.''

Her awareness of his suspicion was clear. She studied him, as though sizing him up. Then she shook her head. ''I don't know what you're implying, but I am not going to let you stand in the middle of my apartment and accuse me of something I didn't do. This is insane.''

He caught the brief flash of anger in her gray eyes, before she turned on her heel. Pulling the hem of her top from the waist of her pants, she stalked from the living room and headed down the short corridor, switching on lights as she went.

''Where are you going?'' he called after her.

''To shower and change.'' The light came on in the room at the end of the hall and through the half-open door Gavin saw a four-poster pine bed with a matching trunk at its foot. And before he could look away, he saw Claudia's naked back as she stripped off her top and pulled it over her head. Even at this distance, there was no mistaking the toned lines of her shoulders and slender back caught in the warm yellow glow of the bedroom lamp.

Gavin tried to look away but couldn't. Either Claudia wasn't in the least bit shy, or, more likely, she was too upset by his accusations to realize she was in plain sight.

"I'll find the journals myself," she called out as the shirt joined the tangle of sheets and duvet piled high on the bed. She moved away from the door, but Gavin could still see her in the reflection of the full-length mirror. Only when she reached behind her for the clasp of her bra, did Gavin at last look away, ashamed at his voyeurism.

"Give me a few minutes and I'll ride over with you," she shouted. "Help yourself to whatever's in the fridge if you want." If she said anything after that it was drowned out by the sound of running water, followed by the hiss of the shower.

Gavin moved to the kitchen and opened the refrigerator, his gaze falling to the near-empty shelves. Claudia needed to do some serious grocery shopping. It was as bad as his own fridge, he thought, reaching for the last can of Coke. Mayo, pickles, several shriveled apples, an unopened bottle of wine along with a couple beers, and some questionable containers of juice and milk. No wonder her place was so tidy; Claudia was probably never home to mess it up.

Snapping open the can, he wandered into the living room. Traces of Claudia's personal life—what little there must be, given the hours he knew she worked—were scattered aesthetically on several side tables and shelving units. Family photos, trinkets and keepsakes—some were precious, while others had obviously been found on the beach. He scanned her shelves of books, wondering where she found the time to read, or if she even did now that she worked Homicide.

The light from the two stained-glass lamps gleamed against the few patches of polished hardwood floor that weren't covered with elaborate woven throw rugs. Pacing the narrow room, Gavin marveled at the sense of home around him—everything from the half-empty cup of tea on the coffee table to the throw blanket flung over the back of the couch. He'd bought his handyman's row house two years ago, and with all the renovations, coupled with his hours, the moving-in process was still very much under way. He'd almost forgotten that a home wasn't normally cluttered with half-unpacked boxes.

He rounded the coffee table and lowered himself into the ample sofa. Exhaustion quivered through his body. He'd been up hours, as well, and were it not for the twinges of suspicion he'd had all day regarding Silver's possible connection to Frank Owens's death, and now to Claudia, he might have succumbed to sleep himself. Certainly given the soft invitation of Claudia's sofa and the immediate comfort of her apartment, it wouldn't be difficult.

Glancing over his shoulder and down the corridor, Gavin saw that the bedroom door remained ajar. A cloud of steam billowed past the opening from the en suite. He turned his attention to the newspapers on the coffee table, hoping to banish the image of Claudia in the shower before it could take root in his mind.

However, it wasn't the *Baltimore Sun* that managed to divert his imagination. It was the unmistakable orange cover of a case file. Only a corner of it peeked out from under the sofa, but it was enough for Gavin to know immediately what it was. With the steady thrum of the shower in the background, he slid the thick file out and understood why Claudia had attempted to hide it.

It was the Owens case. Gavin recognized the incident number instantly.

Had she taken the file out of the office this morning, after going to Evidence Control? Had she felt the need to study it again, believing there to be a connection to Silver's murder? If so, why would she take the risk?

Gavin thought of the case files at his house. IAD files. The most recent one being on Claudia. But then, he *had* to take files home, especially when working a case undercover, so that his comings and goings from the IAD offices were kept to a minimum.

The Homicide unit, however, like others in the Criminal Investigations Bureau, worked under a completely different set of regulations. There were strict rules and penalties for removing a case file.

Gavin opened the binder and his shock doubled. This wasn't even the official file. Claudia had copied the entire contents: case notes, reports, investigative entries, even a complete set of the crime-scene and autopsy photos.

Understandably, Claudia would have a vested interest in the investigation into her partner's death, but surely not to the extent of compromising her career by pulling such a stunt. Unless, of course, she had something at stake in Owens's death. Unless she needed to protect herself with information in the event she was questioned.

"Claudia Parrish was the secondary detective on all three of Owens's bad cases," Lieutenant Randolph had told him five weeks ago. "It could have just as easily been her taking payoffs...it could have been her implicating him."

Again, the niggling suspicion mounted. Gavin leafed through the file. It wasn't anything he hadn't seen many times before—the reports, the photos of Frank Owens dead in his bedroom.

Ten months ago, Gavin had been shocked to learn of the detective's death. Randolph had called him the second the news had hit the police radios that night, and Gavin had demanded to go to the scene. He'd wanted to head the investigation himself. But Randolph wouldn't allow it. He'd been adamant Gavin not reveal himself as the man behind the probe. At that point, though, Gavin hadn't cared if the entire unit found out. He'd wanted to be there. He'd felt responsible.

Now though, Gavin realized it had been for the best. After all, if he had gone to the crime scene that night, he would never have had this opportunity to find the real person behind the evidence tampering.

As if on cue, the shower stopped. Gavin snapped the file shut. He shoved it back under the sofa and turned to the newspapers on the coffee table. In minutes, Claudia's footsteps sounded down the corridor. Her hair was wet, the blond curls dark and weighted. She wore a less formal suit than before, but not at the expense of flattery. The thin fabric of the knit top accentuated each slender curve, and as she slipped on her shoulder holster and buckled the straps, Gavin's gaze lingered on the suggestive swell of her breasts.

Certainly this case would have been easier if he hadn't gone undercover, Gavin decided. Working directly with the detectives he was investigating, particularly Claudia, was difficult. On paper, she looked guilty. But in person...

"I'm ready to go," she stated, interrupting his thoughts. Snatching up her trench coat, she breezed past him to open the door, and in moments they were on their way to headquarters.

EVIDENCE CONTROL WAS LOCATED behind an unassuming steel door down a long corridor in the basement of headquarters on Fayette Street. Claudia's heels echoed along the hollow passageway, a sharp staccato marking her agitation. Gavin had to be wrong about the date books. He mustn't have searched the right box.

Twisting her wrist free from the cuff of her coat, Claudia checked her watch. Eight o'clock. She should be in bed. At least she'd managed to get a few hours of sleep on the sofa before Gavin had woken her...woken her with accusations.

He'd been silent during the ride over, steering the unmarked car past the glittering lights of the Inner Harbor and into the city. And in his silence, Claudia had read mistrust. It was beyond her how something as simple as her name entered in Silver's date book could have led Gavin to believe she would destroy this evidence. Unless, of course, he truly suspected she had something to do with Silver's murder.

Allowing Gavin to hold the heavy door for her, Claudia stepped into the stifling, windowless front room of Evidence Control.

"Hey, Detective Parrish," the technician at the counter addressed her when he looked up from his paperwork.

"Hi, Ned. I'm looking for a box I submitted from the Boston Street scene. Do you think you can lay your hands on it?"

"You got your invoice?"

"No. I didn't stick around for it this morning. They said they'd just send it on up when they were through doing the inventory."

"Well, I'll see what I can find, but it might take a bit."

"Ned, I can handle this." Lori Tobin walked around one of the tall, gray metal shelving units, looking more than ready to call it a day. In fact, she already had her coat on and her purse slung over one shoulder.

"I didn't think you'd still be here," Claudia said.

"We ran late on another scene, but I'm about to head home."

"Well, just my luck that you haven't yet."

"What's the problem?" Lori asked.

"You remember Gavin, don't you?" From the corner of her eye, Claudia caught his nod and then saw the slow smile soften his features as he regarded the technician.

"Of course I do," Lori said, her perfect teeth marking the flawless smile she gave him in return.

It was clear that Claudia wasn't the only woman who found Gavin Monaghan attractive, and she wondered where the twitch of jealousy came from as she watched the two.

Claudia cleared her throat. "Anyway, Lori, I was hoping you could help us out. Gavin was here earlier wanting to go through the material we submitted from the victim's office, but for some reason there seems to be a couple items missing. It's probably just a discrepancy on the submission slip or something. Can you let me see the inventory?"

"Not a problem." Lori took her eyes off Gavin long enough to search under the front desk, then handed Claudia the handwritten list.

A hot wave of dread swept over her as she checked it twice. Gavin was right: there was no mention of date books or journals.

"What about the logs?" she asked. "Has anyone signed anything out regarding the case?"

Again the younger woman checked. She was already shaking her head as she withdrew a clipboard with the log-out forms. "Doesn't look like it. You're the only one listed as submitting the evidence."

A side glance was all Claudia needed to catch the look of suspicion steadily darkening Gavin's features. She saw the quick clenching of a muscle along his jaw, and when his eyes met hers they narrowed slightly.

"I don't understand. There's got to be a mistake somewhere on one of these lists," Claudia suggested.

She didn't take much comfort from Lori's nod, however.

"It's probably a clerical error," she agreed. "Whoever was handling it could have missed it in the inventory. It happens. Why don't I get the box for you? You can look through it yourself."

The minute of silence during which Lori searched for the box felt like a lifetime for Claudia, especially since she knew Gavin's gaze was on her the entire time. Then as she searched the contents of the box herself, she knew he was staring, believing the worst of her. And she almost didn't blame him. The date books truly were gone.

Still she said nothing. She closed the box, thanked Lori when she promised to look into the situation tomorrow, and headed out the door with Gavin at her heels. Only once they crossed the first level of the parking garage did Claudia at last speak.

"This doesn't make any sense," she said, burying her hands in her trench coat. "You put those journals in the box yourself. How can they not be there now?"

"You're right," Gavin offered, but his tone lacked conviction.

Claudia stopped in the middle of the garage. When he turned to look at her, his mistrust was more than evident.

She tried to curb the anger in her voice. "Look, Gavin, maybe you're not keen on it, but Sarge seems determined to partner us up. Now, I don't know about you, but the last thing I need is a partner who doesn't trust me."

"Who said anything about not trusting you?" he asked.

"You don't have to say it. I'm not stupid. I can see it in your face, hear it in your voice. Not to mention the accusations back at my apartment. What are you thinking? That I deliberately didn't submit those journals?" She could hear her voice echo through the concrete structure and immediately lowered it. The severity of her whisper conveyed her ire just as successfully. "Do you think I removed them from the box and shoved them in my car somewhere? Or that I hid them, maybe destroyed them? Would you like to search my apartment, Detective Monaghan?"

Even in the low light of the parking garage, Gavin's stare had a hard edge to it, not unlike his features. His dark gaze was steady, making Claudia feel like a specimen on some entomologist's board, being examined, scrutinized. And when he did finally speak, the calm in his voice infuriated her all the more.

"You can't tell me it doesn't look just a little suspicious. The only piece of evidence that points to a relationship between you and Silver is now conveniently missing," he explained.

"I didn't have a relationship with Silver. I told you, I met him a couple of times. That's it."

He offered nothing more than a speechless stare.

"Did you even stop to consider the fact that I was the one who showed you those journals to begin with?" she asked him. "I found them in Silver's desk, I leafed through them. If I felt threatened by their content, don't you think I would have hidden them from you instead of bringing them to your attention?"

More silent scrutiny.

The light from the lamp mounted on the pillar behind her touched his face, accentuating the strong angles and the chiseled appearance of his mouth. Damn, but she hated that she found him attractive, yet, she couldn't deny it. From the moment she'd opened her apartment door, groggy from sleep, to find him standing on the landing outside, the attraction had been there. And it had only mounted in the confines of the car as they'd driven to headquarters. Even now, angry as she was, it was undeniable.

But there seemed no way to convince him. At last, frustrated with his silence, Claudia threw up her hands. "This isn't going to work, is it? You and me. Forget it. There's no partnership if you don't trust me."

When she tried to shove past him to head to the car, Gavin caught her arm.

Through the material of her trench coat, she felt the heat of his hand. But it was in his stare that she felt even more—a stirring of sorts, a kind of warmth that moved through her as though he had just looked into her thoughts.

Why was his trust so important to her? She should be thankful the partnership wasn't going to work. Yet, in spite of having a valid reason for Sarge to partner Gavin with someone else, Claudia found herself actually wanting his trust. More than anything.

"Just drive me home, all right?" she managed to say.

"I believe you, Claudia."

Did she hear sincerity in his voice this time?

"You do?"

Gavin nodded, his head tilted slightly as if to offer apology.

"Then what the hell were all those accusations about? How can you believe me now and not before?"

"Because now I can see it in your eyes. I needed to see that."

They were standing close enough that just beneath the stench of old car grease and exhaust Claudia could smell the subtle aftershave he wore. She felt his grip relax around her arm and saw the corners of his mouth lift slightly in reassurance.

"I believe you submitted the journals, Claudia. But I don't believe that it was some clerical error or a mix-up in Evidence Control. And I honestly don't think we're going to see those date books again."

"You think someone else removed them?"

He nodded. "Someone with access to the evidence, someone also interested in Silver's schedule and clientele. Maybe someone whose name we failed to see in the books before we submitted them."

Gavin withdrew the car keys from his coat pocket and turned them over a few times in his hands—strong hands, she noted. When she looked back up to find him staring at her, she couldn't resist the admiration she felt. Gavin was a good cop, a cop unwilling to believe in coincidences, and a cop who wasn't about to let something like misplaced evidence be dismissed easily.

"Well, Detective Monaghan, you obviously have some ideas about this case. What's your next move? What do you have in mind?"

"It's more like 'who' do I have in mind," he whispered before ushering her to the car.

GAVIN SLID THE KEY into the Lumina's ignition but didn't start the car. He'd almost lost Claudia just now. He'd pushed her pretty hard with his accusations, but he'd had to. She might have become even more suspicious of him had he not questioned her about the lost journals. And he did believe her. Or, at least, he wanted to.

In the passenger seat, she fingered her drying hair, and then rubbed her forehead as though relieving tension. She still looked tired, but there was a light in her eyes now. It was obvious the investigation energized her as much as it did him, and it was that spark in her that attracted him.

"So who do you have in mind?" she asked.

"Daniel Carver."

A quick glance told him she didn't recognize the name. "It doesn't ring any bells?"

He watched her mull it over in her thoughts a few times, before she said, "No. But it sounds familiar. Should I know it?"

How could she not remember? Gavin wondered. It was Carver's name that appeared at the top of all the autopsy reports in the file she had hidden under her sofa.

"Daniel Carver. *Dr.* Daniel Carver," he clarified.

Claudia's look of puzzlement faded as recognition

took hold. "Doc. Right. Doc Carver. From the Medical Examiner's office."

Gavin rewarded her memory with a nod.

"How is he related to this case?"

"His name was in Silver's last journal."

Even he hadn't recognized the name immediately when he'd seen it in the date book at Silver's office this morning. Working in IAD hadn't given him many opportunities to deal with the Chief Medical Examiner's office, but when he had seen the name, he knew it wasn't for the first time. Not until he saw the name in Frank Owens's case file, did it come back to him.

"I remember," Claudia stated. "I just didn't make the connection to the ME's office. I don't think I ever knew his first name. We always just called him Doc. He's retired now though. He left months ago. Do you think Silver might have met with him?"

"It could be a long shot," Gavin said, turning over the car's engine and putting it in Drive. "But I'm certainly willing to pay Doc Carver a visit to find out."

CHAPTER FIVE

A QUICK CALL FROM Gavin's cell phone up to the office provided them with Dr. Carver's Mount Washington address. From the moment Gavin pulled out of headquarters and steered north, Claudia silently berated herself for not having made the connection herself. She *had* seen the name in Silver's date book, but it had seemed so insignificant.

Nothing is insignificant, Claudia. Wasn't that one of the first things Frank had taught her three years ago when he'd agreed to take her on as a partner? Maybe she hadn't been such a good student after all. Or maybe she was burned out.

"This is it." Gavin pulled the car alongside the curb.

In the light of a street lamp, he double-checked the address. Across the street, set behind several large sycamores, Carver's majestic two-story limestone residence rose up from a tangle of encroaching holly bushes.

"Don't expect too much," she muttered as she took in the austere pillared entrance.

"Why do you say that?"

"Doc Carver was a senile, tight-lipped fuddy-duddy at the best of times. And there are a good many people at the ME's office who'll probably tell you he didn't retire soon enough.''

"So you've dealt with this guy before then?''

"Not on any of my own cases, no. But I've dealt with him.''

She saw the quick lift of one brow as curiosity briefly crossed his face, and she was grateful Gavin didn't press her for details. The last thing she needed was to rehash the memories of the one and only time she'd spoken to the old coroner.

It had been barely two weeks after Frank's death. She'd tried to stay away but couldn't. Even today, she could remember every step she'd taken that afternoon, walking over to Penn Street from headquarters; she could remember every step down that sterile, airless corridor to the morgue where she'd been countless times. Only that afternoon hadn't been like any of the other visits.

She'd gone to see Frank one final time.

In the end though, she hadn't seen him. Doc Carver wouldn't allow it.

Claudia had asked questions, but Carver had been as vague as the rest who were conducting the investigation. The old man claimed he was under explicit instructions not to discuss the case with anyone. After he'd given her that line a half-dozen times like some parrot learning a new shtick, Claudia had left, her exit far from civilized. She'd shoved the stainless-steel doors wide, sending them slapping angrily behind her.

Mounting the steps to Carver's Colonial-style house now, Claudia tugged the edges of her coat tighter around her. There was a chill in the night air. It carried the smell of frost, and in the glaring lights of the portico she saw the faint plume of her breath as Gavin rang the bell.

"We're here to see Daniel Carver," Gavin informed the woman who finally opened the door. She was well into her seventies, her thinning hair teased into a silver bouffant and the skin over her gaunt face taking on an almost translucent quality.

"I'm sorry, sir. This isn't a good time."

"It won't take long."

"It's late. Perhaps tomorrow—"

Claudia reached for her shield, unclipping it from her belt and allowing Mrs. Carver a good look. "It won't take long," she repeated Gavin's words briskly and nodded her thanks as the woman at last allowed them entry.

In keeping with the grandeur of the facade, the home's interior resembled a photo shoot for some architectural magazine. They were ushered through the elaborate foyer, under a glittering crystal chandelier, to a slightly less ostentatious sitting room that oozed tradition.

Unlike his wife, Carver was a big man whose years had not made him frail. He joined them, taking a seat next to the marble fireplace. But although his appearance was one of a healthy, alert retiree, Carver's eyes told a different story. He regarded Claudia slowly, almost cautiously, and she would have sworn there was no recollection behind the rheumy eyes.

"Mr. Silver?" he asked for the second time since

Gavin informed him of the nature of their visit. Carver worried his bottom lip with a thick finger. "Mr. Silver…"

"He was a private investigator," Gavin offered.

"Ah, yes, I do believe I remember him. In fact, I think he was here just the other…no…no, maybe it was last week. He told me he used to work in the police department. Is that true? And you say he was *murdered?*"

Gavin nodded. "What exactly did you and Mr. Silver discuss?"

"Oh, well, we talked about a lot of things, you know. My garden. My roses. It's unfortunate it's dark out, I'd show you them. Then again, I think most everything's finished out there, what with autumn and all."

"Dr. Carver, do you remember why James Silver came to see you?" Claudia heard the impatience in her voice even before she caught the warning glance Gavin shot her. They weren't getting anywhere with the old man. She'd already suspected his senility when she'd spoken to him at the morgue, and it had been confirmed by others at the ME's office since. It certainly didn't bode well for their search for leads today.

"Dr. Carver, please," she said, softening her tone, "it's very important. Do you remember anything that Mr. Silver asked you?"

"Of course, I do." He seemed suddenly taken aback that she should even imply a failure in his memory. "He wanted to know about the Owens case."

"Frank Owens?"

"Yes. That's it—Frank Owens."

She could feel Gavin's eyes on her, but refused to acknowledge it. "Dr. Carver, do you remember me?"

"Of course, dear. A face like yours, I don't forget. You work down at the garden center. You sold me my peonies last spring."

Claudia restrained her frustration. "No, I don't work at the garden center. I'm a detective with the Homicide unit. I was also Frank Owens's partner. Do you remember when I came to see you in January? It was at the ME's office. Do you remember that?"

"Ah, right. Right you are. How silly of me. I *do* recall, Detective. It was just before I retired. Of course. And you had questions about your partner's death."

"Do you recall what you told me then?"

"Not word for word, no. That was months ago. But I imagine I told you that I wasn't allowed to release any information. At least, not at that time."

Now Claudia dared to meet Gavin's gaze as a mutual look of hope passed between them.

"Are you saying you'd answer questions now?"

Daniel Carver shifted his slow eyes from her to Gavin, as though judging their character by appearance. Claudia moved to the edge of the sofa across from Carver, and had it not been for the marble coffee table between them, she might have reached across and taken one of his liver-spotted hands into her own.

"Dr. Carver?" she prompted.

"This would be off the record, I presume?" he asked. And when he returned his focus to her, Claudia was certain she saw more clarity, more lucidity behind those once-wise eyes of his. "Off the record?" he asked again.

"Absolutely. What can you tell us about Frank Owens's death?"

The old man nodded once before proceeding. "The Owens case was one of my last. There were several others on my plate at the time, but I recall that one because...well, because it left me a little confused. The thing is, initially everything indicated he'd died of a self-inflicted gunshot wound."

Claudia was certain her heart stopped. A queasiness clutched her stomach, and for a moment the room became a swirl of rich fabrics and glittering brass.

Had she heard right?

"What do you mean, 'initially'?" she asked, hearing the waver in her voice.

"The reports regarding the bullet definitely indicated a match to Detective Owens's duty weapon. And I don't recall there being any question that the angle of the shot was indicative of a self-inflicted wound. But there was something regarding the gunshot residue results."

"What do you mean?"

"Well, as always with any case of suspected suicide, I ran a GSR test on Detective Owens upon arrival at the ME's offices, swabbing both his hands and sending the sample to the lab for testing. A few days later the results came back to my office. It was late afternoon, I do know that for certain because I was running late to pick up my wife. We have bridge club Wednesday nights. Ten years and we haven't missed a single week. She needs to get out, Mrs. Carver does. It's important, and—"

"Doctor, please." It was Gavin's turn to prompt the old man. "Let's stay on track here. You were telling us about the GSR results from Detective Owens's autopsy."

Claudia watched Carver's expression, the shift in his thoughts almost visible.

"Right. The results. Well, as I said, I was running late that afternoon, so when the initial GSR report came through, I gave it a quick gander. And…well, I was baffled. You know, with a suicide, one naturally expects the results to be positive, but I could have…I could have sworn on first glance that the report indicated a negative result."

"Negative? But that would mean…" She couldn't say it. It wasn't possible. All these months she'd let the reports, her police training, others on the force…she'd let all of them convince her Frank had taken his own life. But what Carver was suggesting… *It wasn't possible*.

Gavin took over. "Are you telling us that Detective Owens hadn't fired his weapon?"

"Oh, there's no question his gun had been fired. The GSR testing was conducted in order to confirm it was Detective Owens who had fired it. Without any residue on his hands though, it's certain he didn't, unless of course he'd been wearing gloves."

Claudia's voice was a ragged whisper. "He wasn't

wearing gloves." In a blink she was at the scene again. How many times had she gone there in her mind during the past ten months? She'd held Frank's hand in hers, still warm. She hadn't been concerned about GSR tests then, but even if she had been, Claudia knew that touching Frank's hand wouldn't have affected anything. If Frank had fired his gun, there would have been traces, no matter what.

She cleared her throat. "Dr. Carver, you referred to it as the initial GSR report. Are you saying you ran a second one?"

He shook his head, lifting a hand to rub his eyes. She wondered if it was fatigue or if the old man's recollection was fading once again.

"Well, no. There is generally only the one test done, but you know, I looked at the report so quickly that afternoon, on my way out the door. It bothered me a bit that night, because I thought I must have misread it. So I checked it again first thing in the morning, and sure enough, the results were as I'd originally expected—positive—indicating that Detective Owens *had* fired his gun."

"So you never questioned the results again, or your initial misinterpretation of them?" Gavin asked.

"No. There was no need. In my haste, I'd obviously misread the report the first time."

"So what did you do with the report?"

"I suppose I filed it along with the rest of the autopsy reports and sent them over to the sergeant in charge of the case."

"Sergeant Gunning?" Claudia asked.

"I believe so." But it was obvious this point, like

many others, was no longer clear in Daniel Carver's waning memory.

"And when you spoke with James Silver, did you tell him any of this?"

"I...I honestly can't remember. Quite possibly."

Claudia mustered a smile she hoped would ease the mild embarrassment on the man's face.

"Thank you, Dr. Carver. We appreciate your time."

Gavin was already on his feet, apparently also realizing the futility in delving further. Daniel Carver rose from his chair and followed them to the front door.

It was Carver's hand on her shoulder that stopped Claudia when they reached the foyer.

"Detective Parrish, I..." He struggled with the words, barely a whisper from his trembling lips. "Are you sure you've never worked at the garden center?"

"No, sir. I'm afraid not."

He nodded thoughtfully for a moment before asking them, "Are you sure you wouldn't like to see my rosebushes?" His voice had altered again, and when Claudia looked at him, his expression had also changed, as though he had no concept of the conversation they'd just shared. It made her wonder if there was more than old age to Daniel Carver's condition.

She was vaguely aware of Gavin graciously declining the man's offer, before bidding him goodnight and ushering her out the door.

CLAUDIA SAID NOTHING as they crossed the quiet street. When she passed under a shaft of light, Gavin saw the tight lines of worry drawn across her face. And as he unlocked the door and watched her over the top of the car, those lines deepened to something that appeared more like anger.

She looked over and met his stare, her lips pursed. "He could have run a second test," she stated flatly.

"A second GSR test?"

She nodded before looking away again, gazing down the dark street. "If he had such doubts about his first reading, he *should* have run another test. How much would it have inconvenienced him to ask the lab to run it again?"

"I don't think it was a matter of inconvenience, Claudia."

"His reputation as a medical examiner?"

Gavin offered her a nod. "Given what I saw in there and what you said the other medical examiners thought of him, it seems pretty clear to me that the man had good reason to worry about his reputation. He wouldn't have wanted to draw attention to any inadequacies on his part if he could avoid it. Coupled with the fact that he'd already had his own doubts regarding his work, something as simple as reading a GSR report would have certainly brought his conduct and ability under question. And being that close to retirement, I doubt Carver would have done anything to compromise his pension or his reputation."

"How could he not?" She shook her head in disbelief. "You know, part of me wants to feel sorry for that doddering old man. But how can I? He questioned those initial results and still filed them with a complete disregard for the truth. More concerned for his own reputation than Frank's—a seasoned and honored detective. He should have ordered that second test.''

Gavin followed suit when Claudia finally opened the car door and got in. He turned the key in the ignition, aware of the anger in her movements as she yanked the seat belt across herself and buckled it. The amber glow of the dash lights did nothing to soften the harsh lines of her expression.

Steering down Everett Avenue away from Carver's house, he managed another sidelong glance. Claudia had wedged her elbow against the window and cradled her temple with her right hand. Her gaze seemed fixed on the taillights ahead of them, but Gavin guessed there was little focus in her wide-eyed stare. He didn't need to see her bite her lip to know she'd been shaken by the implications of the information Carver had just given them, however unreliable it might be.

The retired coroner's admission regarding the confusion over the GSR report hadn't surprised Gavin at all. He'd never been satisfied with the results of the investigation into Frank Owens's death, and his only surprise was that such discrepancies hadn't surfaced earlier. Claudia's reaction, however, was one of surprise. Gavin had seen her mounting confusion as she listened to the doctor describe his doubts and sketchy memories.

''So do you really think the old man read the report wrong the first time?''

She shook her head. "I don't know." He barely heard her whisper.

"Seems unlikely to me," Gavin went on. "I'm sure you've seen your share of reports from the various labs. Some of them are absolute Greek to me. But GSR results? Hard to read them wrong, I don't care how senile you are. They're either positive or negative. The subject either fired a gun or he didn't."

He brought the car to a stop at a red light. When he caught her gaze, Claudia's eyes seemed almost darker than before, her lips drawn a little tighter.

"So what do you think?" she asked him.

He gave a casual shrug, hoping to minimize the magnitude of what he was about to imply. "Just that it's hard to misread those reports. And if Carver saw that it was negative first, and then positive the next morning, I can't help but suspect tampering."

Gavin accelerated through the green light and headed toward Fells Point. Claudia was silent, but he felt her eyes on him.

"I'm sure you've pondered the possibility yourself," he went on. "Carver said he was in a rush that afternoon. If he set the report to one side, waiting till morning to file it, then it's not inconceivable someone could have gained access to his office and the report."

"You mean...someone like Frank's murderer?"

Gavin nodded. "And I'm wondering if Silver was thinking along those same lines. Maybe after meeting with Carver he started digging into the case. And maybe he got someone riled enough that it got him killed."

"James Silver never believed Frank killed himself." This time Claudia's voice was so low Gavin wasn't certain he'd made out the words, but the tremble in her tone was enough to assure him he'd not get a response if he asked her to repeat it.

Pulling up outside her building, Gavin let the silence envelop them for several moments. Eventually he pulled the keys from the ignition and turned in his seat.

"Are you going to be all right?"

Her nod was barely perceptible. She pretended to check her watch, but Gavin could see she struggled with emotions as she bit her lower lip again.

"Yeah, I'll be fine." A shaft of light caught the side of her face, and in it he thought he saw the faint glimmer of tears in her eyes. He heard her shakiness in the deep breath she took.

"It's just…I don't know," she said at last. "I thought it was behind me. I thought it was over."

"What was over?"

"Frank's death. Hearing about it…about the investigation…I guess I figured I'd dealt with it."

"What do you mean?"

"His suicide," she whispered. "Do you have any idea how long it took to convince myself that the reports had to be right? That Frank had taken his own life?"

"You're saying you didn't believe it at first?"

"Of course not. Frank was my partner. My… friend. How could I believe he'd be capable of killing himself? How could I believe that I couldn't…that I wasn't there for him? I had to force myself to-believe. The evidence was submitted, the reports trickled in, then the ruling came down. There was no arguing those hard facts. I'm a trained detective. I work with facts, with evidence.''

Gavin watched her rake her fingers through her hair. Her gaze out the windshield remained unbroken, as though she couldn't bear facing him with her delicate emotions.

''You can't know what it's like,'' she said, her voice as shaky as the hand she lowered to her lap. ''How hard it is coming to terms with your partner's death, especially when everyone tells you it was a suicide. You don't want to believe it at first. You wonder why you, of all people, didn't see the signs. How could you have missed them? Because they must have been there. You think about the things you might have said, could have done…then you struggle with the reasons why. And finally you try to accept the idea that he wasn't the man you believed he was.''

She closed her eyes momentarily before speaking again. Now Gavin thought he heard anger in her voice. ''And after all that, maybe they were wrong. Maybe everyone was wrong. All these months I allowed others, allowed the fumblings of a doddering old medical examiner, to sway me into believing Frank was a quitter.''

He could tell she held back tears.

''And he wasn't. Frank wasn't a quitter.''

''Look, if this is too much…if you'd prefer to not work this case, I'll understand.''

She was already shaking her head, as he'd hoped

she would. Now that he was finally making headway, he needed to stay close to Claudia, needed to find out what she was hiding.

"I don't have to tell you that you should probably remove yourself from the investigation into Silver's murder because of its possible link to your former partner," he said. "But I know it's important to you, on a personal level, so I'm not going to take the request to Sergeant Gunning unless you feel—"

"No, Gavin. I want to see this through. It's important to me. Very important. I have questions concerning Frank's death, and if there are answers to be had, even if they're from some senile old man, I want to...need to find them."

"Well, you do realize that we don't have anything concrete?"

"I know."

"When it comes down to it, how much confidence can we place in Carver's recollection? Even if he could be certain about what he had seen in that report, it's not enough to prove murder, and certainly not enough to reopen the case."

"No, but it's enough for me to know that it's worth searching for answers."

She looked out the passenger window and seemed to gaze up at the dark windows of her apartment on the top floor.

"Would you like to come up for a coffee?"

He wasn't sure why she would ask him—whether she hoped to discuss the case or if she hoped to find out more about him. Either way, he couldn't pass up the opportunity.

Locking the car behind them, he followed her into the row house. He heard no piano-playing coming from the first-floor apartment. In fact, the old building was dead silent. As they neared the third-floor landing, Claudia was already fishing her keys from her pocket. It was when she hurriedly replaced them and brushed back the edge of her coat to unclip her holster that Gavin felt the surge of adrenaline lick through him.

He followed her nod, looking past her shoulder to the door. It stood slightly ajar. He unclipped his belt holster, even as Claudia withdrew her gun. And as he took out his own Glock, Gavin heard the distant thud from within the apartment. In a flash, Claudia was through the door.

CHAPTER SIX

CLAUDIA KNEW GAVIN WAS behind her. He too had his gun out as she quietly edged the door open far enough to allow them entry.

The apartment lay in shadows. The only light was a milky glow slipping through half-drawn blinds from the sodium lamp on the opposite side of the street. Holding her breath, she eased her heel onto the hardwood floor and took another cautious step forward. There was nothing but silence in the darkness. Such silence, in fact, that she thought she must have imagined the muted thud seconds earlier.

But she hadn't.

Another thud, this one louder. It was accompanied by a faint dragging sound, like something against wood. The floor? But the sound was too brief for her to distinguish its source, or its exact location.

Claudia's hand tightened around the grip of her gun. Any exhaustion she may have felt before was lost to the rush of adrenaline. Her heart hammered so rapidly it seemed to press against her lungs, shortening her breath.

If there *was* someone in her apartment, there was no immediate sign. In the pale light, everything appeared in place. Yet, she could sense the presence of someone else.

Then, as she reached the corner of the kitchen bar and was about to step into the hallway, she felt a cool draft. An open window. But she'd not left any open.

A quick glance over her shoulder assured her Gavin was still with her, only inches separating them. The black muzzle of his gun was pointed down, but she could see him stiffen. Either he was reading her, or more likely, he too knew they weren't alone.

Gavin reached for her, placing one broad hand on her hip in an attempt to move ahead of her. Claudia ignored him, taking another step forward. This was her apartment, her home. If anyone was going first it would be her.

In the end, it didn't matter. The second her foot settled on the hallway floor she heard the clamoring of boots against steel. The fire escape.

Claudia muttered a curse and rushed forward. But she was too late. In the three seconds it took to reach the doorway of her bedroom at the end of the hall, she heard the screech of steel against steel as the escape ladder extended down to the alleyway behind the house. And by the time she reached the window, the rusted ladder was already rattling back into place.

Leaning through the open window, she searched the dark alley past the fire escape's landing. She heard the racing footfall before she caught a fleeting glimpse of a figure hightailing it along the cluttered alley. He was wearing black, all black, from his jeans to his baseball cap. The back-porch light of a first-floor apartment halfway down shimmered off the man's leather jacket, and a second later he turned around the corner onto Battery Street and was gone.

She drew back into the room and saw Gavin holstering his gun. Hurriedly he brushed past her, lifting a leg to straddle the window frame.

Claudia caught his arm. "Forget it. He's gone."

He looked out into the night, as if assessing for himself that pursuit was pointless.

"Did you see him?"

"Only a glimpse. And nothing useful." She holstered her own weapon and moved across the room to the light switch.

She expected to find drawers yanked open, and their contents spilled across the floor. Instead, the room appeared untouched.

"We must have come in just in time," she commented, casting a quick glance over the room. "Doesn't look as though he got anything."

Even her nightstand where she kept her off-duty gun remained closed. She moved next to the bed and opened the drawer. The revolver her father had given her years ago lay nestled between a box of tissues and a half-read paperback novel.

"Are you sure nothing's missing?" Gavin asked.

"I think so."

Claudia shoved the drawer closed, then looked up to see Gavin pull his hands into the sleeves of his jacket and slide the window shut.

"Don't bother being careful. There aren't going to be any prints. I'm positive I saw gloves on his hands."

She left the bedroom then, systematically switching on lights and studying each room until she ended up in the living room. Everything was in its place.

"Has anything like this happened in your building before?" Gavin asked.

Claudia shook her head. "There were a couple break-ins last year just down the street. Nothing major though. Small-time opportunists."

After shedding her coat and hanging it in the front hall, she closed the door. Had she forgotten to lock up when she'd left with Gavin earlier? She'd been so anxious about getting to Evidence Control, it was very likely.

As if reading her thoughts, Gavin said, "I'm sure you locked up when we left."

But how could he be? He'd been halfway down the first flight of stairs by the time she'd pulled the door shut.

She turned the dead bolt, and the first feeling of violation quivered through her. No matter what the method of entry, someone had been in her apartment. Someone uninvited. Opportunist, petty thief, local thug...it didn't matter; a complete stranger had let himself into her home.

"Are you all right?" Gavin asked.

"Of course." She tried to control the tremble in her hand as she unbuckled her holster.

"Aren't you going to call it in?"

Claudia shook her head. "What's the point? Nothing appears to have been taken, there's nothing out of place, and I'm pretty certain about the gloves.

Even if I had a team come out, they're not likely to find anything.''

Anyone else might have disagreed with her complacency, but Gavin knew she was right. They'd only be wasting department time and funds.

''Did you want coffee?'' she asked. ''Or would you prefer something else? Frankly, I could use a beer. Are you on shift tonight?''

''No, I'm not. A beer sounds great. Can I use your bathroom?''

She pointed to the door down the hall and went to the fridge. Twisting the cap off one bottle, Claudia took a gulp, wondering if she shouldn't have poured herself something stronger to calm her nerves. It wasn't just the break-in. Carver's revelation had gotten her on edge long before.

It was only when she was about to sit on the sofa that Claudia spotted Frank's case file. A quick surge of panic whipped through her. Had Gavin seen it earlier? He already believed she'd had something to do with the disappearance of Silver's journals, and seeing the copied file would only rouse his suspicions further. Not to mention the fact that he could easily report her and...

With the sound of the bathroom door opening, Claudia kicked the folder completely under the sofa.

''Are you sure you're all right?'' Gavin asked, shrugging off his jacket and draping it over the arm of one chair. ''You seem shaken.''

''I'm fine,'' she lied, handing him his beer and sitting down. ''It was just some punk. He won't be back. I'm sure he saw there was nothing of value here.''

Gavin joined her on the sofa. With his free hand he loosened his tie, slipped it over his head and tossed it on top of his jacket. The white shirt he wore tucked into the waist of his pants billowed, but not so much that Claudia couldn't discern his physique beneath the now-rumpled cotton. Broad shoulders tugged at the fabric as he took a swig from his bottle and lowered it to the coffee table. Unlike her, Gavin obviously found time to work out.

She recalled the admiring look Lori had given him at Evidence Control. And when his dark eyes caught hers now, Claudia couldn't blame the technician for her drooling gaze.

Sitting on her couch with one arm slung across the back, Gavin looked different. Not as formidable somehow. But real. Human. As he unbuttoned his cuffs and rolled up his sleeves, he appeared relaxed, as if he belonged on her sofa.

''In the car,'' Gavin said at last, ''you mentioned that at first you were convinced Frank had been murdered. What made you think that? Was it just that you couldn't bear the thought of your partner taking his own life? Or was there something more?''

She didn't want to discuss this. With Gavin, or with anyone. She wanted it behind her. But if Silver's death was related to Frank's—which now seemed very plausible—then they did need to discuss it, even if that meant reliving those painful memories.

Claudia took another drink of beer and started to pick at one corner of the label. In her mind, she'd gone over that night too many times to count. Every detail seemed as vivid as it had been the second she'd stepped into Frank's apartment. She remembered the cold rain and the sound of it scratching against the windows; she remembered the closeness of the room and the queasiness that had gripped her the second she'd caught her first glimpse of his body slumped in the corner. Most of all, she remembered the smell of Frank as she'd squatted next to him, and the warmth she'd felt in his hand, and finally the dark void that steadily consumed her heart as realization sank in.

"Claudia?" Gavin shifted his hand on the back of the sofa and touched her shoulder, and when she met his eyes she recognized concern there. "Were you on the scene? Was there something that made you think Frank had been murdered?"

She nodded, letting out a deep breath. She needed to tell someone. She'd been silent for too long.

"It didn't feel right," she admitted. "From the moment I stepped into Frank's apartment, it felt wrong. You know that sense you get sometimes?"

She waited for Gavin's nod of understanding.

"I can't explain it exactly. It was just a feeling in my gut. And then when I saw him…I really thought something was wrong with the whole scene."

"Why?"

She held Gavin's gaze, searching for sincerity. And in his eyes Claudia recognized him as someone she could trust, needed to trust.

"The gun…Frank's gun—" she tried to correct

the tremble in her voice "—it was lying in his hand."

"Yeah?"

She took another deep breath, gathering strength. "I've been on a few suicide scenes, and in every case involving a gun, the weapon was never found in the victim's hand. After Frank...I talked to a couple of the doctors at the ME's office...not Carver, though. When I questioned them about such cases, they agreed that they had yet to see a gunshot suicide where the weapon was still in the victim's hand. It has to do with the force of the gun's recoil. And if the weapon *were* found in the victim's hand, it would be clutched tightly, the muscles contracting in death. The gun wouldn't just be lying there."

Claudia watched Gavin absorb this information, his expression thoughtful.

"Did you discuss this theory with anyone?" he asked.

"No. How could I? Everyone was so quick to believe Frank had killed himself, and I was not about to lose my own credibility by screaming 'murder' no matter what I believed at the time. It would have looked personal anyway, him being my partner." She paused long enough to swallow another gulp of beer, feeling the alcohol begin to take the edge off her nerves.

"Everybody was just so ready to believe Frank had folded under the pressure," she said. "IAD had singled him out, and they were relentless. Ruthless. It was wrong. Whoever was behind the allegations pushed Frank to a brink he should never have been on. I'll never forgive IAD, or the department, for allowing that kind of aggressive investigation to go on. At the same time, I don't know if I can ever forgive myself.''

''Forgive yourself? For what?''

''For not being there. For not listening to Frank. We argued the last time I saw him, the night before…''

''Before his death?'' Gavin prompted when she couldn't say it.

She managed a nod, and when she swallowed her beer this time she felt the lump that had settled in her throat. ''We were both pretty angry, arguing about IAD and the allegations. Frank had asked for my help before, but that night he was adamant. He figured the only way he could clear his name was to flush out the real culprit.''

''Frank, we've been through this. I thought you agreed to stay out of it. Just let IAD do their job. You know they won't find anything on you. You'll come clean.''

His apartment had been hot that night, but mostly it was her anger that had gotten her so heated she'd had to strip off her coat and jacket, even though she'd had no intention of staying. She'd come for one reason—to convince Frank to stop his insanity.

''I know you've already started digging around. It's raising eyebrows in the department and surely with IAD,'' she warned him. *''If you keep it up, I… Frank, I'm afraid that IAD's going to view it as an indication of guilt. Like you're trying to cover some-*

thing up. They're going to see you doing exactly
what they're accusing you of."

"*I'm not tampering with evidence, Claudia. I'm
just going to find out who is. IAD doesn't seem to be
getting to the truth, so maybe it's up to me. Don't
you see, it's the only way IAD is going to believe it's
not me. This is my career on the line. Can't you
understand that?*"

Leaning against the arm of the couch, Frank had
reached out and snatched her hand as she paced past
him. And when she dared to look at him, into the
eyes of the man she loved so much, the fear really
took hold. She was terrified of what Frank might get
himself into. Afraid of how IAD might find guilt
when all he'd tried to do was prove his innocence.
And she was afraid she'd lose the only man she'd
ever loved.

"*Listen to me, Claudia. This is serious.*"

"*And so is the potential of falsely incriminating
yourself,*" she argued, wishing there was some way
to break through that bullheaded determination of
his.

She allowed him to pull her to him then, drawing
her into the V of his legs and holding her there.
Eventually she'd cradled his face in her hands, caressing his cheek and searching his eyes, praying to
find compliance there.

"*Frank, I'm begging you. Please don't do this.
Just let it be. Let's get on with our lives. I can't…we
can't take much more of this.*"

She tried to kiss him, sliding a hand to the back
of his neck. But the kiss was brief. He pulled away.

"I love you, Claudia," he whispered. *"And I need you. Not just as my lover, but as a detective. I need your help. I can't do this without—"*

"No, Frank. I can't." It was her turn to pull away, but he hung on to her, and she saw a certain desperation flicker in his eyes. *"I can't help you. It's insane. And it's wrong.* You're *wrong. This is not the way to handle the situation. If the roles were reversed you know you'd tell me the same thing. Just let IAD do their job. If you're innocent, they'll find out and then—"*

"If?"

She watched his entire body go rigid.

"What do you mean 'if'? If I'm *innocent?"*

"I didn't mean it that way. Listen to me—"

"You did *mean it."*

As many times as Claudia played out that last scene in her head, it would always astound her how a simple, seemingly innocent word could lead to such devastating results. And yet, over the months since, she'd often wondered if there *had* been doubt in her mind that had led her to say "if." They'd both been exhausted that night, both of them run-down by the weeks of accusations and allegations, the desperation to find a way out, and to salvage even a semblance of their former happiness.

Frank had pushed her away then and begun pacing. But in spite of the distance, Claudia had been able to feel the anger practically crackle from him. Anger and betrayal.

"God!" he shouted. *"I don't believe this! My own goddamned partner...my lover!"*

She was certain that if the neighbors in the apartment below were home, they'd hear him.

"Even you don't believe I'm innocent, do you?"

"Of course I do. Of course, I do. I just don't think that the way you're going about this is right. I just...I want you to stop."

He shook his head, staring past her to the window on the far wall as though looking her in the eye was impossible. In retrospect, Claudia realized it was at that moment she'd lost him.

"Frank?"

"Forget it, Claudia. Why don't you just leave?"

"No. Let me—"

"Let you what? There's nothing you can do for me. Not when you don't even believe me. Just leave."

He'd grabbed her coat and jacket, thrusting them at her, and only then did his gaze meet hers. The hopelessness she saw there frightened her more than she'd ever been frightened before.

She tried to reach for him, but he stepped back.

"What are you going to do?" she asked.

"What do you care?"

"I do care, Frank. For crying out loud, you know I care. You're the most important person in my life. But the way you're going about this whole IAD thing...it's suicide, Frank."

As long as she lived, Claudia knew she would never forget those words. And how she wished she could have taken them back.

"Yeah, well, maybe it is suicide. But I certainly don't need your help with that, do I? Now leave, Claudia. Just leave."

He threw open the door of his apartment.

"Leave," he said again, this time a whisper in which she was certain she heard his pain. *"Leave."*

And she did. With no more words, she did as he wished. She walked out the door, the scent of him, the memory of that brief, desperate kiss lingering in her senses as she headed down the stairs. She paused on the first landing and turned, but he was gone. The door latched behind him, and she was left in the silence of the stairwell. She wasn't sure how long she'd stood there—seconds, minutes—debating the wisdom of going back.

If only she had.

"So why didn't you?" Gavin's voice shattered the vivid memory. "Why didn't you help him?"

Claudia felt the images of that night slip away to the edge of her memory. "Besides being afraid of how it would make him look? I guess I figured that without me, Frank wouldn't continue investigating on his own. I thought he'd back off and then the whole mess would sort itself out and IAD would realize he was innocent."

"Do you have any idea what he'd been looking into?"

Claudia shook her head. "I don't know for sure. I think he'd gone through other detectives' case files, Evidence Control, different crime labs. He may have even questioned some of the suspects who had benefited from the evidence tampering. I only know he was desperate enough to try anything. But I honestly felt that without my help and support, he wouldn't pursue it."

Still, she'd spent hours that night lying awake, then pacing the floor of her apartment, rehearsing in her mind all the things she might say to Frank to persuade him to stop his investigation. She'd searched for the words that might possibly convince him she did believe in him. And then she'd called. Several times. But she hadn't gotten an answer. Not that night, not the next day. And by the time she saw him again…it had been too late.

"Claudia?" When Gavin touched her shoulder this time, he left it there. "I asked you…did you believe Frank?"

"You mean, believe he didn't have anything to do with the evidence tampering?"

He nodded, and Claudia took another drink. How much did she want to tell Gavin? Hadn't she already said too much?

"At first, of course, I believed in his innocence. Frank and I were…we were close. I knew he wasn't capable of the things IAD accused him of. But as the investigation wore on…wore on his nerves, and on mine…I'm not sure I knew what to believe. The investigation was hush-hush, but there were enough rumors going around to make the allegations seem founded, especially when a lot of the tampering involved Frank's own cases."

"And you've never talked to anyone about this?"

"How could I? If Frank's suspicions were correct and the corruption stemmed from the unit, then I couldn't trust anyone."

"But you work with these guys, Claudia. Surely you know them well enough."

"I may know my squad, but Homicide as a whole…it's a big unit. And in the early stages, when I truly believed Frank had been murdered, I also had to consider the fact that there'd been no sign of a struggle. Not even a struggle for his duty weapon. If it was murder, I can only guess it was someone he knew. Someone he knew quite well. If that was the case, I was hardly willing to rouse that someone's suspicions."

Gavin seemed to mull her words over for a while, taking a couple of swigs of beer before finally looking back at her. "So now what do you believe?" This time his voice took on a more compassionate tone. Without it, Claudia realized, she might not have been so willing to answer.

"Now I don't know what to believe. In the end, after all the reports had been filed and the ruling handed down, I had to believe them. It was actually easier that way. Easier to be angry with Frank for giving up than to wonder how things might have been different if I *had* listened to him. Maybe he would still be alive today if I hadn't just walked away.

"It didn't happen overnight, though—convincing myself of his suicide. It took months. And after all that, now I've got Carver suggesting that maybe it *was* murder."

"You can't put too much faith in the old man's memory."

"I know. But I can't dismiss it, either." The lump in her throat had grown. A single gulp of beer was almost impossible and Claudia set down the half-empty bottle. She didn't want to cry. She'd spent too many months doing that.

As though aware the dam was about to break, Gavin reached over and placed his hand on hers. She looked at the strong fingers folded over hers, broad knuckles with the memory of a deep summer tan and a grip that was sure yet consoling.

It had been a long time since someone had touched her. Not since Frank had she felt the kind of compassion, understanding…camaraderie she did from Gavin as he squeezed her hand. Claudia was almost afraid to look up, afraid of what one gaze into his comforting eyes might do to her. But she already knew.

Even before her eyes met his, she knew she was going to kiss Gavin. It was as if an invisible force moved between them, drawing them together from the moment they shook hands back at headquarters.

She couldn't be certain who made the first move. The distance between them closed. With his other hand he reached over and touched her cheek. So gentle. So intimate.

There was no time to consider her actions. She was heeding a voice stronger than reason. As she felt Gavin's finger under her chin, tilting her face to his, Claudia realized she was lost. There was the warm whisper of his breath across her cheek, and then…Gavin's lips. They brushed hers, tentatively, as though testing her acceptance. But he didn't have to.

Right now she needed Gavin. Needed his strength and understanding. And when he drew back slightly, it was Claudia who reached for him. She put her hand on the back of his neck and trailed her fingers up through his short-clipped hair to guide him to her.

Without a second thought, she surrendered to his skillful mouth. His tongue traced a seductive line along her lips, parting them easily, opening her to him. And as Claudia eagerly returned the intoxicating kiss, she was aware of a warm, flooding sensation that came from deep within her.

She gave herself to him and at the same time, took from him...searching for something she'd been missing these past months. Something far more profound than mindless desire.

Claudia didn't know who closed the gap between them completely. She was only aware of the power of Gavin's body, the strength and solace of his embrace. Her hand slipped to his chest, and she felt the quickening of his heart, beating as fast as her own. Through the thin material of her top, she felt his fingers trace her spine to the belted waist of her slacks. And when his hand slid over her rib cage, across the sheer fabric and cupped one breast, shocks of desire licked through her.

She had no idea if her quiet moan was audible, but she felt it, deep in her throat, filled with so much longing and...betrayal.

Frank.

With a small gasp, Claudia pulled away.

Disappointment flickered behind Gavin's eyes and tugged at the fine lines bracketing his mouth.

"I'm sorry," she muttered, dragging a hand

through her hair and suddenly feeling very uncomfortable.

"It's all right. I think it's been a long day for both of us." He leaned away from her, back into the cushions of the sofa, clearly needing distance himself.

"No, it's not all right. I...I shouldn't have led you on like that." She bit her lower lip, hating the waver she heard in her own voice and trying like hell to control it.

"You didn't lead me on."

She caught his stare, dark and seductive. How was it that she still wanted to kiss him? Still felt that overwhelming attraction?

"No," she said. "You don't understand."

"Then explain."

"It's...it's not you, Gavin. Honest."

"Then what is it? Tell me."

But how could she? Except for Faith, she hadn't told anyone.

And then, Gavin took her hand again. "Trust me, Claudia," he whispered, stroking the back of her hand with his thumb.

It had to be the beer, Claudia thought. The alcohol was clouding her judgment and loosening her resolve. She shouldn't tell anyone. But now Gavin didn't feel like just "anyone."

"Frank and I..." She reached for her beer, needing another swallow. "We were more than just partners. We...we were involved. Romantically. It wasn't until later on, and not for very long, but...I guess the attraction was there from the beginning really."

She swirled the last of the beer in the bottom of her bottle, uncertain whether she should go on, but needing to talk nonetheless.

"When I left Robbery and joined Homicide about three years ago, Sergeant Gunning introduced me to the squad. It was pretty informal, just a quick introduction all around, and then he asked if anyone wanted to work with me. As if anyone really *wants* a new guy. I'd heard about Frank through the grapevine, knew he was a loner who hadn't worked with a solid partner in years, so he was the last person I expected to raise his hand. And yet, he did. I can still picture that morning. He didn't glance up once from the file on his desk, didn't look at me. He just raised his hand and told Sarge he'd show me the ropes."

She remembered the scene—the other detectives on the small squad, including Sarge, all going quiet when they saw Frank's hand go up. It was their silence that had at last caused Frank to meet her gaze. He'd given her the briefest of smiles, more like an acknowledgment, and then nodded his head as though to beckon her over to his desk. It had started then, on that day, with that nod. There had been a bond between her and Frank. And as she met Gavin's intent look of concern now, she realized that the instant connection she'd felt with Frank was not unlike what she'd experienced with Gavin.

"Months later," she said, "Frank admitted he'd reviewed my file. He'd already spoken with others in my squad in Robbery and decided to partner up with me long before that day.

"We worked together for almost two years before

anything happened…I mean, romantically. Not that we hadn't thought about it before then. I guess we just hoped it would go away, that it wasn't true, because it could threaten the partnership. It was only last October when we finally talked about our feelings. And, two months later…Frank was dead.''

Claudia couldn't be certain of Gavin's thoughts as he studied her. His hand had become still over hers, and she saw the quick flex of a muscle along his jaw.

''I'm sorry, Claudia,'' he said at last. ''I had no idea.''

''No one did. We'd decided it couldn't be public knowledge. The partnership would be over. So we swore to keep a professional appearance, and I intend to maintain that.'' She managed a weak smile, hoping to ease the seriousness that seemed to have come over Gavin. But the smile didn't last. ''Frank was the best detective I've ever known. The job came naturally to him. Working with him was the highlight of my career, and I learned everything I know about this job from him. But more than that, he was the best *man* I've ever known.

''That's why Silver's murder is so important to me. I need to know what happened to Frank. Until I do, there's no way I can put it to rest.''

Gavin said nothing. The silence of the apartment swelled around them, broken only by the muffled sound of a passing car in the street below.

''You're right,'' she said eventually, ''it's been a long day. And a hard one at that. The very last thing I should have done was kiss you. I…I'm honestly not ready for anything, Gavin. I hope you understand.''

She waited for his slow nod.

''I also hope what happened tonight, between us…that it won't get in the way of our partnership.'' But she knew the suggestion was a ridiculous one. How could their kiss not affect their partnership? What she'd felt in Gavin's arms wasn't something she could simply forget. She would remember the sensations that had swept through her every time she looked into his eyes or saw that sweet smile lift the corners of his lips.

That same smile touched his mouth now, and Claudia felt another surge ripple through her.

''You worry too much, Claudia.'' He gave her hand a final squeeze and stood up from the sofa. ''I'm a big boy,'' he said, putting on his jacket. ''Are you sure you're going to be all right?''

She nodded.

''I can stay the night if you like. On the couch. I'm only offering because of the break-in.''

''No. I'm fine, really.''

At the door, Gavin gave her another long, hard stare as though seeking reassurance that she was truly all right.

''Are you off tomorrow?'' he asked.

''I'm off the whole weekend. But if anything comes up you can call me.''

''I'll try to let you get your rest.'' His slight hesitation echoed her own sense of awkwardness in their parting. ''Good night, then.''

''Good night, Gavin.''

"And be sure to put the chain on," he told her, before giving her a quick wink and heading down the stairs.

Through the heavy door the sound of his steps stopped, resuming only once she'd done as he'd told her. A minute later, as she put the empty beer bottles on the kitchen island, Claudia heard the car start up on the street outside her windows.

Exhaustion rippled through her. Coupled with the beer, she considered herself lucky to have managed enough lucidity to back out of their kiss when she did. She had to be nuts: first instigating their intimacy, and then so eagerly returning her passion. Gavin was her partner. Had she learned nothing from the past?

At least she'd been honest with him, Claudia thought, turning out the lights and walking down the hall to her bedroom. There was no way she could move forward, no way to have any semblance of a relationship with anyone until she was able to uncover the truth behind Frank's death. And now, more than ever, she wanted to move forward.

COMPARED TO CLAUDIA'S APARTMENT, Gavin's row house was an absolute shambles. He cast a disparaging glance around the narrow living room, his gaze falling on box after box. Some were still taped shut, while others had been opened in numerous and aborted attempts to unpack.

When he'd bought the fixer-upper two years ago, he'd decided to start renovating the upstairs and work his way down, but that ambition had resulted in half-finished living quarters. Every project he'd taken on seemed to have been interrupted by some case or departmental crisis. The kitchen, in spite of dazzling new cupboards and appliances, was still awaiting a new floor and counter. The door to the downstairs bathroom had remained closed since he'd moved in, yet the upstairs one gleamed right down to the faucets. The spare bedroom was stuffed with more boxes, along with camping equipment that hadn't seen use since he'd joined IAD, while the master bedroom could have been a showpiece were it not for the laundry spilling from the hamper.

Gavin shoved aside several outdated newspapers and lowered himself onto the leather couch. Closing his eyes, he let out a deep sigh, but it did little to relieve the tension knotted along the tops of his shoulders.

What the hell had he been thinking?

That was just it, wasn't it? He *hadn't* been thinking.

If he had, he would never have kissed Claudia. He would never have submitted to the fantasies that had been playing themselves over and over in his head since he'd first laid eyes on her. Not only did it complicate things, and completely jeopardize his investigation, but that one kiss made him want Claudia all the more.

He could still smell her perfume. The delicate traces of jasmine sent quick shocks of desire through him again as he remembered the softness of her lips and the undeniable response of her body to his touch.

It was just a kiss, he tried to convince himself.

Claudia had said herself it was wrong, had apologized for it, and told him she wasn't ready for anything. As though *he* was!

And yet, the attraction was there. It must have started the day he'd opened her file. How, in just one day, could he be more attracted to Claudia than any woman in his past? Not that there had been a lot of them, especially since he'd joined IAD.

He admired Claudia's strength and stamina, her sharp mind, her professionalism and quiet courage. And now, he could add resilience and stoicism to that list of character attributes. Her love for Frank Owens was amply clear, not just in her words but in her entire demeanor as she had—almost painfully—described her former partner. She'd said that no one else knew of her relationship with Owens; she'd kept it secret all these months, mourning on her own in silence. Gavin couldn't imagine the kind of strength that took.

He understood why she'd risked copying Owens's file. Gavin's first suspicion was that she'd been involved in Owens's death. But she couldn't be; not after he'd seen for himself the love she had for her former partner. No, she'd copied the file because she'd been determined to find his murderer, if, in fact, Owens had been murdered.

Not that it seemed to matter on an emotional level to Claudia. Murder or suicide—she blamed herself. Probably as much as she blamed Internal Affairs.

Gavin sat up. From the cluttered coffee table he took the file Lieutenant Randolph had given him on Claudia. He couldn't begin to imagine what she'd do if she ever found out his real reason for joining Homicide. Then again, in the end, how could he possibly avoid it? Once his investigation was over and the results submitted, Claudia would know. The entire unit would know who Detective Gavin Monaghan really was, and they'd resent him for it. He should be used to it by now; he'd become a "rat" the day he'd joined IAD. It hadn't bothered him before; he'd justified it by doing the best job he could, by being one of the most thorough and scrupulous agents in the department. And yet, with the memory of Claudia's kiss still on his lips, for the first time, the stigma associated with IAD bothered him.

Opening the file, he leafed through the reports from Owens's past cases. Claudia had been the secondary detective on all three of the cases that had gone sour due to evidence tampering. And then there was her own case, thrown out of court just yesterday. The implication certainly didn't play in Claudia's favor, especially since IAD's first prime suspect had been dead for ten months now.

Three other IAD investigators had tried to uncover the corruption after Gavin's initial attempt a year ago. All three had come up with nothing and been asked to hand over their findings. There hadn't been enough to charge any one particular detective or unit. In the end, there could only be silent finger-pointing, and all three investigators had pointed directly at Claudia.

Even he had agreed with them that as Owens's partner she was the most likely suspect. That's why he'd switched to Claudia's squad, why he'd talked

to Gunning about wanting to work with her...
wanting to work with one of the best Homicide had
to offer, he'd told the sergeant.

But now, how could he believe Claudia responsible? His heart told him otherwise. It was as if all
suspicion had been melted with a single kiss.

Where was his head? If nothing else, he should
suspect Claudia all the more; she'd had primary access to Silver's journals. And now they were gone.
Evidence, once again, had been tampered with...lost.

No, Gavin thought as he closed the file and tossed
it back onto the coffee table. No, he had to keep his
wits about him. He couldn't let one kiss, no matter
how passionate, influence his investigation. Facts
were facts, and those were what he'd have to work
with. He had to find out who was behind the corruption, even if it meant charging the same person who
now filled his thoughts with fantasies the likes of
which he'd never entertained before.

CHAPTER SEVEN

BEYOND THE WINDOWS of the Homicide offices, the sky brooding over the city had darkened another shade. All morning the forecasted rain had held off. It could only be a matter of time though, Claudia thought as she turned back to her desk.

Ignoring the sounds of the office around her, she tried to focus on a report from the State's Attorney Office. But it wasn't the noise that prevented her from concentrating. She lifted her gaze to Frank's desk. Or rather, Gavin's desk. The calendar in the blotter was fresh; last December's, with all of Frank's doodles and dates, was gone. As was the box of Cracker Jacks and the reading glasses. Only paperwork remained.

She could have used the weekend to do some of her own. Silver's was just one case on her plate. There were others, from as long as a year ago, requiring typing and organizing of reports and investigative updates. But instead of working she'd used her days off to the fullest, staying away from the office entirely.

Gavin, on the other hand, had obviously put in his hours and then some. Reports from the Silver case were all typed and the orange case folder was already sitting there with the occurrence number stamped across its front. She'd taken a peek at the file when she came in this morning, and admired the precision and organization of his work. He had certainly been busy over the weekend.

Not only that, but he'd obviously made himself at home. Claudia pushed back the quiver of resentment.

"Detective Parrish." Tony flashed her a playful grin as he crossed the office. "Finally decided to join us, huh?" he asked, folding his arms over his chest and coming to a stop at the corner of her desk.

She returned his smile.

"Glad to see you took advantage of your weekend off. I hope it was good."

"Restful," she answered, remembering the lazy mornings in bed, and her disappointment at having to get up with the alarm this morning. "Just sort of took it easy. Went up to Westminster to visit my sister. That's about it."

"Well, we sure could have used you around here, let me tell ya."

"I heard on the news."

"Four homicides over the weekend, and of course I'd get the double. I've been swamped. Looks like your partner's been hard at it, too." He nodded to the paperwork across Gavin's desk. "I was surprised he didn't drag you in to help him."

Claudia shrugged. It didn't surprise *her* that Gavin hadn't called over the weekend. Unless something urgent had come up in the Silver investigation, why would he? Even then it would probably have to have been something crucial. He'd told her he would let her get her rest, but Claudia knew there was more to it than thoughtfulness on Gavin's part. No doubt he felt as awkward as she did over the kiss they'd shared Friday night. In fact, she was almost relieved they had not run into each other yet today. She wasn't sure how she was going to handle seeing him again. Not after she'd spent the weekend thinking about him, remembering how he'd made her feel.

"Claudia, in my office." Sergeant Gunning's voice boomed above the din. His hulking frame filled the doorway momentarily before he disappeared back into his office.

"Sounds serious," Tony mumbled as Claudia pushed her chair back. "Good luck."

She gave him a wry glance and headed to the open door. Sarge did have all the appearances of seriousness. He lifted a somber gaze in greeting as he scratched at his chin and waved for her to take a seat.

"So where are you with the Silver case?" he asked. His steel-framed chair creaked in protest as he leaned back and laced his fingers behind his head.

"What do you mean, Sarge? You assigned Gavin as the primary, remember?"

There was no question that Sarge caught her mocking tone. A brief spark of humor flashed in his eyes, even though he didn't crack a smile. Three years of working under him afforded Claudia the luxury of ribbing the man from time to time.

"All right, where is Monaghan with the investigation?" he asked.

"I'm not really sure. I haven't actually spoken to him since Friday."

"And how are you two working out?"

Claudia wondered if the heat she felt rise within her revealed itself in her face as the memory of their kiss flitted through her mind. She cleared her throat, managing to say, "Fine."

"You think you're gonna be okay partnering with him then?"

"As I recall, you didn't exactly give me much choice in the matter."

"I'm serious, Claudia. Can you work with this guy?"

"Sure I can." Of course, it would be a hell of a lot easier if she could put an end to the rampant fantasizing that accompanied any thought she had of Gavin.

"So is he any good?"

Again she felt a quick flush. "Yeah," she replied. "He's very professional, both on the scene and with witnesses. He's a thinker, and his experience is pretty obvious."

"He's all right to handle this investigation then? Silver being a former cop and all, there's bound to be some heat on this if we don't get somewhere fast."

"I think Gavin will do fine. He's on top of things."

"But you said he doesn't have any leads?"

"No, I said I haven't spoken to him since Friday. I'm not sure where he's at with the investigation or what leads he might be following. You haven't talked to him yet?"

His chair squealed again as it snapped back into

position under his great weight. ''I haven't had a chance.''

Then obviously Gavin hadn't told Sarge of the possible connection between Silver and Frank, Claudia thought. Nor would he have had the opportunity to relate to him their meeting with Dr. Carver and the possible implication behind the old man's comments. Well, if Gavin hadn't told Gunning, she certainly wasn't going to. Maybe Gavin hadn't had the chance to speak with him yet, or more likely he hadn't wanted to share information until it was more concrete. Either way, it was Gavin's investigation, not hers.

She watched Sarge prop his elbows against the desktop. He closed his eyes and massaged his temples as though attempting to stave off a headache. When he reached for his glasses, she recognized his dismissal.

''All right, then.'' He nudged the glasses firmly onto the bridge of his nose. ''I just wanted to be sure you're doin' okay.''

''I appreciate it, Sarge.''

''But I want you to keep me posted on what's happening with this Silver case. Every step.''

''I'll let Gavin know.''

As she stood, a look of understanding passed between them. She would not overstep her boundaries as the secondary detective on the case; any information would have to come from Gavin.

''Good,'' Sarge said gruffly before turning his attention back to his paperwork.

It was only once she had her hand on the doorknob, that Claudia decided to ask him. All weekend she'd considered the possibility that Frank might have left something behind: a clue, a reference to Silver, something that might give them a direction or, better yet, a probable cause with which to reopen the investigation into his death. It wasn't until she'd seen the way Gavin had moved into Frank's desk that she thought about the drawers' possible contents.

She stopped, turning to him one last time. "Sarge, I wanted to ask you...about Frank's stuff."

"What stuff?"

"From his desk. I know you cleared it out. I was just wondering where his things were. Would they still be in Evidence Control?"

"I guess so. Why?"

She couldn't tell if it was confusion or concern that brought his hard gaze up one more time. She shrugged, attempting to make the query appear casual.

"No reason really. It's just with Gavin using the desk now, I thought I'd clear out the rest of Frank's stuff. I wasn't sure if it should go with the other things." But the truth was, Claudia had no idea if there was even anything left in those steel drawers. She'd never dared open them for fear of the emotions she'd stir up.

"Well, I think I removed anything pertaining to work or the department. If you do find anything beyond supplies, I guess just pass it by me and I'll let you know if we need to submit it."

"Thanks, Sarge."

She imagined that he watched her leave his office,

probably wondering why, after all these months, she'd questioned him about the contents of Frank's desk drawers. But he said nothing.

After closing the door behind her, she stopped. Gavin sat at his desk. His attention was fixed on his paperwork, and then, as though he sensed her, his gaze came up. Claudia couldn't put a name to the warm sensation that spread through her when his eyes caught hers—embarrassment or attraction, or more likely, both.

Gavin on the other hand appeared unaffected as she crossed the office and joined him.

"How was your weekend?" he asked, a charming, effortless smile curving his lips as he tapped several reports against the top of his desk to straighten them.

"It was fine, thanks."

"Do anything exciting?"

Small talk, Claudia thought. Maybe Gavin didn't appear uncomfortable after the intimacy of their last encounter, but his polite conversation was a sure sign.

"Not much," she answered. "Just some family stuff and catching up on sleep mostly."

In the same way that Faith had looked at her expectantly when she'd mentioned having a new partner, Gavin held Claudia's stare now as though awaiting more details. And, in the same way she'd not told her sister anything more about Gavin, Claudia was reticent to share her personal life with him. Maybe if they kept everything else in their relationship strictly professional, she might manage to quell the more personal desires that had taken hold of her.

"So, it looks as if you've been busy," she said, determined to change the subject.

"Well, I like to keep up with my paperwork. You know how it is."

She nodded. "You haven't talked to Sarge yet, have you?"

"About the case? No. I really don't have anything to tell him that isn't already in my office report, do I?"

There was no mistaking the message behind the knowing look he gave her.

"So you're not telling him about our visit with Dr. Carver or the possible link between Silver and Frank, then?"

"Nope." He lowered his voice. "That's the way I work, Claudia. I don't go around voicing hunches until I've got something solid to back them up. I hope you don't have a problem with that."

"No problem." She offered him an assuring smile. "So, Detective Monaghan, you working on any new hunches?"

"As a matter of fact..." He set down his paperwork and took up his notebook. "It's not exactly a hunch. More like a potential lead. Are you interested in going back to Boston Street with me?"

"What have you got?"

Gavin was already wheeling away from his desk. He stood, slipping the notebook into his jacket pocket, enthusiasm shining in his eyes.

"I finally received all the officers' reports from the canvass of the area around Silver's office. Seems like we might actually have a witness."

MR. GOUCHER WAS A SMALL, roundish man, with an equally round and polished head, giving him the appearance of a middle-aged gnome. And the plaid flannel bathrobe cinched around his bulbous waist contributed greatly to the image, Claudia thought as she pulled her gaze from their witness to scan his shabby living room.

"Look, detectives, I told everything to the officer the other day."

"I understand, Mr. Goucher," Gavin placated him. "And as I said, we appreciate your patience. But you know these officers, they don't always get their details right. It's routine to have detectives follow up. So if you don't mind going over it one more time, could you tell us exactly what you saw that night."

"When Silver got killed, you mean?"

Gavin nodded and quietly clicked his pen before flipping to a fresh page in his notebook.

"Fine," Goucher grumbled, running a hand over his bald pate. "Like I told the officer, I work the midnight shift down at the Domino Sugar Plant. I was gettin' ready for work, had the TV on, watchin' the eleven-o'clock news, see? Then I heard somethin'."

"What kind of something?"

"I don't know exactly. Maybe a car backfiring. Maybe kids just out screwin' around in the alley. Just somethin'. It was only afterward, once I found out what happened to Silver, that I realized it musta bin the gunshot I heard. Like I said I had the TV on.

Anyways, I hear this noise, so I go to the window, see? Look out and nothin'."

"Did you happen to notice if there were any lights on in Mr. Silver's office windows at the time?"

Goucher appeared to think for a moment, then said, "Yeah, I guess there were."

"Do you know Mr. Silver's car?"

"Yeah. He drives an old Bonneville. Kinda beat-up."

"Was it parked on the street?"

"Nope. Pretty sure it wasn't."

"So you didn't see anything?"

"Not right away. I looked out and there was nothin' there, so I went upstairs and got dressed. Then, I dunno, maybe ten...fifteen minutes later, I'm about out the door, and I walk past the window here, see?" He waved one fleshy hand at the wide window overlooking Boston Street. Venetian blinds hung askew over the dingy pane, several of the partially open slats dented and bent. "And that's when I see this guy come outta the old mattress building."

"You told the officer that you thought it was Silver at first, is that correct?" Gavin asked.

"Well, yeah. He's the only one who comes 'n' goes that late at night there. So of course, I'm thinkin' it was him. I met Silver a coupla times. Nice guy. Polite. Anyways, this guy was kinda his size and build. But then I see this guy's walkin' kinda fast, kinda like he's in a hurry to get outta here, you know what I mean?"

"And where did he go?"

"Down the street." He nodded his head indicating

the direction, and when his gaze met Claudia's she offered him a smile of appreciation.

From the moment he'd opened the front door to find them standing on his narrow stoop, Mr. Goucher had been more than forthright in his resentment at being dragged out of bed to be asked questions he'd already considered answered. It was only Gavin's sincere apology that seemed to have won the man over enough to invite them in.

The place smelled of cooked onions and old grease, with a pervasive mustiness characteristic of many of the run-down row houses in Baltimore. As Claudia studied the cramped room again, she wondered when Mr. Goucher had last opened a window for air.

"Did this man get into a car?" Gavin was asking.

"Yeah, but if you're gonna ask me what kind, I dunno. It was down the street a ways."

"Mr. Goucher, was there anything at all unique about this man?"

He shook his head. "I can tell you he was white. That's about it."

"Do you remember what he was wearing?"

"Yeah. Black. Black jeans, black jacket, black gloves. Hell, he even had on a black baseball cap."

"Was it a leather jacket, sir?" Claudia asked.

"Yeah, I think so."

It was too close for coincidence. Gavin shared a quick glance with her before snapping shut his notebook and shoving it into the pocket of his coat.

"Mr. Goucher." He shook the man's hand. "I

want to thank you for your patience. You've been very generous with your time.''

"You won't…well, you know…be needin' me to testify or anything, will you?''

"It's a possibility, sir,'' Claudia told him, trying to soften the notion with a smile. "But not terribly likely. I wouldn't worry about it if I were you.''

"Yeah. Whatever,'' he mumbled skeptically as Gavin opened the door.

"Thanks again, Mr. Goucher.''

Gavin said nothing until they reached the car and he settled in behind the wheel. "So what is your gut telling you?'' he asked. "Obviously you're the one working a hunch now.''

"The guy I saw running from my place the other night—same outfit. I don't know about you, but the coincidence is a little too much for comfort. Sure, whether someone's going out into the night to shoot someone or break into an apartment, the attire of choice might be black, but right down to the baseball cap and leather jacket?''

Gavin turned over the car's engine. "We're still no further ahead,'' he said as they headed down Boston Street.

"Sure we are. Now we can wonder if the person who killed Silver might actually be the same one who was in my apartment Friday night. And if that's the case, then I feel pretty certain all of this is directly related to Frank's death.''

"All right then. Working on those assumptions, what was this guy looking for in your place? You said nothing was taken.''

"I have no idea what he was after. But obviously we interrupted him. Silver's office had been thoroughly searched, whereas my apartment wasn't even touched."

"He might be back."

"Yeah, well, I'm locking my windows these days. What about Silver's apartment? Have you checked that out?"

"Where do you think we're going?" Gavin asked, flashing her a smile. Unexpectedly, a flutter of desire went through her. He followed the stirring smile with an even more charming wink. "Great minds," he added.

As he steered onto Jackson Boulevard, Claudia studied his profile, watching that enchanting smile fade as the detective in him took over once again. "I went by Silver's place on Saturday, but the super was away for the weekend. He called me this morning. He's expecting us."

GAVIN HADN'T ASSUMED answers would simply pop out of the woodwork and slap them in the face, but at the same time he'd hoped for at least something, given their efforts. As promised, the superintendent of James Silver's building had been waiting for them. Since letting them into Silver's one-bedroom apartment on the top floor of the four-story walk-up, Dwight had kept a watchful eye. For more than a half hour the super had stood in the doorway, a can of Milwaukee in one hand and Silver's mail in the other. Now, however, with the beer can apparently empty, Dwight seemed anxious for them to wrap up their search.

"I don't know what you expect to find. I already told ya, Jimmy never brought no work home. Never."

Crouching over the open bottom drawer of an antique chest in the living room, Gavin gave the man an impatient glance when he tried unsuccessfully to hold back a low belch.

"I used ta ask Jimmy why he didn't—why he always hung out at that office of his till the wee hours of mornin' when he coulda sat here in the comfort of his own home. But he said he liked to keep the two separate. Work and home. Nope, wait...*work and life,* he used ta say. Same with when he was on the force. He never brought home stuff then, neither."

Not like Claudia, Gavin thought, remembering the file tucked under her sofa. Looking across the small apartment past the open bedroom door, he saw her pause as she rifled through the top dresser drawer. And when she caught his stare briefly, he was certain that she was also thinking of her copied file on Frank. Probably wondering if he'd seen it.

She slid the drawer shut. "There's nothing here, Gavin," she stated, coming back into the living room. "We're wasting our time."

"Don't say I didn't tell ya," Dwight offered.

"So, you said Mr. Silver's mother asked you to take care of all his stuff?" she asked the super.

"Yeah. No way she's coming all the way up from

Florida to do it. The old lady's gotta be seventy-something.''

"And he doesn't have any siblings, is that correct?''

"Nope, just me.''

As Gavin stood, he caught the quizzical look that registered on Claudia's face.

Dwight recognized it, as well, and clarified. "What I mean is, I'm the closest thing to a brother Jimmy's got. He's bin in this place over twenty years. Since he started as a beat cop. I've known him all that time.''

Gavin joined them in the apartment's front hall. Just beneath the lingering stench of Dwight's beer, he could smell Claudia. It was an intimate smell now, Gavin thought. One that transported his memory to three nights ago in her apartment. He'd spent all weekend trying like hell to put the incident out of his mind, trying to convince himself that what he'd felt...what he'd wanted, when he'd finally kissed her, hadn't really happened.

And with a single whiff, he was right back where he'd been when he'd driven away from her place, swearing he wouldn't get involved and at the same time wondering how on earth that was going to be possible.

As he had ever since he'd watched her step out of Sergeant Gunning's office a couple of hours ago, Gavin tried to focus on their work.

Claudia beat him to it.

"Dwight, can you tell us where Mr. Silver's car

is? We noticed it wasn't anywhere in the vicinity of his office.''

Gavin watched the super eye her warily, before pulling his key chain from his pants pocket and removing a key.

''It's parked out back. Blue '84 Bonneville.''

''Have you been in it?'' she asked. ''Have you driven it since the murder?''

''Can't,'' he replied, crushing the empty beer can in one hand. ''Needs work. Jimmy cabbed it to the office last Thursday and Friday. Was planning on taking the car to his buddy up in Hampden to work on it over the weekend. You guys aren't gonna take it, are ya? Impound it or somethin'? I sorta was fixin' on getting it looked at, you know? See what I can get for it?''

Claudia snatched the key from him and muttered an impatient thank-you. With a nod, she headed for the door, and Gavin followed her past the super and down the stairs.

In the front entranceway, she shoved one of the doors wide to a virtual downpour. Gavin had heard the storm on the roof of Silver's apartment but hadn't expected the sheets of rain that washed the street. Already, gutters spilled over as small rivers raced to swelling storm drains.

Claudia paused, but he sensed it wasn't the rain that stopped her. When she turned to look at him, he could see she was upset.

''Was it just me, or does this Dwight character seem just a little too eager to claim his inheritance?''

she whispered harshly. "God. With friends like
that…"

Turning up the collar of her trench coat, she
stepped through the door and into the driving rain.
By the time Gavin caught up with her alongside the
building, water had already snaked past his own collar and slid coldly down the back of his neck. "Just
ignore him, Claudia," he suggested, keeping up with
her quick stride. "There're always going to be people like that." He settled one wet hand onto her
drenched shoulder. "It's going to be dark soon. Let's
just find Silver's car, all right? Then we can get the
hell out of here."

Silver's leaf-plastered Bonneville sat at the east
corner of the potholed lot, conveniently located under
an overgrown dogwood that provided them with at
least some shelter. Still, they were getting wetter by
the second, and after ten minutes of searching the
garbage-littered car, both of them were so soaked
shelter meant nothing.

The hammering of the rain on the old car's roof
was relentless, almost deafening, Gavin thought as
he slammed the door shut. "Did you find anything
yet?"

If Claudia had answered, he didn't hear her over
the rain. He moved to the open driver's side door,
bracing his hands on the roof and standing over her
as she sat half in half out of the cluttered car. Unlike
Silver's apartment, which had been relatively neat
and organized, his car bore all the characteristics of
a private investigator's surveillance car; his home
away from home.

"I guess Silver spent more time in here than he did in his apartment," he said. The front of the PI's car was worse than the trunk and the back combined: a mess of empty soda cans and potato-chip bags, receipts, notes, crumpled sections of the *Baltimore Sun,* several pieces of surveillance equipment.

Claudia, however, seemed unfazed by the filth. Her hair was soaked now, the curls heavy and drizzling rain over the car's worn and cigarette-burned upholstery. She stretched across the bench seat and blindly searched with one hand beneath the passenger seat, then the driver's.

When she'd first asked Dwight about Silver's car, Gavin had been impressed with her detective work, and figured her insightfulness would pay off. Now, as rain soaked through his coat and he felt his shirt cold against his skin, he was ready to throw in the towel. Claudia, on the other hand, was far more determined.

She slid off the seat and Gavin stepped back to give her room. Rain pelted against her back and shoulders as she crouched next to the open door to dig farther under the driver's seat.

"Do you believe this sty?" he asked.

"Long hours," she replied, as she pulled out even more scraps of paper and paused to examine each one. "I never could understand why anyone would leave the force for PI work."

She turned her search to the seat, sliding her hand along its rear and withdrawing several more items. "It's a horrible profession. Spending nights in your car, spying on adulterous husbands and wives, and then having to—'' She stopped. In her hand she unfolded a piece of creased notepaper.

''Now, this is interesting.''

''What is it?''

He took her hand, helping her to her feet. And when she showed him the scrap, Gavin stared at the scrawled handwriting as rain soaked the flimsy paper. There was no mistaking Silver's handwriting: LORI TOBIN. EVIDENCE CONTROL.

CHAPTER EIGHT

EVEN WITH THE CAR'S HEAT blasting, there had been no cutting the chill. Nor had either of them managed to dry off much. After finding nothing else of interest in Silver's car, Claudia had driven them back to headquarters. Practically dripping a trail behind them, they'd headed straight to Evidence Control, only to find that Lori had gone home for the day.

Now, riding the elevator up to the crime-scene technician's apartment, Claudia caught sight of herself in the mirrored panels of the elevator doors. Her hair was hanging in limp, wet tresses that framed her pale face. Her coat was heavy with water, and beneath it her shirt clung to her skin.

Gavin looked drenched, as well. His shoulders seemed to slump under the weight of his rain-soaked coat, and in the unforgiving light of the elevator's fluorescents, he appeared almost as pale as she did.

When he met her gaze in the reflection, Claudia looked away, embarrassed for staring.

"Are you sure about this?" he asked. "Just showing up on Lori Tobin's doorstep is not exactly protocol."

"I don't much care about protocol when I'm working a hunch."

He returned her grin.

"Besides," she asked, "do you really want to wait until tomorrow to find out why Silver might have written her name down on a scrap of paper?"

"We might have called first."

"It was on the way," she reminded him as the elevator stopped and the doors slid open. "Don't worry, Gavin. I think I know Lori well enough for her to forgive the intrusion."

The comment didn't seem to ease his discomfort as they headed down the corridor to the apartment number they'd gotten from the clerk at Evidence Control.

"She may not even be home."

But within seconds of them knocking, Lori swung open her apartment door.

"Claudia. Gavin." Her face was an instant mask of quiet alarm. "What's wrong?"

"Nothing, Lori. Nothing's happened."

The technician's face calmed by a degree. She cinched the sash of her robe and tugged the edges of it tighter over her chest.

"I'm sorry to intrude like this. I guess we caught you at a bad time."

"Sort of, yeah." Lori shot a glance over her shoulder, back into her apartment—a gesture that assured Claudia that Lori had company. Intimate company, no doubt, given the woman's attire. Taking a step into the corridor, Lori pulled the door partly shut behind her.

"I'm sorry," Claudia said again. "It's just that Gavin and I are working this Silver case, and we really needed to ask you something. We went to Evidence Control first, and…well, look, Lori, this might be personal. I don't know.''

Confusion rippled across Lori's face.

Claudia took the damp scrap of paper from her pocket and held it out to her. ''I found this in James Silver's car. We were hoping that maybe you could explain why he might have written down your name.''

She watched Lori's gaze drop to the note and then back up again, the concern at last fading from her expression.

''He came to see me.''

''Silver did?''

''Yeah. About a week ago. He came to Evidence Control. Asking for me specifically.''

''Do you know why?''

''Why he asked for me? I have no idea. I just assumed he'd gotten my name from one of his former colleagues. I knew he used to be on the force.''

''What did he want?''

''Information. He wanted me to release some evidence to him.''

''Which case?'' Claudia asked, but didn't need to. She already anticipated the answer.

''Frank Owens.''

''Do you know what exactly Silver was after?''

''Not really. He asked if I'd release Detective Owens's personal notes and evidence. Said he just wanted a quick look, that I could stand over him while he went through it.''

''And did you let him?''

Lori crossed her arms over her chest and looked from Gavin back to Claudia. "Of course not. I couldn't. Silver's not with the department anymore. I can't just release evidence to him, especially in a police shooting. I told him he'd have to get permission from the Chief, or at the very least he'd have to talk to the investigating sergeant, and then he left."

"Lori, why didn't you tell us about this at the scene on Friday morning?"

"Why would I? I mean, it's not related to Silver's death, is it?"

Lori looked to Gavin as though seeking reassurance that she hadn't screwed up.

"No," Gavin told her. "No, you're right. It's not related." But one glance from him, and Claudia knew he said this only to avoid raising suspicion. He hadn't voiced his suspicions to Sarge; he certainly wasn't about to do so with Lori.

"Thanks," Claudia offered when she realized Gavin was ready to leave. "And again, sorry to have bothered you at home."

"It's not a problem."

"Oh, one more question," she said. "The evidence...the personal items from the investigation into Frank's death, they are still in Evidence Control, right?"

"I think so. But you'd have to check the records. I honestly couldn't say for sure."

IT WAS DARK BY THE TIME they got down to the car. The rain had let up marginally, but Claudia was wet beyond caring. As she steered the Lumina back toward headquarters, she had no trouble convincing Gavin that they should at least check for Frank's personal effects before going home to dry off.

As Sarge had suggested it should be, the single box of evidence was still logged, even though it had taken the clerk a good fifteen minutes to find it. Gavin signed for the evidence, telling Claudia that he didn't want her to have to take any flak should someone find out and consider it inappropriate for her to be looking into her former partner's death. With that in mind, Gavin refused to take the box upstairs to the offices in order to examine the contents. Instead, he carried it to the parking garage, set it in the back seat of their unmarked car and took the wheel.

Now, as they drove across the city, past the harbor and all of its lights, Claudia thought about the box. When the clerk had slid it across the counter toward them, it had been Gavin who'd opened it and taken a fast survey of the items to be sure they weren't wasting their time. She hadn't been able to bring herself to look inside.

"You know, since we're going through all of Frank's things, you might also check his desk," she said, remembering her conversation with Sarge earlier.

"Already did that over the weekend. Whoever cleared it out was thorough. I'm hoping everything's in the box."

Gavin slowed for a red light. Looking out the rain-smeared windshield, she was aware he was staring at her.

"You know, I can go through his stuff myself, Claudia." The concern in his voice was unmistakable. "There's no need for you to if you're not—"

"No. I'll be fine," she lied. "Of course I'll help. I want to. Besides, you'll probably need me to decipher Frank's handwriting."

They fell into silence again, and Claudia watched pedestrians with their umbrellas, scurrying along the glistening sidewalks to the trendy shops and bars lining the waterfront. Beneath her she felt the wheels of the car drum rhythmically against the old cobblestone. The "charm" that the city tried to maintain in Fells Point was certainly lost in the wear and tear of vehicles, Claudia had thought from the day she'd moved down to the area.

It was Gavin who broke the silence next, but this time his voice held a darker concern.

"I think we're being followed," he said flatly.

In the passenger-side mirror, she could see only headlights. The vehicle was at least forty yards back, bobbing and jarring along the rough street just as they were. She watched until the other vehicle passed beneath a street lamp, but it was too far back for her to discern anything about the vehicle.

"Are you sure?"

"Not entirely." His eyes locked onto the rearview mirror, the reflection of the tailing headlights causing him to squint slightly.

"How long has it been behind us?"

"I don't know. But I noticed it just after we left headquarters. At least, I think it's the same car. Hard to tell."

"Well, there's only one way to find out." Claudia scanned the street ahead of them. Gavin slowed the car as though knowing what she was about to suggest. "Take this next right."

He followed her direction, turning onto an even rougher street, the sound of the tires thumping across the cobblestone drowning out the slapping windshield wipers. Claudia watched the passenger-side mirror. Seconds later, the headlights reappeared.

"It's too dark," she said. "I can't make out the model, or even tell if it's the same car."

When she looked to Gavin, his hands tightened around the wheel as he studied the ill-lit street ahead of them. A muscle twitched along his jaw and he squinted again when he looked to the mirror.

They were headed back to the water, leaving the activity of Fells Point behind them and driving past the old shipping yards and abandoned warehouses. The headlights of the trailing car remained in the side mirror. Gavin slowed, probably expecting the other car to catch up, or possibly pass them. It didn't.

At the end of the street, Gavin took another right, heading along the waterfront. Sure enough, seconds later, the headlights appeared again. This time, instead of slowing, Gavin gunned the engine, disregarding the poor condition of the road. The Lumina bucked, sending up sprays of water from deep puddles and hammering across railway crossings. Claudia grabbed the armrest to brace herself.

"What are you going to do?" she asked.

The tension in Gavin's expression was fixed. "Find out who the hell this is." With one more glance into the rearview mirror, he mumbled a warning to hang on.

Even so, she wasn't ready for Gavin's maneuver. The brakes threatened to lock as he pressed down on them. The car lurched, starting to slide across the slick street, and in the same instant, he spun the wheel into a sharp 180-degree turn. Claudia felt a stab of pain along her right cheek even before she realized she'd struck herself against the passenger-side window.

Ahead of them, easily a half block down, the tailing vehicle appeared to slow. The headlights splintered across their rain-spattered windshield for a split second, and then, suddenly, the other vehicle veered around a corner and disappeared entirely from sight. Gavin accelerated, and this time Claudia gripped the armrest even tighter, prepared for whatever he might do next. Instead, Gavin braked as they reached the side street.

But the street was empty, the mysterious vehicle gone.

Claudia brought a hand up to her face. Her cheek felt tender to the touch. Out of the corner of her eye, she saw Gavin looking at her.

"Are you all right?" he asked.

She gave him a brief smile. "It's nothing."

He turned up the deserted street and pulled over.

"What happened?"

"I guess I wasn't exactly prepared for your tactical maneuver back there."

"Sorry about that. Here, let me take a look at it." She should have expected the warmth that spread through her when he placed a finger under her chin to turn her face.

In the light of a street lamp, she saw concern in his expression when he tilted her head to better examine her.

"It's really all right," she said to reassure him.

"Why don't you let me be the judge of that."

Gently he touched her cheek, carefully circling the spot that was tender. His touch reminded her of the feelings that had swept through her when he'd held her in his arms, and it made her realize just how effortlessly she could fall under Gavin's spell.

It would be so easy to take that hand in hers, to put her own against *his* cheek and draw him close.

But this wasn't the place, she thought. Nor was it the time…if there would ever be one.

"Well, I have to admit," she said in an attempt to cool the deep longing she felt, "that stint with the commissioner's office sure paid off for you."

"What?" He backed away from her enough that she could see his face. He looked puzzled.

"Driving the commissioner's car? The way you handled yourself back there?"

"Oh, right." He settled further into his seat, composure erasing the brief flicker of confusion she was sure she'd glimpsed. "A lot of it is just instinct, you know."

She nodded, almost certain his hesitation hadn't been her imagination.

"You're going to be all right," he said finally. "You might have a slight bruise if we don't get some ice on it though. I'll get you home."

With that, he jammed the car into Drive and drove back to Fells Point.

GAVIN REACHED INTO the evidence box on the coffee table for yet another handful of loose notes and papers. Settling back into the soft cushions of Claudia's sofa, he shuffled through them in the same manner he had the previous handfuls. But nothing leaped out as immediately obvious. He paused, taking a long swallow of rapidly cooling coffee from his mug.

When he'd parked outside of Claudia's apartment, he'd once again offered to look through Frank's personal effects by himself, but Claudia had been adamant that she would hold up her end of the investigation. He admired her courage but wondered how well she would handle going through the effects of her dead partner...her dead *lover*.

Behind him, down the corridor, he could hear the shower still running. She'd let him use the en suite first, setting out towels and dry clothes—no doubt Frank's—for him before making coffee and icing her cheek. After a weekend of convincing himself that there could be nothing between him and Claudia, he probably shouldn't have come up to her apartment. He should have acknowledged his inability to keep desire at bay, especially after what he'd experienced in the car less than an hour ago. He'd examined her cheek. Nothing erotic in that, and yet it had taken more restraint than he'd imagined to not kiss Claudia.

If he'd come so close then, what in the hell was

he doing in her apartment? *Working the case,* he tried to convince himself as he examined the papers.

So far nothing to imply innocence or guilt. And at this point in his investigation, no matter how much Claudia admired and respected her former partner, Gavin couldn't say Frank was innocent. It was still possible that the detective had been responsible for the corruption; he might have sought out Silver to help him cover up instead of expose, and his death might have been a suicide in spite of old Doc Carver's uncertainties.

The shower stopped, and silence filled the apartment. Gavin inhaled deeply.

As a detective, he knew he shouldn't—couldn't—rule Claudia out as a suspect in the evidence tampering, as well as in connection with Silver's, and possibly Frank's, death. Try as he might, though, he couldn't bring himself to believe that Claudia was anything but the upstanding and honorable cop depicted in her file. Not to mention an alluring woman. One look at her, and every last shred of suspicion, no matter how warranted, vanished. She came down the corridor now and into the living room, stopping at the side of the couch when she spotted the open box. She wore a pair of drawstring pants and a flowing shirt. Where the buttons stopped at her chest and the fabric flared back, her skin seemed to glow with a warmth that made it far too easy to imagine its softness.

Her hair had been towel-dried and pushed behind her ears so that the damp curls brushed the top of her collar. But her face was what held his gaze—so fresh, her skin almost luminescent, and those wide silver eyes that projected nothing but absolute, undeniable innocence.

One look into those eyes, and the detective in Gavin was lost. Suspicion was the last thing he could conjure up in his mind. Claudia was utterly incapable of the corruption he had been sent in to investigate, nor could she be even remotely responsible for Frank Owens's murder.

Gavin cleared his throat. "How's your cheek?"

"It's fine. The ice helped." The smile that graced her lips and lit up her eyes was fleeting. Her gaze locked onto the papers in his lap.

"I poured you a coffee." He indicated the mug next to his.

"Thanks. But actually, I think I might prefer something a little stronger. Would you like a drink?"

"What have you got?"

"How's Scotch?"

"Great." He nodded, and she went into the kitchen. He watched her take out two glasses and some ice. She grabbed the bottle from the corner of the counter and brought it with her to the couch before pouring him a generous shot.

"So what about the car tonight?" she asked, handing him his drink. "What are your thoughts?"

Gavin swirled the amber liquid over the ice for a moment then took a sip. Almost instantly the warmth of the liquor moved through him, melting the last of the chill. "It's hard to know for certain whether it was following us, or if it was even the same car."

"Do you think it might have something to do with this case?"

He offered her a shrug. "Who knows?" Of course, they would have known had he been just a little faster, Gavin thought. He should have anticipated the side street when he'd spun the car around. If there had actually been a trace of the other vehicle, he would have pursued it. But with so many alleyways and side streets, it would have been pointless.

"Guess we'll just have to keep an eye out from now on," he suggested.

Again Claudia's gaze dropped to the items in his lap, and again her discomfort was obvious.

"Do you want to call it a night?" he asked.

"No, Gavin. I'm fine." She took another drink of her Scotch. "Come on, let's see if there's anything in this box."

IT WAS A CHRISTMAS CARD that finally stopped Claudia. For almost an hour, she'd managed to keep her emotions in check. Not an easy task. Going through the personal items she'd seen on or in Frank's desk during their partnership, had done nothing but whip up a fountain of memories.

The Christmas card had been the last straw. Not that there was anything exceptional or profoundly personal about it. She and Frank had only been partners at the time, even though Claudia had already been wishing for a lot more.

Seated at one end of the sofa with her legs drawn up beneath her, she held the card she'd given Frank two years ago. It was a simple, humorous card, nothing that would have raised anyone's suspicions, least of all Frank's. "Merry Christmas, Partner. Hope it's a good one. Here's to another great year ahead. Claudia." And yet, she could remember what she'd really wanted to write back then.

Obviously, she wasn't the only one. Frank hadn't been a pack rat. He wouldn't have kept the Christmas card unless it had meant something more to him. It didn't surprise her, though. Hadn't Frank told her that he'd entertained romantic thoughts for a long time before they'd done anything about it?

"You want to know something, Claudia?" he'd asked her on the morning after they'd made love for the first time. *"This...right here, with you...this is where I've imagined being. Ever since I met you."* He'd held her even closer, and she remembered wondering if he'd lain with her in his arms all night. *"It's hard to believe it's real."*

"Claudia?" It was Gavin's touch more than his voice that drew her out of the memory. He'd reached across to place one hand on her shoulder and squeeze it gently. There was concern on his face. "Are you okay?"

She closed the card and discarded it along with the rest of the items she'd already sorted through. "I'm fine."

"I was saying, I think we're about finished with this. We've been through everything, and there's nothing here."

She nodded in agreement, scooping up the piles she'd looked at.

"I think we should call it a night," he said. Her

silence must have concerned him as they returned Frank's things to the evidence box, because he asked again, "Are you sure you're all right?"

Biting her lower lip, she wished like hell that she had let Gavin search through the box by himself. From the moment she'd first seen Frank's handwriting there had been an ever-mounting sense of self-reproach.

"You know," she admitted at last, hating the sound of the tremble in her voice, "all this time, all these months, I've been blaming myself because I hadn't listened to Frank. Because I hadn't seen the signs. But now…"

Daniel Carver's words flitted through her thoughts, as they had ever since he'd told them about the possible negative results on the GSR test.

"Now…what if Frank *was* murdered? I'm almost *more* to blame for that."

"That's nonsense," Gavin said quietly.

"Is it? I don't think so. If I'd stayed that night, if I'd heard him out and agreed to help him with whatever angle he was working, maybe we would have uncovered the truth. Maybe we would have flushed out the real culprit, the person who probably killed Frank."

"Claudia, you can't beat yourself up this way. You can't think about 'what if.'"

"But Frank might still be alive today if I'd given him the benefit of the doubt and done what he'd asked."

"Or you might be dead, too. Murdered because of

what you knew. Did you ever stop to think about that possibility?''

She shook her head, not knowing what else to say. She felt cold, numb. Even tossing back the rest of her Scotch did nothing to soothe her.

''You did the right thing,'' Gavin added softly, giving her shoulder a comforting touch. ''You stayed out of it.''

''But I could have saved him.''

''There's no way for you to know that. And you certainly can't spend the rest of your life wondering how you might have done things differently. You can't live in the past. You're here. Now. Yes, Frank's dead. I'm very sorry about that. I have no doubt that it was a great loss, but you're alive. You have to move on.''

When she dared to lift her gaze to meet Gavin's, she was moved by the compassion she saw there. Reaching to her shoulder, she took his hand into her own, finding strength in the encouraging squeeze he gave her in return.

''Listen to me, Claudia. You did what you thought best at the time. You can't go on blaming yourself.''

She nodded reluctantly. ''You're right. I know you're right.''

It had to be the Scotch, she thought. The liquor dulled the edges of her inhibitions, made her not only welcome his embrace then, but actually seek it. She wanted his arms around her, needed to feel Gavin's strength and compassion surround her.

He moved beside her, taking her into his arms, pulling her tight against him. ''Claudia, I swear to you, if someone killed Frank, we'll find them. Even if it's not related to Silver's murder, I'll help you.''

She nestled her cheek against his chest, listening to the slow, strong rhythm of his heart while he quietly stroked her hair. It was a comforting touch, one that felt natural and right.

When he spoke again, his voice was barely a whisper. ''But I want you to promise me one thing,'' he said.

She remained silent. Waiting.

''Promise me you'll move forward. You have a life. And given what you see in your job every day, you know it's too damned short to waste by clinging to the past. Frank died. You didn't. You have to move on.''

Even her own sister had never challenged her like this, never spoken such a jarring truth. It took someone who barely knew her to point out what she'd been doing the past ten months.

''I should probably go,'' he murmured.

''No.'' She sat back, bracing herself with one hand against his chest and feeling the shift of muscles beneath her palm as she held his gaze. ''Please, Gavin, stay. I need...I mean, I'd like you to stay.''

She didn't have to say anything else. In Gavin's eyes, she could see his understanding, combined with a desire that she guessed had been building steadily since that first kiss. Maybe even earlier.

''I'm not exactly sure what it is...or why, but please, I don't want to be alone right now. I—''

Gavin stopped her. Lightly he pressed one finger against her lips. He studied her for a moment as if uncertain what to do next, but she knew he was going to kiss her.

They'd been here once before, only this time it was different. She felt an urgency from him that hadn't existed in their first kiss. It was as though he'd thought about it…hoped for this very situation.

And why not? Hadn't she also wanted to kiss Gavin again? Hadn't she considered the possibility over and over all weekend?

Shifting on the couch, she reached behind his neck and drew him deeper into their kiss. With her tongue she traced the softness of his lips, tasting Scotch, and then tasting his own desire.

She gasped slightly, wondering if she'd forgotten to breathe. He eased back, but not out of reservation, Claudia guessed. As his hands traveled down past her rib cage and to her hips, she was certain that Gavin too wanted to savor each sweet sensation.

He brushed back the edge of her shirt, exposing her shoulder, and pressed his lips to her neck, sucking on the sensitive area just below her ear as if knowing the reaction it would entice from her.

Raking her fingers through his short-cropped hair, Claudia pulled him to her, welcoming the hot kisses that trailed downward. There was nothing she wanted more in this instant than to feel Gavin and everything his kisses promised.

When he reached her bra, he moved back slightly. Looking into his dark eyes, Claudia could see the hunger that sparked there as he ran a finger just under the lace and then nestled one breast into his palm.

She wondered if he was second-guessing himself.

Fearful he might change his mind, Claudia placed her hand over his. She pressed it tightly, urging him to caress her, as she guided his mouth back to hers.

The desire was excruciating. She wanted more. *Needed* more.

"Gavin." She wasn't sure if she'd actually whispered his name between their kisses, until he looked into her eyes. "Gavin, I..."

She took his hand, entwining her fingers through his. "Come with me," she said quietly, easing herself off the couch.

Wordlessly he allowed her to lead him to her bedroom. The small lamp atop the dresser was still on, and it cast soft shadows about the room. When she reached the side of the bed, Gavin stopped her. With one hand on her hip, he turned her. He caressed her cheek with the soft pad of his thumb, and as the warm light touched the angles of his face, she marveled again at the strong lines. More than that, she marveled at the deep yearning she saw in his eyes.

A heat swept through her when he brushed aside the edges of her shirt. Even deeper shocks of desire coiled inside her as he traced the column of her spine, slowing when he reached the small of her back and pulled her tight against him. She didn't need to feel the hard bulge that pressed against her belly to know Gavin wanted her.

This time when he kissed her, his mouth crushed hers with a ferocity that she was incapable of resisting. Not that she wanted to. Even if what they were about to do amounted to nothing, Claudia didn't care. It was the here and now that mattered.

"You have to move on," Gavin had said.

And in his passionate embrace, Claudia felt more alive than she had in a long, long time.

She'd anticipated the hard play of muscles along his torso and back, but the feel of them snatched her breath. He obliged her when she lifted the sweatshirt over his head and let it drop to the floor. She trailed her fingers over his strong shoulders and across his chest, admiring the definition of muscle under the slight smattering of black hair.

Taking her cue, Gavin swept her shirt off her shoulders and let it fall to the floor. Appreciation rippled across his face then as he unclasped the snap on her bra. It too dropped to the floor.

He cradled one naked breast in each palm, the heat of his hands sending shivers racing through her. The sensation only amplified as his hands glided downward.

Untying the drawstring of her pants, Gavin slid them easily from her hips, and in one fluid movement she drew back the duvet and guided him onto the bed with her. He kissed her, his mouth answering her hunger with his own. Breathless as well, he braced himself on his elbows and she felt his fingers tangle through her hair as he lowered himself over her.

Yes, she needed Gavin. She needed everything he could give her—comfort, understanding, support and, most of all, the passion she felt now.

Sliding a hand between their bodies, her own ache heightened as she felt his unrestrained erection through the fleece of his sweatpants. She stroked him, taking pleasure in the moan that rumbled deep inside his broad chest.

She tugged at the waistband, and in seconds Gavin had managed to remove the sweats. He lowered himself onto her again, completely naked, and the sheer power of his body caught her breath. Her heart raced even faster, and when she felt his erection, hard against her belly, Claudia thought she might climax at the mere anticipation of Gavin inside of her.

Slowly she rotated her hips beneath him, a gentle motion that she knew aroused him even more. Maybe too much. He drew back slightly, just enough for him to reach down past her hip and between her legs.

His fingers found the small nub and circled it teasingly. Pleasure shot through her, and just as she thought she could take no more, Gavin shifted. His mouth left hers and again sought the sensitive skin on her throat. It was when she felt the full length of his erection rub against her that Claudia experienced the fiery release.

She opened her eyes. A gentle smile played on Gavin's lips as he gazed down at her. She saw it in his eyes as well—a look of tenderness and affection, in spite of the desire she could feel tensing every muscle as he restrained his own passion.

"Gavin." His name rasped from her throat as her fingers fluttered to his hips. "I want…"

But she didn't need to say more. With one hand, she reached behind her to pull open the nightstand drawer, and Gavin withdrew one of the foil packets.

"Are you sure, Claudia?" he asked softly, caressing her lips with his thumb.

She could barely manage to nod. She ached to feel him inside her. If she'd had the time to think about it, she might have believed herself insane to want to give herself so freely and completely to him. But she trusted Gavin. And she wondered whether she'd ever trusted anyone this much in her life.

The next few moments were pure fire. He began to enter her, and Claudia reached for him, lifting her hips to meet his, clutching at his flesh with a delirious desperation. He kept her there for as long as he could, until at last, he plunged into her fully. She'd thought herself ready for him, but nothing could have prepared her for this.

In the last moment, before Claudia felt his body go rigid, before she heard his deep-chested groan echo hers, she looked up into Gavin's eyes. In that split second of rapturous calm came a quiet sense of peace she'd thought she'd never again experience.

CHAPTER NINE

GAVIN SQUINTED as a single shaft of morning sunshine pierced the blinds. He shifted slightly, careful not to wake Claudia. With one slender arm draped over his chest, she pressed the length of her body against his. A quiet sigh of contentment slipped from her lips; the sound of it sent an involuntary shiver of desire through him.

He watched her sleep, her eyes closed, her golden hair spilling across the pillow, and remembered last night. He hadn't had many lovers during his years with IAD; even so, Gavin considered himself experienced. But none of that experience came close to what he'd felt with Claudia. There had been no other woman so sensual, whose body had moved in the same erotic way Claudia's did and could do the things she'd done to him. And there certainly hadn't been any woman in his past who'd made him feel as many emotions as Claudia could in a single glance.

They'd fallen asleep in each other's arms after the first time. Then, in the middle of the night when reason had seeped in and Gavin had tried to slip from her bed, Claudia had reached for him again. They'd made love a second time, even more fervent than the first. Nothing had ever seemed more right.

But in the light of morning, reality loomed.

Gavin let his gaze travel across Claudia's body, admiring the gentle curves that molded so perfectly against him and feeling the softness of her skin along his. He drew the sheets up and again she nudged closer. Yes, this was right. Being with Claudia.

He had to be crazy! Crazy and very stupid.

No question: he had feelings for Claudia. Deep ones. If he hadn't believed it before, last night had proved it to him. Nor was there any lingering doubt in his mind of her innocence concerning Frank Owens or the ongoing corruption.

But none of that mattered. He was IAD. Even once he proved her innocence, even if she ultimately forgave him for lying about his true identity, there could never be a relationship between them. Not now, not ever. If anyone found out, even long after the fact, his entire investigation would appear biased, and would probably lead to a reopening of the case…or worse—charges of misconduct.

Maybe that's why it had been so easy to fall for Claudia, Gavin considered, and why being with her was so exhilarating. Claudia was the forbidden fruit. Maybe he was head over heels for her simply because he knew that ultimately he could not have her.

Gavin glanced around the bedroom. Their clothes were strewn across the floor and at the foot of the bed; the covers were mostly in a tangle at their feet, and the drawer of the nightstand was still open.

Gavin closed his eyes. What had he done?

When he opened them again, his gaze stopped on

the framed photograph on the nightstand. Frank Owens, frozen on celluloid, smiled back.

"He was the best man I've ever known," Claudia had said only a couple of nights ago. But she needn't have. Hearing her describe her partner had been enough for Gavin to sense her undying love for the man.

Gavin held back a bitter laugh. It was ironic really. Frank Owens was the very reason they were together. He was their link—Claudia's love for the man, and Gavin's investigation into him. And yet, the same man who had brought them together could be the very reason they might never stand a chance, regardless of the conflict created by IAD. After all, what man could possibly come close to comparing with Frank Owens in Claudia's mind?

For that reason, Gavin expected to find extreme regret in Claudia's face when she finally woke next to him. It might have been better if he had left last night.

This time, when Claudia stirred in his arms, her eyes opened. He waited for the moment of realization to strike her, for surprise and then disappointment to wash over her, but there was none. A contented smile lifted the corners of her lips as she calmly nestled closer, pressing her face against his neck and placing a soft kiss along his jaw.

"Good morning," she whispered. "Have you been awake long?"

"Uh-uh." He shook his head, feeling another wave of longing coil through him at the mere sight of her smile.

Propping herself on her elbows, she shifted so that her body covered his. Her smile only widened when she felt the product of his mounting desires. A seductive sigh slipped from her lips, and she backed it up with a slow kiss.

"Are you all right?" he asked only after he'd taken greedily from the kiss she offered.

"Of course I'm all right. Why wouldn't I be?"

When he studied her this time, Gavin was certain he saw a shadow of betrayal behind that bright face of hers. A flash of pain as she no doubt considered the last man she'd shared her bed with. There was no mistaking it, no matter how glowing her smile.

"I just wanted to be sure," he said.

"Well, I'm more than all right," she murmured, moving over him in such a way that he could feel every curve of her body melt into his. She rocked slightly, just enough to drive him mad with wanting her, and when she kissed him again, Gavin was certain he would be lost.

If it hadn't been for the pager's piercing alarm, he knew he would have made love to her, and still it wouldn't have been enough to sate him.

"I'll get it." Frustration laced her voice as she got up and began to search the clothes she'd draped about the bedroom to dry.

Gavin couldn't help but stare. He liked the fact that she wasn't the least bit shy in her nakedness. Seeing the morning sunlight washing over her curves, he couldn't imagine that he'd ever get enough of Claudia.

"It's yours," she said, at last locating the pager and tossing it to him.

One glance at the display was all Gavin needed to know that their morning had just ended.

"I'm sorry," he said, sitting up.

Claudia came to the side of the bed, disappointment darkening the sparkle he'd seen only moments ago in her eyes.

"It's important." He reached out to touch those downturned lips, and followed it with a kiss he hoped displayed the full extent of his own disappointment, a kiss that he also hoped would stop any questions she might have regarding the reason behind the early-morning page.

When she got up from the bed this time, she put on her robe. "Grab a shower," she told him. "I'll start the coffee."

CLAUDIA SHOULD HAVE EXPECTED that Jimmy's would be deluged with the late-breakfast crowd.

"I'm sorry I dragged you here," she told Tony, trying without success to wave down their waitress for a refill. "We probably should have tried someplace else."

"It's all right. I can't stay long anyway. This coffee'll do me." He lifted the stained mug to his lips and leaned back into the bench seat of their window booth. "So tell me what it is that's got you so worked up?"

"Who said anything about being worked up?"

Tony barked a short laugh. "The second we're through with roll call you're tugging at my sleeve, needing to talk, bribing me with breakfast. Like you've ever done *that* before. Come on, Parrish, what's up.''

''Nothing's up, Tony.'' Nothing more than her suspicions, she thought, giving the restaurant another casual scan. ''I just need you to check something out for me.''

For a second his eyes narrowed. ''What exactly?''

She swallowed hard. ''Well, not *what* so much as *who*,'' she managed to say.

She hadn't imagined asking would be so difficult. She'd only known she had to. It had started last night, down near the waterfront, just after Gavin had lost the car they thought might have been tailing them. She'd made a crack about his chauffeuring for the commissioner, and it had taken him too long to comprehend what she'd said. It had been enough for her to begin to wonder.

Then this morning, when she'd tossed Gavin his pager and he'd looked at the display, she hadn't imagined the darkness that had come over his expression. It was a darkness that had left her wishing she'd at least glanced at the pager's display herself before tossing it.

And now she had no idea where Gavin was. She'd covered for him at the office, making excuses for him when he still hadn't shown by roll call.

''Who is it you're so interested in, Claudia?'' Tony stared at her across the table.

''I just thought that maybe…well, you've got six years over me, Tony, you know more people on the force.''

"Not necessarily."

"I figured you might know someone, maybe at the commissioner's office. Maybe someone down in D.C."

"Ah, so it's Monaghan, is it?"

She nodded, feeling her stomach churn at the thought of what she was doing.

"You don't buy his story, is that it?"

"I don't know, Tony. I'm curious, that's all."

Tony studied her intently, and Claudia felt unsettled. But then, she felt unsettled about suspecting Gavin in the first place.

Over the years, her sister had continually pointed out that Claudia's downfall in relationships was her inability to trust. Now Claudia was beginning to realize just how much truth lay behind Faith's criticism. In the end, she hadn't trusted in Frank, and look where it got him. And now Gavin...

Last night, though, she'd trusted Gavin. More than she thought herself capable of trusting anyone. It had been the page that had done it. Even when he left her apartment with a coffee in hand and a quick kiss at the door, Gavin hadn't given her an explanation about the early-morning page or the reason for his abrupt departure.

Tony reached across the table and laid a steady hand over hers. She hoped he didn't feel her tremble.

"I need you to be discreet, Tony. Like I said, this isn't anything serious. I certainly don't want to be setting something off or stepping on anyone's toes."

"I hear ya," he replied calmly, adding a smile of encouragement. "Don't worry, I'll look into it. I don't know how much I can get for you, but I promise you I'll be discreet.''

She felt queasy. The memory of making love with Gavin was still so fresh...and now she was doubting everything he was. She should hate herself, Claudia thought. Yet, the cop in her, the training that had taught her to question everything and have complete faith in nothing, could not settle until she knew that Gavin was who he claimed to be.

''I TOLD YOU BEFORE I ACCEPTED this assignment, Lieutenant, I am not going to rush this.''

Lieutenant Randolph rocked back in his over-stuffed leather chair and tapped a silver pen on one armrest. He'd done exactly that for the past forty minutes as he listened to the update on the case, and Gavin had long since grown impatient with the display.

''I just thought you'd have something a little more concrete by now. Thought that you'd be a little further along.''

''Further along? How much further along can I be? I've not only gotten assigned to Gunning's squad, but I've managed to get myself partnered with your prime suspect. What more can you want?''

''Evidence,'' Randolph said, as though it could be found by simply opening a file and reading a report. ''I just don't want you getting wrapped up in some homicide investigation.''

Gavin barely managed to swallow his caustic laugh. ''And how else did you expect me to work undercover in Homicide?''

"I didn't think you'd be on the street with the squad so soon. I figured you'd have answers for me before it came to that." With the end of his pen, he scratched his chin and seemed to regard the files on his desk. "This dead PI, Silver…you're wasting your time, Monaghan. You're wasting IAD time."

"You have got to be kidding me. You don't see the potential for a connection between Owens and Silver? A connection to the corruption?"

He'd filled Randolph in on everything except his meeting with Dr. Daniel Carver. He knew the kind of reception he'd receive from the lieutenant on that one. As far as his boss was concerned, the Owens investigation was over. If Gavin even whispered the fact that he was considering the possibility Frank Owens may have been murdered, Randolph would almost certainly have him off the case. He'd view it as Gavin's continued obsession with the case he'd always believed he'd bungled.

"It's a long shot," Randolph replied. "I'd rather have you focus on the corruption. I'd rather have you focus on Claudia Parrish."

Gavin fought back the mental image of Claudia in bed this morning. Focusing on Claudia was not the problem.

"That's why I worked so hard to get partnered with her. And the Silver case is ours. The best way I can investigate her is to work this homicide. If you want it done right, it's going to take time. I told you that from the start. There's no other way. I am not going to let you rush this investigation like the last one."

Randolph regarded him long enough that Gavin felt the need to get up from his chair and pace to the windows. The city had come alive; traffic streamed off the Jones Falls Expressway and snarled into the city streets as pedestrians scurried to their offices. It was after eight o'clock. He'd already missed morning roll call. Claudia was bound to be wondering what had happened to him.

He'd have to come up with some kind of explanation. He hadn't said anything back at her apartment, hadn't been able to bring himself to lie to her after what they'd shared. Yet, there was no way he could tell her the truth.

"All right," Randolph grumbled at last. "I'll give you more time, but only because I trust you. Only because I know that if anyone's going to get to the bottom of this mess it's you."

"Thanks, Lieu," he said. Unwilling to give Randolph the opportunity to change his mind, Gavin snatched up his jacket. "I'll get back to you the second I've got something."

"I count on it."

"And just to be safe, sir, I suggest that when you need to meet with me again, we do it elsewhere. I don't like the odds of being spotted coming in here."

"Understood," Randolph said as Gavin walked out the door.

Gavin kept his head down as he crossed the IAD office, unwilling to be drawn into any conversation with fellow agents. Only when he passed his own desk did he pause.

He'd not sat there for almost a month. Whatever

current files he had were at home. Working undercover, he'd wanted, as much as possible, to stay out
of the lion's den...or, in this case, Gavin thought, the
rat's nest.

The sight of the desk that had been his for five
years was a cold reminder of who he was, what he
was. And by the time Gavin reached the street reality
had taken a firm grip.

He filled his lungs with the crisp morning air, letting it bring him to his senses. He was an IAD agent.
He had an investigation to conduct. And Claudia was
his primary target. It didn't matter that he believed
her innocent; the guilty party still had to be found.
And he could hardly do that with his emotions in the
way.

No, Gavin thought as he turned up the collar of
his jacket and started the short walk to headquarters...no, he could not allow his emotions to affect
his investigation. He'd told his lieutenant that working as Claudia's partner made it easier to investigate
her. But that was a lie.

Still, it didn't matter. He would stay on the case.
And he would stay *out* of Claudia's bed. No matter
how impossible that might seem.

CLAUDIA SAGGED into the cushions of her couch and
kicked off her shoes. Her gaze fell on the closed
evidence box on her living room floor.

They'd found nothing last night. At least, they'd
found nothing related to Silver.

She eyed the bottle of Scotch and the empty
glasses on the coffee table, half-tempted to pour her-

self a drink. Instead, she reached for the remote control, turning on the TV with the slim hope of taking her mind off Gavin.

The day had been long. After her coffee with Tony, she'd headed to the State's Attorney Office and spent several hours reviewing her next case due for trial. From there she'd gone back to headquarters. And still, there'd been no sign of Gavin although someone had mentioned seeing him.

It wasn't until well after noon that she'd glanced up from her desk to see him wander into the back office. She'd tried to read the emotion behind the look he'd given her, but couldn't. And for the remainder of the afternoon, Gavin's standoffishness led her to believe that he'd decided last night was a mistake after all.

He'd worked at his desk the rest of the day, putting together his case folder as she struggled to focus on other cases demanding her attention. What little discussion they shared was brief and pertained to the reports in the Silver case—ballistics and lab results that were still forthcoming. After three hours, when his silence had gotten the best of her and she'd been set to confront him about it, Gavin told her he was going out. And when she offered to come along, he'd declined…again with the same mysteriousness as he'd had that morning.

"Gavin, do you want to tell me what the hell is going on?" she'd finally demanded. Her whisper had been harsh, but not loud enough for others in the bustling office to hear.

"Nothing's going on." He at last came around to her desk. "I'm just going to check on a few things."

"Where did you go this morning?"

The question seemed to have taken him off guard. Or perhaps it was her bluntness that surprised him. "Can we talk about this later?" he'd asked.

"You've had all afternoon to talk to me about it. I just want to know if…if it's about last night."

"No." He gave the office a quick scan and lowered his voice so as not to be overheard. Then he took her hand for the briefest of moments and gave it a gentle squeeze for reassurance. "Really, Claudia, can we talk about this later?"

"Where are you going now?"

"To run down a couple of things."

"Regarding the Silver case?"

"Yes."

"And you don't think I should be involved?"

"I can take care of it. Besides, I can see you're swamped with prosecution reports. I'll call you tonight. We'll talk more then."

Resting her head against the sofa's back, Claudia envisioned the last look Gavin had given her in the office, the small smile of encouragement before he'd thrown on his jacket and walked out. She tried to believe in his apparent sincerity, tried to push away the shadow of suspicion.

So why hadn't he called yet?

Turning off the TV, she tossed down the remote and stood. She unbuttoned her shirt and tugged it from the waist of her pants as she headed down the hall to her bedroom. She'd take a shower and—

The phone shattered the silence of her apartment and Claudia started. Backtracking to the kitchen, she grabbed the receiver. But it wasn't Gavin.

"Claudia. Tony here."

"Hi, Tony." She was unsuccessful in curbing the disappointment in her voice.

"Expecting someone else, were you?" he asked. "Well, look, I can't talk long. I'm in the middle of something, but I wanted to get back to you about what we discussed this morning."

She felt the quickening of her pulse. "You have information for me already?"

"Probably not as much as you'd like, but it's as much as I'm going to be able to get. I talked to an acquaintance of mine who did a stint at the commissioner's office for a couple months last year. She never heard of Monaghan. Now, that isn't to say her time didn't correspond with his, you know? But I called down to D.C...."

Claudia didn't really need to hear the rest, she already suspected what Tony had discovered.

"...a friend of a friend," he went on. "I don't know how reliable this guy is, but he's never heard of anyone named Monaghan working Homicide down there."

Cold reality wrapped itself around her. Her hand felt frozen on the receiver, as the apartment began to tilt and threatened to spin.

"Claudia? Are you still there?"

"Yeah. I'm here."

"So what's this guy about? How is it that he's got you worried?"

"I...I'm not worried, Tony. It's probably nothing."

"Nothing? Crap. If this partner of yours isn't who he says he is—"

"Trust me. It's nothing. Probably just some crossed wires."

There was a brief silence over the line, before Tony said, "You want me to dig some more? I'm not making any promises, but someone's gotta know who this guy is."

"No, Tony. Thanks. I can take care of it."

Claudia hung up. She needed to handle this one herself. How, though, she had no idea.

She'd had only the slightest, niggling suspicion, one that she hadn't actually believed would amount to anything. Her hand lingered on the phone as shock continued to course through her. She wanted to believe there was some kind of explanation, but she knew...

There could be only one reason Gavin's background was a lie. *Internal Affairs.*

The thought sent a cold, angry shiver through her.

Should she have seen it before? Should she have suspected?

No, Claudia thought as she snatched her keys from the kitchen island. There was no way for her to have guessed. No way for anyone to have guessed. IAD almost never went undercover.

Almost never. Only this time, they had.

GAVIN HUNG UP THE PHONE. Unclipping his holster and his pager, he deposited both on the coffee table.

Shrugging off his jacket, he lifted a hand to his shoulder and massaged the knots of tension that had taken root there the moment he'd received the lieutenant's page this morning.

He should have known his day could only get worse after that.

He'd tried to put the morning's meeting behind him. He'd spent the day pretending he hadn't heard the warning tone in Randolph's voice. But he knew. Randolph's promise for more time meant nothing. If Gavin didn't make some documentable progress soon, the next meeting would be far worse than the one this morning. And after that…well, after that he might even be removed from the case.

The thought of someone else handling the investigation sent a shot of dread through him. With Claudia being such an obvious suspect, there was no telling where the case could end up.

The chime of his doorbell startled him. It wasn't a sound he heard often.

Pausing at the coffee table, he opened the side drawer. When he reached for his holstered gun, intending to put it out of sight, someone began to hammer against the solid oak of the front door, even as the doorbell persisted ringing.

Gavin slid the empty drawer shut and removed his gun from its holster. The hammering continued as he unlocked the dead bolt, and by the time he swung the door open, expecting a confrontation, his hand was tight around the grip of the gun concealed at his thigh.

"Claudia?"

She stood on his stoop, her hands balled into fists. She wore no jacket, and the wind tugged at her hair and the folds of her shirt. Glancing past her shoulder, Gavin saw her old Volvo across the street, parked with one front tire half-up on the curb.

"Can I come in?"

He wasn't sure what to make of the tension that was so visible in her face, and for a second he tried to believe it was just a result of the chill in the night air.

"Sure." He ushered her in, closing the door behind her. "That was fast," he said jokingly. "I just called your apartment and left a message."

"Why?" The coldness in her voice banished the last trace of his smile. "So you could get even more information from me?"

Her expression said everything. Her mouth was a tight line, and her jaw flexed a couple of times. But mostly, it was her wide eyes fixed on his, glistening with what he could only imagine were tears of anger, betrayal, maybe even hatred.

He should have expected suspicion. He should have expected that eventually Claudia might check his story. But how was he to know it would come so soon?

"Why didn't you tell me?" she demanded, struggling to control her voice.

"Tell you what?"

"Oh please!" She stepped back then, probably trying to distance herself from his lies. "Do *not* play me for stupid. I'm not some dumb cop fresh out of the academy. Do you think I'd show up on your doorstep unless I knew for sure? Do us both a favor, and don't even think about continuing the charade.''

Gavin's grip loosened around his gun. He crossed the room and put it on the coffee table. When he turned, Claudia hadn't moved.

''Why didn't you tell me who you were working for, Gavin?'' Her voice trembled, but he knew she wasn't about to shed any tears in front of him.

''I'm supposed to be undercover. I can't just go around telling people.''

''Oh, so it's all right to sleep with me, but you can't tell me who you're really working for, is that how it works?''

He wondered if she'd avoided mentioning Internal Affairs deliberately.

''I did want to tell you. But I had to be careful. Trust me, I *wanted* to tell you.''

''Trust you? Please.''

The short, biting laugh that slipped from her lips was colder than anything he could have imagined from her. But he deserved it, as much as he deserved her next statement.

''You wanted to tell me, but you wanted to sleep with me first, isn't that the way it goes?''

''That's not it at all, Claudia.''

''So tell me the way it is then. Tell me what you're investigating...who you're investigating.''

He held her stare for what seemed like minutes. Still she stayed her ground, betrayal tearing at the usually soft lines of her face.

''*Tell me!*''

''I can't.''

She shook her head, her eyes narrowing for an instant before she turned from him. Her hand was on the doorknob.

"Wait, Claudia." Taking hold of her arm, he spun her around. In that brief touch he could feel her muscles taut with anger, and he knew that if he didn't start talking she'd be gone. Maybe forever. "It's about the corruption on the force," he admitted finally. "But you already knew that. You had to at least suspect it."

She waited for him to release her arm before nodding.

"The tampering of evidence," he said. "It's been going on for more than a couple years now. It continued even after Frank's death."

"So you suspect me, is that it? Is that why you couldn't tell me?"

"No. No, I don't suspect you, Claudia." He swallowed the partial lie. He couldn't tell her the truth. Not the absolute truth—that he couldn't *not* suspect her. "I couldn't tell you, because I couldn't tell anyone. That's what undercover means."

The quip didn't play well with her. She closed her eyes as if unable to look at him any longer. When she opened them again, she scanned the living room instead, perhaps searching for something to say, and Gavin could only pray that she didn't spot the file on his coffee table—the file compiled on *her*.

He'd expected her anger eventually. He just hadn't expected it so soon. Nor had he anticipated its depth. Then again, given what he knew about her relationship with Frank, why *wouldn't* she be fuming? Even though she didn't know the whole truth about him, she knew he was Internal Affairs, and that was enough. After spending the past year hating IAD, blaming the department for her partner's death, how could she bring herself to stand here and look at him?

When she did turn her gaze onto him again, there was no mistaking the condemnation in her eyes.

"You IAD sons of bitches are all the same," she said at last in a voice so full of hurt and contempt that his heart felt as though it had stopped.

She turned then, grappling for the knob and swinging the door wide to a blast of cold air. He moved fast, snatching her arm again to stop her, although he had no idea what he could possibly say to keep her there.

She tore herself free of his grip, and he could see that she was losing her battle to keep back her tears.

"Damn it, Gavin. I trusted you."

Then she was gone—down his steps, crossing the street and slamming the door of her car. The Volvo's engine roared to life and the tires let out a short squeal as she drove away. He cursed softly, the vapor from his breath curling into the cold night air as he watched her taillights disappear.

CHAPTER TEN

CLAUDIA HAD LET FAITH CHOOSE the restaurant, especially since their dinner date was due entirely to her sister's persistence. She'd called two nights ago, within minutes of Claudia coming through the door of her apartment after her confrontation with Gavin. Faith had recognized the tremble in her voice instantly and had refused to take no for an answer to her invitation to an early dinner.

After a full day of trial preparations and many hours hunting down lost witnesses for the State's Attorney Office, Claudia was actually grateful for Faith's arm-twisting. She needed to sit back and unwind. And the relaxed, intimate atmosphere of Donna's Café in Mount Vernon, several blocks up from headquarters, was the perfect place.

Now, as she stirred cinnamon through the dying foam floating on her half-drunk cup of cappuccino, Claudia felt the stress of the day begin to fade. Across the small round table, Faith fingered a stray blond wisp that had slipped from her otherwise-tidy French braid.

"So have you actually spoken to him since storming out of his place?" she asked, regarding Claudia with a look she might have expected from an older sister.

Claudia shook her head, pondering the wisdom of having told Faith as much as she had about Gavin. For a short time, before their waitress had come to clear their plates, Claudia had watched her sister's expression come alive, practically glowing with delight, as Claudia mentioned the night she'd shared with Gavin. But Faith's glow had dimmed when she heard the rest of the story. And now Claudia could tell that Faith was about to do her damnedest in the repair department.

"You've only seen him around the office?"

She nodded. "A couple of times yesterday, but it was after roll call and then later as I was leaving. I haven't had a chance to talk to him."

"What you mean is you *could* have talked to him, but you didn't."

Claudia exhaled her frustration. "And what am I supposed to say to him, Faith?"

"An apology might be a good start."

"Apology?"

Faith's shrug was so casual that Claudia wondered if her sister had absorbed even half of what she'd told her about Gavin and his connection to IAD.

"What am I supposed to apologize for?"

"Oh, come on, Claudia. It's not as though you haven't already figured it out yourself. It's so obvious. You're blaming Gavin for everything that went wrong with the investigation last year."

Yes, she had certainly considered that.

"It's understandable you'd do so, but it doesn't

make it right. I know you still feel Frank's loss. And you'll never find me disagreeing with you that the investigation was totally unjustified. You have every right to blame IAD for the way they bungled things. But don't blame Gavin. It's not as if *he* had anything to do with it."

A silence fell over their table and the sounds of other patrons—clinking glasses, the rasp of cutlery and muted conversations—seeped into Claudia's awareness as she considered Faith's words. Of course, she'd thought the very same thing herself, tossing and turning in bed the past two nights, lying awake and watching the glare of headlights pass over her bedroom ceiling. But hearing that same logic spoken out loud by someone else, instead of the anxious, heartbroken voice in her head, gave it more credence.

"I gotta ask you," Faith continued, "what exactly is it you feel for Gavin? And don't you dare sit there and tell me it's nothing, because I know you too well, big sister. You've never moved this fast, so it's got to be something."

The foam was long gone from her cappuccino. Still, Claudia swirled the spoon through the cooling liquid. She remembered the way Gavin had made love to her, the way her body had responded to his, and the way he'd made her feel…so alive.

"I'm not sure what I feel for him," she said at last, but knew Faith would detect the lie.

"You slept with the man, Claudia." Thankfully her sister lowered her voice. "And if there's one thing I know about my sister, it's that she doesn't jump into the sack with *any* man unless she has some damn strong feelings for him.''

It was a valid observation. She had never taken relationships lightly. Three years younger than her, Faith had been dating in high school ages before Claudia had even had her first solid crush. All the more reason for her to question why she'd slept with Gavin so quickly.

''Well,'' Faith said, tossing several bills down to cover the check as she'd been determined to do, ''if you feel so much for the man, why don't you try trusting him? You always did have an issue with trust. I swear, it's being a cop that's done it to you.''

''I did trust him, Faith.'' Claudia heard defensiveness edge her words. ''More quickly than I've trusted anyone in my life. Maybe *too* quickly.''

''And you're saying that now you don't, simply because he's an IAD agent who's doing his job? Honestly, I don't think you can view this as Gavin breaking your trust. He admitted the truth when you confronted him, right? In fact, given that he's supposed to be working undercover, he probably told you far more than he should have. The way I see it, he wouldn't have taken that risk unless he had some real feelings for you himself.''

How many times had Claudia's mind conjured up the image of Gavin standing in the entranceway of his house, a look of hurt in his eyes? She hadn't been able to identify the emotions glimmering behind his pained expression. So perhaps Faith had a point. Maybe she hadn't given Gavin enough credit; maybe his feelings for her were deeper than she'd thought.

Abandoning her cold cappuccino, Claudia retrieved her coat from a wall hook and followed Faith out of the restaurant. The silence that fell between them as they strolled toward St. Pauls Street where Faith had parked her car was the comfortable kind that Claudia imagined only sisters could share. But in it, she knew Faith was working on something. She could almost sense her sister's struggle as she searched for the exact words she needed.

She was right. After Faith opened the door of her Subaru, she turned once more to face Claudia, her expression solemn in the dusk that had settled over the city.

"You know what this is really about, don't you, Claudia? This mistrust and anger toward Gavin?"

"I'm sure you're going to tell me."

"It's Frank."

Claudia waited for the explanation that was sure to come.

"Look, I know you're the older one here, and in my books you'll always have full credit for being the smarter of the two of us. So I'm sure that what I'm about to say isn't something you haven't already considered yourself over these past months. But I'm going to say it anyway because I'm worried about you. And because I'd like to see you happy again. The way you were when you had Frank in your life."

"Faith, I'm fine."

"No, you're not. You still haven't let go. I can see it in your eyes. Whenever anyone even mentions Frank's name, I can see the pain. It's been ten months, and, yes, I know they've not been easy. But

it's as if you've built this kind of pedestal to place
Frank's memory on. You've let all these months of
silent mourning make him into something that no
other man could possibly come close to matching.
He was an incredible person. I'll never deny that. But
he was only human, Claudia. And so are you. You
deserve to be happy. To have someone love you.''

A crisp fall breeze whistled up St. Pauls Street and
rattled through the dried leaves clinging to the
branches of the sycamore above them. Claudia worried her keys through her fingers. She was about to
agree with Faith, but her sister spoke first.

''I just want you to be happy. And I'm worried
that as long as you keep Frank on that pedestal,
you'll never be able to fall in love again.''

Claudia studied her sister's serious expression.
Fine lines creased at the corners of her eyes as she
squinted against the sharp wind, and worry traced
several deeper lines across her forehead. She certainly wasn't the tomboy of their youth anymore.

''How did you get to be so wise?'' Claudia asked
her, watching Faith's smile mirror hers.

''I had a good teacher.''

They said good-night, hugging each other in the
cold street, and finally Claudia watched Faith drive
away. She stood for several moments, churning
Faith's comments over in her mind before she tugged
the edges of her coat around her and headed south.

Not until she reached headquarters did Claudia de-
cide to go back up to the office instead of getting
into her car and driving home. She would put in another hour or so on paperwork, she thought, even

though she realized it was a pretense. There was only one reason she took the elevator to the sixth floor—she hoped to see Gavin.

There was a lot of truth in what Faith had said. She couldn't dismiss the possibility that Gavin *did* have some feelings for her. She'd let her anger cling to her over the past two days, blocking her ability to see the truth. And she'd never know the whole truth unless she talked to Gavin.

At her desk once more, Claudia tried to focus on her files, checking her watch periodically and wondering if perhaps Gavin had already come and gone. It wasn't until an hour later that her work was interrupted.

"Detective Parrish?"

Corky Ellis, a gaunt, stooped man in a lab coat who had probably spent too many years hunkered over a microscope, stopped at the corner of Gavin's desk. Under one arm, he clutched a folder. "Is Detective Monaghan here? I'm not sure I know what he looks like."

"No, Corky, he's not in. Is that the ballistics report on the Silver case?"

Corky gave her an abrupt nod. The quirk had always given the ballistics expert a nervous appearance; it was a tic that never failed to elicit a desire within Claudia to place a calming hand on the man's shoulder whenever she saw him.

"You're the secondary on the case, aren't you?" he asked.

"Yes."

He handed her the report. "Have you found the murder weapon yet?"

Claudia shook her head. "Not yet."

"Well, at least now you'll know what you're looking for." A rare smile crept onto the expert's thin lips. "You got two slugs. The one from the body was too mangled to get anything off of. But I got lucky on the one they dug out of the wall. Must have gone clean through the victim and been buried in the plaster. Without that slug, I probably wouldn't have had anything for you guys. You know these .44s—"

She passed a quick glance over the results and her heart started to race.

"There's no telling where a slug of that caliber is likely to stop or what kinda damage it'll sustain before it does. Plaster's good, though. The density helps stop a slug before it can get much farther."

Claudia looked at the bottom of the page. "You were actually able to determine the make and model of the weapon used?"

"Well, you're just lucky I'm so good."

She looked up in time to catch his wink.

"That's why it took me a while. I wanted to be sure," he added.

"A Smith & Wesson .44 Magnum?" she asked, reading the bottom of the report.

"No question."

She scanned the report again, her thoughts tumbling over the possibilities. Was it merely coincidence? *Only dumb cops believe in coincidences,* Frank had told her early on. *Nothing's a coincidence until you've ruled out every possibility.*

"You're good, Corky," she whispered as her mind whirled.

"I keep telling you guys that."

"Do you think you're good enough to do me a favor?" she asked, the quiver of suspicion deepening.

"Depends on what it is. We're pretty backed up downstairs."

"I know you are. So what if I begged?"

It was a struggle to smile, but it was definitely worthwhile. Corky surrendered. "All right, what is it?"

"I wonder if you could compare this slug to the ones from the Lamont Brown case."

"But that case is over a year old."

"I know."

He studied her, as if preparing to argue about the merit behind such a task.

"It would mean a lot to me if you could do it as soon as possible."

Finally he gave her one of his characteristic nods and let out a breath. "All right, I'll look into it."

"And listen, this is only a hunch I'm working on, all right? I'd be a bit embarrassed if it doesn't pan out, so maybe you could keep it quiet?"

Mistrust pursed his lips, but another smile won him over. "Fine."

"I'm off tomorrow, so if you do manage to get results by then, could you page me?"

"No promises, Detective. I'll see what I can do."

"Thanks, Corky."

And with that the ballistics expert turned from her

desk and scurried out, perhaps anxious to avoid any further unexpected work in the form of favors.

Checking her watch again, Claudia stood and reached for the jacket on the back of her chair. Six-thirty and still no sign of Gavin. She'd call it a day. Maybe try phoning him at home tonight.

Waving to several detectives, she headed to the elevators and down to the parking garage. Fatigue rippled through her. She imagined she could fall asleep the second she got home, but no, she needed to talk to Gavin first.

And then, Claudia spotted him. Rounding the corner to the second level where she'd left her car, she saw his tall figure. She called out his name, and the bottom of his coat swirled behind him as he spun around to face her.

He held his ground, waiting for her to get to the top of the ramp, his hands buried deep in his pockets, his face revealing no expression beyond what she guessed was mild surprise at the fact that she was actually speaking to him.

"Gavin, I...I wanted to talk to you," she said when she reached him.

One glance into those dark eyes and Claudia felt the now-familiar pull. She was drawn to him, no question. In spite of the anger, in spite of the questions, there was still that undeniable thrill when his eyes met hers. She hated it, even though it exhilarated her.

"I've been thinking about the other night and I want to apologize. I shouldn't have said the things I did. I was out of line."

His silence was unnerving.

"I'd like us to talk, Gavin. Can we go somewhere?"

When he nodded at last, a wave of relief flooded through her. "I've got some paperwork to type up," he said. "But I can pick you up at your place when I'm through."

"That would be great."

"Fine. I'll see you in a while."

She caught the briefest hint of a smile on his lips before he turned from her, and she tried to take hope from it. But when he reached the elevator and looked over his shoulder, Claudia wasn't sure what to make of the worry she saw in his expression.

GAVIN COULDN'T COUNT the number of times he'd wanted to pull Claudia aside, to say something... anything in order to break their two-day silence. But what could he have said?

Even now, as he reached the landing outside Claudia's apartment, he wasn't sure what he could possibly do to regain her trust. He knew he didn't deserve it. And he couldn't begin to guess what would come of their meeting. He only knew that he wanted to see Claudia, needed to see her. The past two days had been unbearable. Over and over again in his mind he'd replayed their lovemaking. And over and over again he'd remembered her angry words.

It wasn't until then that Gavin understood what it was about Claudia that had so consumed him. She filled a deep void in his life and in his heart, one he'd been too busy over the years to even realize was there until he'd held her in his arms. When she'd stormed out his front door, he'd felt for the first time the full extent of that void, and he longed for her to fill it again.

She answered on the first knock, greeting him with a nervous smile. She wore a plain white T-shirt tucked into faded, well-fitting jeans. After all the suits he'd seen her in, it was a refreshing look. Gavin let his gaze take an appreciative sweep as she lifted a hand to push back her thick blond curls and let him in.

"So where would you like to go?" he asked, unable to think of anything else to say.

"Actually, I was hoping we could talk first." There was a slight tremble in her voice. He wasn't the only one who felt awkward and uncertain.

Shedding his coat and holster, he followed her to the couch, spotting the wine bottle on the coffee table. It had been opened, and one of the two glasses she'd set out was already half-empty. Gavin wondered if she'd needed the drink to loosen up. If so, it hadn't done the trick. Her tension was visible as she seated herself stiffly on one end of the couch.

He nodded when she offered him a glass, and watched her pour the crimson liquid. She looked and smelled fresh. She'd taken a bath, Gavin thought, groaning inwardly as he tried to stop the involuntary image of her naked in a tub of bubbles.

"Sorry about the heat," she said at last, settling back into the cushions. "My superintendent started up the furnace the other day. I can get you a T-shirt if you'd like."

"No, I've got one." He took off his sweater and straightened the T-shirt he wore underneath. When he looked over, he caught her stare and wondered if the color on her cheeks was really from the heat.

"So…have you gotten anything new in the Silver investigation?" she asked after he picked up his wineglass.

"Not really. The lab reports are just starting to come in, and without any witnesses there's really not much to go on right now. I've been talking to a few acquaintances of Silver's, but no one was really aware of what he'd been up to, or who might have had it in for him."

"Well, you already know who had it in for him— the same person who's behind the evidence tampering."

"That's the most likely suspect, yes."

"Kind of fortuitous that you were on shift the night Silver's body was found."

He wasn't sure what to make of her tone but heard the residual bitterness.

"True," he said. "But even if it had gone to another squad, I would have found a way to work the case. You didn't ask me here to discuss the Silver investigation, though, did you, Claudia?"

She let out a tense breath and took a swallow of wine.

"No, not really. Look…the other night…I was wrong to come down on you the way I did."

"Not really."

"Yes, I was. You have a job to do. I…I understand that now. I know about being dedicated to the force. I respect you, Gavin, as a cop, and as a person. My accusations the other night were not entirely warranted."

"Claudia, it's—"

"No, please, let me say this. I was hurt by the secrecy, but I do respect you for doing your job, and for your commitment. I think I know you well enough to realize that you carry your detective's shield with a lot of pride. And still, you were willing to risk that loyalty by telling me the truth. You didn't have to trust me with your identity, and now that I've had a little time to think about it, I realize my reaction was wrong."

"It was understandable."

"But wrong. I let my anger get the better of me. The thing is, I've spent almost a year blaming IAD for Frank's death, for the wrongful accusations and the unjustified persecution. I shouldn't have taken it out on you. I can't hold you responsible for someone else's incompetent investigating."

"Claudia, I think…" He swallowed hard, tasting the bitterness of even more suppressed lies. How could he tell her that she was wrong? That she had every right to blame him for what had happened a year ago?

Setting down his wineglass, he reached over to take her hand in his. He was grateful she didn't pull away, but at the same time, she placed a finger against his lips before he could say another word.

"No, let me finish. See, the thing is, I have an issue with trust. I didn't trust Frank in the end, and my lack of faith was what probably got him killed.

But I want to trust you, Gavin. If we are to have any sort of relationship, any chance at being together, I need to trust.''

She shifted closer to him on the couch, and Gavin wanted to scream at her *not* to trust him, to run away before he hurt her with the truth. But he didn't have the chance.

''And I do hope for something between us. I really do,'' she said. ''I feel something for you…something I can't describe right now, but it's there.''

Rain scratched at the dark windows, yet he barely heard it. Every sense was focused on Claudia. His body was alive with wanting her—wanting to feel her in his arms, to taste her, to smell her, and let the heat of her desire envelop him.

''I've missed you, Gavin,'' she confessed, her voice barely a whisper. ''I'm not sure what it is about you, but…''

When she kissed him, there was no denying the truth behind her words, or the intensity of her longing. Nor was there any denying his. In the past two days he'd thought of Claudia and little else, but even recalling their passionate lovemaking, he hadn't imagined he'd missed her this much. The touch of her hands, moving down his chest to the waist of his pants was almost more than he could bear. The hunger it sent through him overrode any reason he may have had left. He knew he should stop her, tell her the truth, but the urgency of her desire obliterated all ability to protest. And when she eased her hand even farther down, pressing it against his already mounting erection, Gavin couldn't contain his low moan.

"Claudia…" It was a halfhearted attempt to stop her.

"Shh, Gavin." She held a finger to his lips, still tingling from the heat of hers. "No more words. I want to be with you. Come on." She took his hand, about to lead him to her bedroom, when her mouth claimed his again.

Unable to end this, Gavin lifted her from the couch and into his arms. He wasn't sure how he made it all the way to her bedroom, but when he reached the side of her bed, Claudia was still kissing him. There was a desperation in her kiss, a hunger that mirrored his own.

He lowered her onto the tangle of sheets as she clung to him. She tore at his T-shirt, pulling it over his head, as he yanked hers loose from the waist of her jeans. Beyond the rain-spattered windows of her bedroom, a street lamp shone through the half-open slats; pallid fingers of light touched Claudia's skin, raking across the exquisite curves of her body as she lay before him. She hadn't been wearing a bra, and Gavin paused to suckle each dark, firm nipple.

He unzipped her jeans and tugged them from her waist, taking her panties with them, before he moved over her again.

He knew she was going to be wet even before he touched her, and the thought of burying himself deep within her sent a shudder of yearning through him.

Claudia, too, seemed desperate to feel him inside of her. When she reached for the nightstand drawer, her fingers were at his belt. Groping, struggling, twisting free the buckle, she then eased the fly over his erection. With a deep groan that could have come from either of them, she wrapped her hand around him.

"I've missed you so much," she murmured, her breath hot against his neck.

There was no sweet, languid foreplay this time. Only the driving need to be with each other. There was no holding back, no restraint. But there needn't have been. She was as ready as he. Gavin felt Claudia tighten around him, and then they cried out together.

HE WASN'T SURE how long they lay there, unmoving, both spent. But eventually he rolled to his side, and Claudia nestled her cheek against his chest and wrapped herself around him.

It had been only two days, he tried to remind himself.

And yet, during those two days apart, when he'd believed he'd lost her, Gavin realized that Claudia had come to mean everything to him. It didn't matter that they'd known each other less than a week. The connection between them was vital, alive and undeniable.

"Claudia?"

Her response was barely a murmur, and Gavin wondered if she was asleep.

"Claudia, I think I might be falling in love with you."

The second the words left his lips, Gavin knew he shouldn't have spoken them. It was the absolute truth, but it wasn't fair to Claudia. How could she possibly face him once she found out he was the IAD agent who had investigated Frank? And given the indescribable peace he felt right now, lying next to her, how could he tell her?

He wondered if he imagined the subtle stiffening of her body then, but she said nothing in response to his admission.

He knew he should leave but couldn't. He said nothing after that, letting the silence embrace them as he stroked her hair, feeling her breath fan across his bare chest.

For a long time she said nothing, and when she did finally speak, nuzzling against him, he started slightly.

"Gavin, I wanted to ask you..." Her voice was barely a murmur, its soft tone awakening desires all over again. "I wondered if you could do something for me."

He didn't know why he should feel the spark of dread that shot through him then, until Claudia continued.

"I thought maybe you could find out who headed the IAD investigation."

Instantly, every muscle in his body tensed. She had to feel it; she had to sense the chill that crept over him in that second. But when she raised herself up onto her elbows to look at him, she seemed unaware.

"Why?" he asked, the word almost choking him.

In the yellow glow of the street lamp, he could see her eyes glisten with restrained tears. Yet her voice was as strong as her determination.

"I want to know," she answered him simply. "I

need to know who was behind the allegations, who handled the case."

He watched resolve settle across her face and wondered how long she'd been waiting to ask him, or whether she had just thought of it now.

"And what would you do with the information, Claudia?" he asked her at last.

"I'm not sure really. I just want to know. I've always wanted to know."

How could he tell her? His stomach twisted and bile rose to his throat at the thought of confessing the truth. *How could he* not *tell her?*

"All I'm asking is that you look into it, Gavin," she prodded. "See what you can find out."

"Even if it wasn't against policy, and even if I *could* get you a name, what would it prove?"

"Nothing, I guess. It's just that maybe I'd be able to put the whole issue behind me if I actually had a name, if I actually knew who was responsible for Frank's death."

Tension clenched along his jaw. He tried to calm it by tucking one loose curl behind her ear.

"Then we should focus our energies on finding the person who really *was* responsible for Frank's death...whoever killed him," he told her. "If he *was* murdered."

He wasn't sure what to make of the expression on her face, and for a moment he thought—hoped—she'd given up on the notion.

But she hadn't.

"Please, Gavin. Can't you just look into it? For me?"

"You realize that the agent might not even be with IAD anymore, don't you?"

She lowered herself again, pressing her warm curves against his body as her cheek nuzzled his chest. "I don't care. I need to know who it was."

After that, there was only the sound of the rain pelting the windowpane and the occasional rev of a car's engine down in the street. As he listened to her breathing deepen and felt her body gradually relax, Gavin held her tighter, afraid that it might be his last chance to do so.

CHAPTER ELEVEN

OVERNIGHT, THE CLOUDS HAD dissipated, giving way to a brilliant blue sky. Morning sun flooded into the apartment, stretching its rays across the bed as Claudia closed the last section of Friday's *Baltimore Sun*. The rest of the paper, already read, lay scattered among the sheets as she sipped her coffee.

While she'd slept, Gavin had showered and put on the same clothes he'd worn yesterday. He'd woken her with a kiss, then handed her the paper and a steaming mug of coffee.

She'd kissed him back, wrapping her arms around his waist and feeling the heat of longing wash through her. She told him she wished he had the day off, as well, and made him promise to come over right after he finished his shift this afternoon.

Gathering the sections of the paper and dropping them to the floor, Claudia lowered herself into the warm sheets again. This afternoon seemed a lifetime away.

There had been an undeniable urgency behind Gavin's lovemaking last night, an urgency that confirmed the emotions she'd seen in his face the night she'd stormed out of his house. And any question regarding his feelings for her had been put to rest after they'd made love.

I think I might be falling in love with you, he'd whispered in the darkness. Too afraid to admit her own feelings, she hadn't known what to say in response. So she'd said nothing. Instead, she'd asked him about the agent behind the initial corruption investigation.

She was grateful for Gavin's eventual compliance, even though she knew he was right—knowing the name of the person responsible was not the way to put Frank to rest. The only way she could do that was to find out who really had killed him. Then she could at last get on with her life, which now appeared to include Gavin.

Claudia reluctantly left the bed. Maybe she would go in to the office after all. She could check with Corky herself on the ballistics tests, see where he'd gotten with them. Tying the sash of her robe, she padded barefoot to the living room.

Claudia stopped as her gaze fell on the box next to the couch. She hadn't opened the box from Evidence Control since Gavin had closed it several nights ago. She hadn't been able to bring herself to go through the contents again even though she knew she should before returning it to headquarters.

Lowering herself onto the couch, she dropped one hand to the cardboard lid. She traced her fingers across the smooth surface, uncertain if she could open it.

She didn't hear the footfall on the stairs outside her apartment; if she had, the sudden hammering at the door might not have startled her as severely as it did. Her heart skipped a beat as she shot up off the couch, and before she could get to the door, the pounding started again.

Rarely did she use her peephole, but the insistence of whoever was on the other side of the door demanded it. Confusion gripped her when she viewed the convex image of Gavin. He had raised his fist again when she swung open the door.

Not even his impatient hammering could have prepared her for the anger that sharpened his features. She was reminded of the first time she'd opened her door to find him on her landing, demanding to know where Silver's journals were.

But this anger was even darker than the last. So dark, it frightened her now.

"What is it, Gavin? What's wrong?" Unconsciously she drew the collar of her robe tighter over her chest.

He brushed past her into the apartment, each step punctuated with a simmering rage. When she closed the door and faced him, a muscle along his jaw twitched and clenched.

"Gavin, you're frightening me. What the hell's going on?"

From his breast pocket he took out a piece of paper. He unfolded it before handing it over.

"I think this was mistakenly put on my desk instead of yours. Do you want to explain it?"

When she managed to tear her gaze from his, she looked down at the report in her hands.

A combination of shock, relief and panic swept through her. It was the report from Corky.

"Claudia?" Gavin prompted her harshly. "What is this about?"

She scanned the report. Corky's handwriting had never been the easiest to decipher, but the results were amply clear—a match.

"It was a hunch."

"A hunch?"

She looked back at Gavin and was startled once again by the anger and the suspicion that lingered in his eyes.

"Talk to me, Claudia, because I'm starting to believe the worst here."

"When I saw the report yesterday afternoon on the slugs from the Silver murder and that the presumed weapon was a Smith & Wesson .44 Magnum, it…it just seemed too coincidental. It was a hunch, Gavin. Nothing more. I swear."

"So what do these results mean then?"

Claudia took a deep breath, trying to absorb the implication behind Corky's report in the onslaught of Gavin's ire. "I'm not entirely sure. I wasn't actually figuring on the two cases matching."

"The Brown case?"

"Yes. The murder weapon that went missing was a .44 Magnum. It's not exactly a popular street gun, so I figured…well, as I said, it was a hunch, so I asked Corky to run the comparison."

"And this report proves that the gun used to kill James Silver was the same weapon that supposedly disappeared. What does this imply to you, Claudia?"

There was no mistaking the accusation that lowered his tone, but she had no time to take offense. She was too excited.

"It implies that our theory was right. Silver *was* investigating the corruption and Frank's death."

"Uh-huh." He prompted her for more.

"It implies that whoever shot Silver is connected to the evidence tampering. The .44 Magnum from the Brown case was stolen from Evidence Control. Whoever has been behind the tampering obviously took the gun and received a good payoff from Lamont Brown or one of his gang for the weapon's disappearance. Then, I guess, this same person somehow discovered Silver was looking into Frank's death. Maybe Silver even approached the person himself, confronted him, because whoever it was obviously panicked and killed Silver for fear of exposure."

"And the gun?"

"Well, presumably the killer used the stolen Magnum so that the weapon wouldn't be traced back to him."

"Or her," Gavin suggested with a coldness she'd not seen from him before.

She felt herself go limp, the report almost slipping from between her fingers as she stared back at him. Had she heard him right? He couldn't possibly mean...

"That's *it,* isn't it? That's why you stormed over here." Disbelief gripped her, almost stealing her voice. "God, you suspect *me,* don't you?"

Even if he'd had a response, Claudia didn't give him a chance to voice it.

"Do you realize how insane that is? If I had *anything* to do with this, why would I have run the comparison on the slugs? It would just draw attention to the connection between the Brown case and Silver's murder."

"Unless you knew that eventually someone else would." Gavin's tone was almost too calm. "And as long as you did it first, as long as *you* were the one who ran the comparison that proved the connection, you would have the appearance of innocence."

"So you do suspect me."

"No, Claudia. *I* don't. But others may. I wish you'd told me about this." He took the report from her. "This all points to you—Silver, Frank, the Brown case and the missing Magnum. People are going to suspect, especially since you were the last person to sign for that .44 before it went missing."

She could barely speak as she saw what his words really meant. "I don't believe it. *I've* been your primary target from the start, haven't I? You haven't been investigating the unit. You've been after *me*. You couldn't have known I was the last person in the chain of evidence on that case unless you'd looked into it specifically. God..."

She shook her head, incapable of saying more as she watched him return the report to his breast pocket.

"Claudia, I have to tell you something."

"No." She held her hands up. "No, Gavin. You've told me quite enough."

"Hear me out."

"I don't want to hear anything you have to say. I want you to leave."

"Claudia—"

"Leave, Gavin. Now!"

If he'd protested again, she might have screamed at him. Instead, with a final flash of those dark eyes, he turned from her and didn't look back.

With the door ajar, Claudia listened to his fading footfall accompanied by the sound of Mrs. Cuchetta's piano-playing.

She felt paralyzed, and the effort of crossing the foyer to close the apartment door was almost impossible. She tugged the edges of her robe tightly around her, but the chill that went through her had nothing to do with the draft from the stairwell. It went deeper than that.

On shaky legs, she started back to the bedroom, but not before her gaze fell on the evidence box one last time. *So this was how you felt, Frank,* she thought. The false accusations, the suspicion, the utter absence of faith, and the desperation to be believed. Except that Frank hadn't known who was investigating him. At least for him it hadn't been personal.

She needed to get out of the apartment. The memory of her night with Gavin was too much to bear. With anger spurring her, Claudia went to the bedroom to dress.

AFTER THROWING ON A PAIR of jeans and a sweater, Claudia left her apartment and drove around for over an hour, running errands. She didn't dare go to the office, afraid she'd run into Gavin. After returning to Fells Point, she saw the crush of the lunch crowd at Jimmy's and walked around the corner to The Daily Grind instead.

Sitting at one of the side tables, she leaned her head back against the rough stone wall of the former mill. She closed her eyes, blocking out the din of the coffee shop, and replayed her conversation with Gavin. How could she possibly work with him now? What was she supposed to say the next time she saw him?

"So this is where you come on your days off, huh? Hanging out with the younger, hip crowd?"

She recognized Tony's voice immediately. Opening her eyes, she attempted a smile, but he obviously noticed the effort it took.

"Whoa. What happened?" he asked. "Your dog die?"

She didn't respond but gave him a smirk.

Never one to need an invitation, Tony pulled out a chair, its legs rattling across the centuries-old floorboards. He set his takeout cup on the table and straddled the chair.

"I never figured you for a trendy place like this," she joked.

"Hey, a guy's gotta have his coffee. I don't care where it comes from, as long as they don't go putting all that cinnamon crap on it. I'm actually just passing through. Heading up to the Northwest. They think they might have a lead for me on this latest case of mine."

"Congratulations." But she could barely manage a smile.

"Seriously, Claudia, what's going on? You okay?"

"Sure. I'm fine."

"You don't look it." His gaze was fixed on her as he lifted the plastic lid of his cup with his thumb. "This doesn't have anything to do with what you asked me to check into earlier this week, does it? About Monaghan?"

She needn't have nodded. Tony had to know he was right the second she let out the breath she'd been holding.

"What's going on, Claudia?"

Gradually she nodded. It was anger toward Gavin, coupled with a sadness she just couldn't shake, that made her want to talk to Tony. And why not? Why shouldn't she turn to a friend?

"Your leads were right about Gavin. He never worked D.C. Homicide or drove the commissioner's car."

"So what's his story then?"

Claudia paused to take a drink from her mug. "He's IAD."

When she lifted her gaze, Tony seemed at a loss for words.

"Internal Affairs? No shit." He lowered his voice to a harsh whisper. "You're kidding me, right?"

If only she was, Claudia thought, shaking her head.

"Are you sure? How do you know?"

"He admitted it to me. I confronted him the other night after you told me what you found out."

She watched Tony nod slowly, obviously absorbing her revelation, and she was grateful that he didn't ask why Gavin would admit such a thing to her.

"I don't know what to do, Tony. I mean, I can hardly keep working with him, knowing he's IAD. But what do I say to Sarge? What reason do I give him? And what about the Silver case?"

Tony was shaking his head. "I don't know, Claudia. As far as Sarge goes, you know he's not going to listen to any excuses. And the Silver case, well, Monaghan's the primary, right?"

"Yes."

"Then I'd say you just leave it to him. Let him do the work and you stay out of his way. These IAD guys...I don't trust the slimeballs. Cripes, especially if they're resorting to working undercover." He lowered his voice even more and leaned across the table closer to her. "Listen to me, Claudia. I'm going to give you the same advice I gave Frank a year ago—*stay out of it.* Don't fall into the same trap he did, okay? Most of all, C.Y.A.—cover your ass. And stay the hell away from Monaghan."

He stood then, shoving the chair back under the table and scooping up his coffee cup. "I gotta go. I've got witnesses waiting for me. But I'm telling you, Claudia—don't trust him."

Claudia watched him leave. He swung open the door and stepped out into the sunshine. Through the café windows, she saw him check for traffic before sauntering across the street to his car.

Tony was right to warn her. It was the same advice she'd given Frank herself—let IAD do their job, and they'd do it right. They'd find him innocent.

But where had that advice gotten him? Not only had IAD continued to target Frank, but the pressure had merely increased in the last few weeks of his life.

Claudia turned back to her coffee. What choice did she have? She had to back off, let Gavin do his job. Soon enough he'd find out she was innocent. Not that her innocence was going to make any difference to their relationship. There had been too many lies, too much suspicion and too much hurt, for her to believe there was even the slimmest chance left for them.

THE WARM AROMA of fresh bread from the H&S Bakeries combined with the smells of the harbor and wafted through the open window of the Lumina. Behind the wheel, Gavin surveyed the comings and goings of patrons to The Daily Grind.

Claudia had been there for almost an hour. He'd seen Tony go in, only to come out fifteen minutes later with an oversize cup. Gavin hadn't doubted that the detective had stopped to chat with his colleague.

And still, Claudia hadn't come out.

He felt ashamed at having followed her here. In fact, he'd followed her since she'd left her apartment a couple of hours ago. He hadn't planned on it; it had been opportunity more than anything.

After leaving her apartment, he'd sat in the car for almost twenty minutes, going over their heated argument and pondering her theory regarding the results of the ballistics test. Then he'd spotted her coming out. And when she steered her Volvo down the street, he'd followed.

He had no idea why. He only knew he wanted to talk to her, to explain. He wanted to convince her that everything was going to be okay, and that he wasn't going to listen to his superiors, who were anxious to point the finger at the first available suspect. He wanted to tell Claudia that he'd take his time and do whatever was needed to prove her innocence.

Yet, after two hours of following her around, he still hadn't been able to bring himself to approach her.

Why? Did there remain a small part of him that actually believed Claudia could be guilty of the evidence tampering, as well as Silver's murder?

It was the IAD agent in him, forever suspicious, that was unwilling to rule her out entirely as a suspect until there was concrete evidence of her innocence. Ever since finding the folded-up report mistakenly put on his desk instead of Claudia's, Gavin had harbored a complex battle between his head and his heart—his heart disbelieving Claudia could have anything to do with the corruption, and his head refusing to totally dispute the evidence.

As he sat outside The Daily Grind, his heart was the louder voice. But how reliable was that? If he put some badly needed perspective on this, he could see that his emotions had cost him a good deal of the professional objectivity he'd always managed to retain in the past. When it came down to it, how well did he know Claudia? He might feel as though he knew her better than any woman before, but the fact remained, he'd known her all of one week.

When Claudia stepped out of the coffee shop, Gavin slumped behind the steering wheel. Not that she could have seen him. Her car was parked down the street. Without even a glance in his direction, she turned up the collar of her leather bomber jacket and crossed the cobblestoned street. The breeze off the harbor ruffled her short hair, and Gavin remembered its silkiness between his fingers.

He remembered a lot of things from last night and then this morning.

He'd have to hang on to those memories, he thought as he watched her get into her car. Memories might be all he'd have of Claudia now.

SHE HADN'T KNOWN what else to do. By going to the office, she ran the risk of running into Gavin. So instead, Claudia returned home.

With her T-shirt knotted at her waist and the sleeves rolled up over her shoulders, she directed her energies at cleaning. Every last trace of him had to be wiped away. She'd already washed last night's glasses and poured the undrunk wine down the drain.

Now Claudia focused on her bed. Tearing off the sheets, she balled them into a crude bundle and shoved them deep into the hamper. If only she could do the same with her emotions, she thought, turning back to the dismantled bed. But even without the linens, the memories of their night together lingered.

She started to remake the bed, each tug of the fitted sheet over the mattress accompanied by another whispered expletive. Then she found his sweater draped over the trunk at the foot of her bed. Without thinking, she lifted it to her face, feeling the bite of wool against her skin. It took no effort to recall the way he'd held her, the way his body had felt against hers.

With another curse, she tossed it onto the bed along with the duvet.

No! She was not going to do this to herself. She had to put Gavin out of her thoughts. She need only remind herself of the suspicion she'd seen flicker in his eyes this morning to eradicate any residual feeling she had for him.

Angrily she switched on the vacuum cleaner. If nothing else, she'd at least have a clean apartment to show for all her hurt.

For almost ten minutes she vacuumed, shoving furniture aside with steadily rising bitterness. Lifting the bed skirt, she drove the vacuum's head underneath several times. She was still swearing when she felt it strike something.

Immediately she shut off the vacuum. Just over the whir of the dying motor, there was the unmistakable sound of an object skidding across the hardwood floor.

Confusion gripped her as she eyed the gun that had come to rest on the opposite side of the bed. The feeling turned to dread when she recognized the model.

A ray of late-afternoon sunshine caught the chrome muzzle of the Smith & Wesson .44 Magnum. Not just any .44 Magnum, Claudia realized as she stood over the weapon, but *the* .44 Magnum.

CHAPTER TWELVE

THERE WAS A BUZZING in Claudia's ears, and her pulse began to race. She wasn't sure how long she stood over the gun, staring at it, her mind clamoring to put the pieces together. It wasn't until the buzzing was replaced with the shrill ring of the phone that she was able to move.

She picked up the receiver just before the answering machine clicked on, her gaze riveted on the gun in the middle of her bedroom floor.

"Claudia. Sergeant Gunning here."

"Sarge." Shock seemed to have stolen her voice and Claudia had to clear her throat.

"I'm sorry for calling you on your day off. But since I'm away this weekend, I needed to check with you on this Silver case."

"Sure. What's up, Sarge?"

"I just had a friend of mine from the Eastern District drop in. Apparently he worked with Silver years ago and was asking how things were going with the investigation."

"Mmm-hmm."

"So I gave him what I could. Said we didn't have any suspects yet, that I had two of my best on it, and then he told me something very interesting. He says

Frank was once Silver's partner. Were you aware of that?''

"Yes, I was."

He seemed to take a moment to digest her response.

"So, I take it then that you and Gavin aren't ruling out the remote possibility of a connection between the two cases?''

"Well—"

"The thing is, I got to thinking. You had asked me about the contents of Frank's desk the other day, so I called down to Evidence Control,'' he continued, the unoiled squeal of his chair punctuating the tension she heard in his voice. "I figured I'd look into it myself, so I asked for the box and was told that your partner had already signed it out.''

"Yes, sir."

"Is there anything you want to share with me?''

"It's Gavin's investigation, Sarge."

"Yes, but it's *you* I'm talking to. I want you to fill me in on whatever angles you two are working.''

"I really think you ought to speak with Gavin."

"If you've got any suspects—"

"None that I know of, but Gavin has been working the case more than I have, I really think—"

"Do you know where he is?''

"I'm sorry, Sarge. I don't."

There was another silence, followed by a loud exhale. "Fine. But when you see your partner, tell him I want the both of you in my office first thing Monday. This case is going to start catching media attention if we don't get some answers soon. I want to see what kind of strategies we can come up with.''

"I understand, Sarge.''

He hung up before she could wish him a good weekend.

She fumbled with the receiver, missing the cradle several times as her gaze returned to the gun.

Only a few hours ago she'd theorized to Gavin the relevance of the .44 Magnum. She'd explained her belief that someone had stolen it from Evidence Control for a payoff, then used it to kill Silver because it was handy and couldn't be traced.

The last time she'd seen the gun was shortly after they'd wrapped up the Lamont Brown crime scene. Not three days later, when she'd had the arrest warrant signed, the gun was gone. They'd turned Evidence Control upside down with no luck. She never believed she'd see the .44 again.

Let alone in her own apartment.

So who had put the gun there? The only person she'd had in her apartment in weeks was Gavin, and he'd certainly been the only one she'd invited into her bedroom.

But the suspicion was fleeting. She knew exactly how long the gun had lain under her bed, waiting to be discovered by her or by someone else. Her memory raced back to the night she'd come home with Gavin and startled the burglar.

Only he hadn't been a burglar. He hadn't broken in to steal anything. He'd come to plant the incriminating weapon. She remembered Mr. Goucher's description of the man he'd seen leaving Silver's office building the night of the murder…a description that matched her intruder. More than likely the same man who had shot and killed James Silver.

Taking a pen from the top of her dresser, she hooked it through the trigger guard and carefully lifted the weapon from the floor even though she was certain she wouldn't find any prints on it.

She dropped it onto the bed and stared at it. She needed time to think. Someone had gone to great effort to set her up. Someone desperate, Claudia thought, otherwise they would have simply disposed of the murder weapon. Then again, they'd been desperate enough to kill Silver, so why *not* plant a gun?

But who?

And who could she turn to?

Internal Affairs? How could she take it to Gavin when he already harbored such doubt in her innocence? Claudia sat next to the gun. No, handing it over to Gavin would be the equivalent of signing her own arrest warrant.

She needed a plan. Maybe she'd have to take care of this herself. In order to prove her innocence to Gavin and to IAD, she'd have to find the guilty party herself.

But wasn't that exactly what she'd begged Frank not to do? God, how could she even contemplate such foolishness? It was professional suicide. She'd lose everything.

A knock on her door shocked her into action. She bolted up from the bed, her heart pounding. Panic surged through her as she stared at the gun. The knocking sounded again. With no choice, Claudia hurriedly yanked the duvet over the Magnum and headed to the door.

GAVIN COULD TELL the second Claudia opened her door that something was wrong. Her expression was tight and her complexion pale. She seemed more than a little apprehensive at finding him on her landing, but he had trouble believing it was entirely due to their confrontation this morning.

"Are you all right?" he asked before she could even greet him.

"Yes, I'm fine." The hand she lifted to brush back one unruly curl trembled slightly, as did the awkward smile that struggled to her lips. "I just…I wasn't expecting company."

"Obviously." He nodded to her attire.

"I was cleaning."

"Oh. I was hoping we could talk," he said, half-expecting her to slam the door in his face.

She didn't respond. Instead she held his gaze, gripping the door as though it was the only thing holding her up.

"Claudia, please. Let's discuss this."

"Why do I get the feeling I should ask to have my lawyer present?"

"You know that's not necessary. I trust you. You're not under suspicion."

Still she blocked the door.

"Can I come in?"

Again a nervousness flickered over her face. He wasn't sure what to make of it, and for a second, he wondered if she already had company.

"I won't stay long," he added.

She let him in at last, closing the door and following him into the middle of the apartment. She certainly had been cleaning. Other than the unmade bed he glimpsed down the corridor, the place was spotless.

He exhaled deeply, but it did little to release the tension that gripped him. What could he say when he saw such mistrust in her eyes? How could he convince her?

"Claudia, I want...I really need you to believe me when I tell you that everything's going to be okay."

"Are you referring to your investigation or us?" she asked bluntly.

"Both. But I think, at this point, you're probably more concerned about my investigation."

She remained silent.

"I want you to know that I'm going to do whatever it takes to get to the bottom of this. I'm going to find the truth. You have to understand, though, that my lieutenant and his chief are both pushing me to resolve this. There've been too many cases lost because of the evidence tampering, and they're ready to point the finger at the first available suspect. But I want you to know you can count on me to be fair and not to jump to conclusions *and* to go the full distance to find the guilty party."

Still, she said nothing.

"Claudia, please, say something."

"What?"

He ran a hand through his hair. "I don't know.

Maybe tell me you have faith that I'll get to the bottom of this.''

She crossed her arms over her chest. "Pardon me if I don't ooze faith in the person who's got me targeted in a major IAD investigation."

"You're *not* my target, Claudia. No one is. I'm not investigating you. I'm investigating the corruption."

"Right. Whatever you say."

But simmering beneath that calm surface of accusation, there was no mistaking her nervousness. Then he saw the twitch at the corner of her right eye. He'd seen it once before, when they'd first arrived at Silver's office, and he remembered wondering if it was some kind of a nervous tic.

"Do you want me to leave, Claudia?"

"I…yes, I think that would be best." Her hesitation made him question the sincerity of her response.

"Fine, I'll go." Involuntarily his gaze went to the bedroom and the unmade bed where, just last night, they had shared such passion. He cleared his throat. "Let me get my sweater," he said, spotting it atop the tangled duvet.

He was already stepping past her before she objected.

"I can get it for you," she said abruptly, but he was halfway down the hall with Claudia at his heels.

When he stepped through the door, she barged ahead of him, reaching for the sweater before he could. And when she handed it over, she placed herself firmly between him and the bed.

"What's the matter with you?" he asked.

"Nothing. I just…I'd like you to leave."

He cast a glance over the bedroom, almost expecting to find someone there, someone she intended to hide from him…or perhaps some *thing*. But there was only the aftermath of major cleaning. Or "purging" as the case might be.

He *was* too late. No amount of explanation was about to bring her around. She'd already done her best to get rid of every last trace of him.

Still, he would have staked his career on the fact that Claudia was desperate to keep something from him.

"What is it, Claudia? What are you hiding?" Maybe he'd been a cop too many years. He'd looked too often into the faces of the guilty, searching for the lies, and always expecting the worst of people. He wondered if he'd ever lose that suspicious heart.

"Never mind," he said at last, ignoring the gnawing suspicion, *wanting* to trust. "I'll go."

But he got no further than the doorway.

"Gavin, wait. I…"

When he turned to look at Claudia again he wasn't sure what to make of the tension that twisted her expression. Her eyes darted from him to the bed, and then back again. And as she lifted a hand to rub her forehead, there was no mistaking the violent tremble that had taken hold of her.

"I have to show you something," she said haltingly.

She stood motionless for a moment. Finally, when he thought for sure she'd changed her mind, Claudia reached for the duvet.

Nothing could have prepared him for what he saw when she swept it off the bed.

"What is this?" he asked, studying the lines of the weapon, the wide chrome muzzle, the heavy walnut grip and the Smith & Wesson insignia. "Is this yours?"

"Not exactly."

His pulse quickened, and he forgot to breathe. Frantically he searched the top of Claudia's nightstand and found a ballpoint pen. With it he hooked the gun by its trigger guard, holding it up and examining it more closely.

It couldn't be…

"This is a .44 Magnum, isn't it? This is *the* .44. From the Brown case."

"I think so. Yes."

"But it…" No, there was no explanation. Not beyond the obvious. Rapid fire, the scenario played in his mind: the gun from Claudia's case, the gun that was last signed for by her before it went missing, the same gun that had been used to kill James Silver…and now it was in her possession.

"Oh God, Claudia…what have you done? What are you—"

"It's *not* how it looks." Her voice was thin, with a kind of desperation he'd not heard from her before. "Let me explain."

"What's to explain? Especially after this morning, after you laid everything out—the comparison of the slugs, and the rationale behind using this gun to kill Silver. How can it *not* look bad? Do you realize that by possessing this weapon you can be charged with

Silver's murder? Not to mention a slew of other things.''

She stepped away from him then, pacing the bedroom floor as though needing to put space between them. When she turned to look at him again, anger tightened her mouth and narrowed her eyes.

"You are *so* Internal Affairs, aren't you, Gavin? So quick to suspect. So damned ready to point a finger.''

"I'm just telling you how it looks.''

"God! I know how it looks! And I'm sure that whoever planted that damned gun under my bed knew how it would look, too!''

"You're saying this was planted?''

"Oh, come on, Gavin, you can't honestly believe *I'm* behind this? What was all that you said only moments ago about trusting me? About me not being under suspicion?''

"Then tell me how it is you've got this gun in your apartment.''

She came within a couple feet of him.

"The break-in last week... Not only was nothing taken, but the intruder matched the description of the man leaving Silver's building the night of his murder. Haven't you wondered why he came here if he didn't take anything?''

"Then why didn't you bring the gun to me?''

"Because I *just* found it.''

"But you weren't going to give it to me at first, were you? You tried to get me out of the apartment, so I couldn't find it.''

"I was afraid.''

"But it's evidence, and you tried to hide it."

"It wasn't like that."

"You didn't exactly offer it up as new evidence."

"And it's *not* exactly evidence when it's been planted, is it? Not to mention that it's hardly a lead. You don't actually believe you'll find any prints on that, do you?"

He shook his head. This time he took the step back, unable to stand so close to the woman he had such mixed feelings about. He cast his gaze to the floor, no longer able to meet her challenging stare, but he was certain she'd recognized his skepticism.

"For crying out loud, Gavin, if I wasn't innocent would I have even shown you the gun?"

Too many possibilities charged through his mind, each one clamoring to be heard. He needed time to process all this.

"Gavin, do you honestly believe I have something to do with all this? The corruption? The tampering? Silver's murder?"

He looked up to see desperation cloud her anger. It was her turn to shake her head, and he thought he saw tears beginning to well in her eyes.

"Is that what you honestly believe?"

"Honestly? I don't know what the hell to believe anymore."

From the first moment he'd looked into Claudia's eyes, he'd seen something that made him sense a connection with her. And he'd feared that sense. Even then, he'd worried about the potential for his emotions to get in the way of his investigation.

And he'd been right to worry. His feelings for her

had made him blind to the truth. Seeing her now, as he dangled the incriminating weapon from the pen, Gavin felt as though someone had driven a knife through his heart. More than anything he wanted to believe what she was telling him. But how could he?

Gavin knew he needed space. He needed to get away from the seduction of Claudia's gaze so he could think straight. So he could regain his focus.

"I've let my emotions cloud my judgment. I've allowed my feelings for you to mislead me, Claudia," he admitted at last. "But that doesn't really matter now. What I feel or believe isn't the issue. The facts are…and the evidence. As a cop, you can understand that. And right now, combined with everything else IAD has on you, this doesn't look good."

"What do you mean by that? Exactly how much false evidence *have* you compiled against me?"

There was no mistaking the betrayal that swam in her eyes now. Beneath that, though, Gavin could see something new—fear.

Claudia feared him.

And in that moment, Gavin wanted nothing more than to take her into his arms. He wanted to hold her, as though feeling her body against his might convince him that everything she was saying was the truth. But he couldn't.

He had to go. There was nothing left to say.

Taking one last look at her, feeling the knife twist at the sight of her pain, he started for the door, the .44 still dangling from the pen he gripped securely in his hand.

It was her voice that caused him to stop.

"What are you going to do, Gavin?" she asked, her voice a ragged whisper.

He didn't look back.

"My job."

CHAPTER THIRTEEN

IN THE FRONT SEAT of her Volvo, Claudia shivered against the chill. With no cloud cover and a full moon hanging in the sky overhead, the temperature had plummeted since sunset. Now, at ten o'clock, it was close to freezing. Curling her hands up into the sleeves of her leather bomber jacket, she considered turning over the engine and cranking the heat. But if she did that, she knew she'd only end up driving away instead of doing what she'd come here to do.

For half an hour, she'd stared across the empty street, watching Gavin's house. Lights were on both upstairs and down, and several times she'd seen his silhouette behind the curtains. She wondered how much longer she had to sit out here before she found the words she needed to persuade him.

But she knew time wasn't going to offer her any answers. She'd had time—all last night, all today...and still she didn't know what she could possibly say to convince Gavin of her innocence. Even seeing him at the office hadn't brought her any closer to knowing; it had only made the tension worse.

Then again, she'd taken a certain amount of comfort in his presence at the Homicide offices today. If he hadn't shown up for shift she might have believed he'd concluded his investigation, especially since he had enough evidence—false or not—to charge her.

But she might have found more comfort if Gavin had actually made eye contact with her even once during the entire shift. He'd worked mainly on the computer in the other office, doing his best to avoid her, and by the time they'd been relieved by the following shift, Gavin had vanished.

Claudia exhaled, her breath fogging up the driver's side window momentarily as she watched Gavin's shadow move behind the first-floor window again. She had to talk to him. There was no alternative.

The only way she'd convince IAD that she wasn't guilty was to give them the responsible party. Finding that person, however, after the failed attempts by IAD themselves, was certainly not something she could do on her own. She needed help. Gavin's help.

Just like Frank had needed hers, Claudia thought, leaning against the headrest.

Now, more than ever, Claudia knew how Frank had felt in those last days—the anger, the helplessness, and the desperation to convince someone to believe. The same someone who claimed to love you.

In the end, she hadn't helped Frank. Why should she expect Gavin to help her?

Her fingers toyed with the keys hanging from the ignition. She should just leave, drive away before he realized she'd come. Maybe she should take Tony's advice and stay out of it, let IAD…let Gavin do his job.

But how could she?

Watching Gavin walk away yesterday while she

stood helpless in the middle of her bedroom, she'd
known it was over. There could be nothing between
them after the deep wound of betrayal she'd seen in
his eyes, after the suspicions she knew he harbored.
But feelings aside, she wasn't here expecting any
kind of resolution in their relationship. Any chance
for love between them was gone now; she wasn't
about to kid herself otherwise.

No, she was here because her job was at stake.
Her entire career was in Gavin's hands. Even if she
had to beg, she would convince him of her innocence. Because without her career, she had nothing.

Finally she opened the car door. Pocketing the
keys, she crossed the street, each step shakier than
the last. She remembered her previous visit to
Gavin's, how she'd stormed out his door in a rage
after discovering he was IAD. Her performance had
to be better this time. She needed to win Gavin
over…at whatever cost, she thought as her finger
trembled over the buzzer.

There was no way she could have anticipated the
emotions that swept through her when he opened the
door. He wore a plain cotton shirt and well-worn
jeans, and his chin sported a five-o'clock shadow.
Claudia couldn't remember anyone looking so good
to her. She released a tense breath.

Gavin didn't smile. Nor did he look at all surprised. Wordlessly he ushered her inside.

"I ordered a pizza," he said after he'd closed the
door. He gestured toward the coffee table. "It's a bit
cold, but I can heat it up if you'd like some."

Claudia's gaze went from the closed pizza box to

the clear plastic bag on the other corner of the table. She recognized the evidence bag immediately; more importantly, she recognized the .44 Magnum inside.

"I don't think so," she answered him. "I don't have much of an appetite."

Beside the gun were several file folders. She had no doubt one of them was dedicated to her. But she didn't get a chance to see as Gavin covered them with yesterday's edition of the *Sun.* It was a solid reminder of how easily he could turn her in, and she tried to take heart in the fact that he hadn't done so yet.

"Gavin, I…" She jammed her fists into the pockets of her jacket and glanced around his living room, unable to bring herself to look into those dark eyes that held such seductive memories.

"Would you like to take off your jacket? Stay a while?"

She shook her head. "No. I don't think so. I just came over to… Gavin, I…I've never begged for anything in my life. But my entire career is on the line here." She hated the weakness she heard shake her own voice.

"I know." His tone, in contrast, was calm. He was about to sit on the couch, but when she didn't make any move to join him, he crossed the floor to stand before her. "Why else do you think I haven't done anything yet? Why do you think the gun is still sitting on my coffee table?"

"I've been a cop for fourteen years, and in all that time, I've been trustworthy. I think I've set a good example. I'm hardworking and dedicated. You won't find a single complaint anywhere in my file. Hell, I haven't even taken one sick day in all those years. I've given everything I have to the department. I've given my life. And I'm a damned good detective, Gavin. One of the best.''

''I know.''

Of course he knew. He had a complete file on her.

''And now I'm being framed. Just like Frank was. I had nothing to do with that .44 going missing. Nor did I have anything to do with Silver's murder, or his missing date books, or any of the evidence tampering that's been going on. Someone put that gun under my bed knowing it would incriminate me.''

''Claudia—''

''It's probably the same someone who tried to set up Frank. Who let him take the heat for the tampering. This is history repeating itself. I know what Frank went through now. I know the helplessness he felt. To have your entire career…your life…threatened by false allegations. I'm telling you, Frank had nothing to do with any evidence tampering. He was as dedicated to the force as I am, maybe even more. He could never have done the things IAD accused him of. Whoever headed that investigation was relentless. Unjustly relentless. I'm begging you, Gavin, don't make the same mistake that agent did. Don't let IAD point a finger at me just because I'm the easiest suspect. Give me the benefit of the doubt Frank wasn't granted.''

''Claudia, I have to tell you—''

''No,'' she interrupted. ''Hear me out. Please. You said you let your emotions cloud your judgment. You said your feelings for me had misled you. But they haven't, Gavin. If there's one thing I learned from Frank's death it's that you have to listen to your feelings. If I'd done that instead of listening to reason, I would have helped Frank, and he might not be dead today."

She swallowed back tears, feeling the painful lump that had swelled in her throat.

"I'm begging you. I need your help. I need your trust. Please, listen to your feelings, if you still have any for me. Let them guide you, so you can believe me when I say I'm innocent."

"I *do* believe you."

She hadn't expected such quick compliance, and for a second she wondered if it was some trick.

"I do believe you," he said again. "I was wrong to even doubt you. I misread the situation, your nervousness, your attempt to keep the gun hidden. My immediate response was to suspect guilt. It's a job hazard of IAD. I've become cynical...skeptical of everyone. I'm sorry, Claudia."

"You don't have to apologize. Your reaction was understandable. After all, how well do we really know each other? I mean, it's only been a week."

"Actually, I disagree. I feel as though I know you pretty well."

He took her hand in his, and she couldn't deny the surge of desire that moved through her.

"I know it hasn't been that long," he went on. "But I think I have a good sense of what drives you, what it is you stand for, and what you want out of life. Now, maybe it's not the same for you, but I think there's a connection between us, Claudia. And maybe I shouldn't be saying this, but I meant what I said the other night.''

''You said a lot of things,'' she murmured.

''I'm referring to the part about falling in love with you.''

She took a step forward, closing the gap between them. His breath fanned lightly across her cheek as he gazed down at her. She expected him to kiss her, but he didn't. Instead, she saw disquiet in his dark expression. She couldn't identify its cause, though. Hesitation? Uncertainty?

''I don't know if you want to hear this, or if it's even right for me to admit it given the situation we're in,'' he ventured, ''but I don't just think I'm falling in love with you, Claudia, I'm *sure* of it. You make me feel things I've not felt for anyone in my life before. You make me want things that I've never even contemplated. Now, maybe you're right about our not knowing each other that long, but in this short time I can say that I truly respect you. I admire so much about you—your strength, your determination, and especially the courage I know it took for you to come here tonight. You're an excellent detective, Claudia. I don't need your file to see that. And you're a remarkable person. You have a warmth and generosity that cops too often lose. But most of all, there is a light about you. I can't describe it, but it's drawn me from the very moment I looked into your eyes.''

She didn't know what to say. What could she? Nothing had prepared her for the depth of his words.

She'd come here tonight for the sake of her career. Not for one moment had she figured there was hope left for anything between them. And now, more than ever, she wanted to kiss him.

Claudia didn't give him a chance to say anything else. Reaching up, she pulled him to her. Her breath was lost in the intensity of her own longing, and as their lips parted she welcomed the intimate familiarity of their kiss. A deep ache trembled through her, the same one that had led her into his arms more than once in the past week. The same one that sent her heart clamoring over itself.

Lurking beneath that hunger, however, was something stronger. Something that threatened to overwhelm her drive to be with him.

It was fear. A fear of trusting. A fear of loving. But most of all, a fear of losing all over again.

She couldn't be certain if it was Gavin's hesitation or her own that slowed their kiss. But it was Gavin who broke it.

"No. Don't pull away, Gavin. Please. Not now." Her whisper sounded more like a whimper. She may have known it before, but until now, Claudia hadn't acknowledged it. She did have deep feelings for Gavin, feelings she hadn't dared to name. And if she was completely honest with herself, Gavin was the real reason she'd driven over here tonight.

"I need you," she said. "More than ever, I need you, Gavin."

"Claudia…"

She thought it was a flash of pain she saw in his eyes before he closed them. Exhaling a long breath, he lowered his forehead to hers, resting it there as she caressed his cheek with the pad of her thumb.

"Claudia," he murmured again. "I have to tell you something. It's—"

"Shh…no, Gavin. No more words. I want…no, I *need* to be with you. I need to *show* you how I feel."

When he drew back this time, he studied her for several moments as one finger traced the line of her lips, numbing the tingle his kiss had left.

"Please, Gavin," she whispered again. "Take me to your bed. Make love with me."

She took his hand—strong and warm—and led him to the base of the stairs. She was only vaguely aware of her surroundings as he followed her up. Like the living room, the rest of the place looked in need of repair. No doubt it was the hours of the job that kept him from dealing with the renovations.

Then Gavin took the lead at the top of the stairs, ushering her into the master bedroom without turning on any lights. The moonlight was more than enough illumination to see the gleaming hardwood floors and the pine wainscoting, and she didn't doubt Gavin had done the renovations himself. Even the huge oak bed looked as though it had been stripped and oiled by hand.

To her left, her eye caught the low green glow of a banker's lamp in what appeared to be an adjoining office. It sat atop a mahogany desk littered with papers. She wasn't surprised at the idea of Gavin bringing work home.

She studied the bedroom again. Laundry overflowed the wicker hamper in the corner, and a shirt and jacket were draped over the ladder-back chair under the window, giving the room a lived-in look. A sense of comfort and home, Claudia thought.

"This is beautiful, Gavin."

She turned in the circle of his arms, her hands settling on his hips. He lifted one hand and toyed with a curl of her hair, twirling it around his finger a couple of times before tucking it behind her ear. Pale moonlight touched the side of his face, accenting his square jaw and the strong line of his nose. She could only wonder what he was thinking, his gaze so serious, but just beneath that earnestness there was no mistaking the desire she saw in his eyes. Seeing it inflamed her own.

She would have thought herself ready for their kiss then, but her breath caught in her throat when his mouth took possession of hers. As his fingers fanned back through her hair, following the line of her throat to move steadily downward to the V of her shirt, Claudia thought she might cry out with longing.

Deftly he opened her shirt, one button after the next. And when he finished, he tugged it from the waist of her jeans. She shivered against the soft warmth of his hands when they brushed the worn cotton from her shoulders. He traced the line of her bra and cupped one breast in his palm. Slowly he pulled back the lace with his thumb. Shocks of yearning gripped her when he circled the nipple with his tongue, urging it into a hard, sensitive nub.

She was only vaguely aware of her bra dropping to the floor and of Gavin's hands moving over her ribs and across her stomach to the top of her jeans.

His kisses, each one burning with promise, trailed down her neck and across one shoulder.

"Oh, Claudia," he whispered, "what you do to me...the things you make me feel...do you even realize how much—"

"I think I do," she answered before he could finish.

Anxiously she reached for his shirt, each button sliding easily through her fingers until he, too, stood topless before her. She caressed his shoulders, chest and strong torso, and reveled in the quiver of anticipation that seemed to ripple beneath her palm where she touched him.

"Show me," she murmured into his ear as she nuzzled it. "Show me what I do to you, Gavin."

His eyes never left hers as he guided her to his bed. Even when he lowered her onto the sheets his gaze was riveted. He unzipped her jeans and slid them quickly over her hips, dropping them to the floor. He reached for her again, letting his hands make a slow journey across her flesh, exploring each angle and curve as though he feared it might be their last time.

But it wouldn't be, Claudia decided. Seeing the emotion in his eyes, she knew that theirs was no casual fling. She could trust Gavin with her career, with her life, and most of all, with her love.

Taking hold of the waist of his jeans, she rose to sit on the edge of the bed before him. She pressed her cheek to his stomach, and he threaded his fingers through her hair. His heat mingled with hers, his smell filled her senses, and his caresses assured her that this was right. There had probably never been anything in her life *more* right than Gavin.

She kissed her way to his abdomen until she reached the denim barrier. Sweeping her hand over the taut material, she bit back a small gasp. She'd barely begun to touch him, and already he was aroused. Like her, it took no more than the idea of their lovemaking...

She unbuttoned his jeans and eased the zipper down over his erection. He helped her tug the jeans from his hips, and she felt his shudder as she slid her fingers under the waistband of his shorts and pulled them off as well.

Wordlessly, Gavin joined her on the bed, covering her body with his, but then he propped himself up on his elbows. She recognized hesitation in his eyes again.

"Gavin, what is it?"

Even in the dim light, there was no mistaking the slight furrowing of his brow as he brushed back her hair...restrained, even though she knew he must be aching to be inside of her.

"What is it?" she repeated.

He shook his head, closing his eyes. And when she touched his lips, he kissed her fingers.

"Tell me," she urged him.

He exhaled quietly. "I'm just worried."

"About the investigation?"

"No. About us. About our future."

"I know," she admitted softly. "But—"

"What kind of future can we have? You and me? After this investigation, even once I've proved your innocence, there will be questions. Even if I leave IAD, if anyone finds out about our relationship, people will question my conduct during the investigation.''

She nodded slowly.

''We can't hide this, Claudia.''

''Right now, Gavin, I don't care about any of that. I just want to be with you. We'll figure out the rest later. I'm not willing to let this slip away because of police politics. We'll figure it out. I promise.''

Talking this way made her desperate to have him inside of her. She wanted to see the worry gone from his face, leaving behind only the love he proclaimed to have for her.

He moved away, and for a moment, Claudia thought he was stopping, until she realized he was searching for a condom.

She reached for him and still sensed his restraint. He entered her slowly, and she couldn't be certain if he was testing, teasing or simply taking pleasure from the feel of their bodies uniting. She raised her hips to meet his. She clutched at him, her fingers grasping hard muscles, urging him into a fervor that matched her own.

But Gavin needed no urging.

There was nothing between them now, Claudia thought—no lies, no secrecy.

She arched against him, the first white-hot burst flooding rawly through her. She gasped, hearing Gavin's own deep-throated moan. It whispered in her ear as he pressed his face against hers. And just when she knew she could hold out no more, when his name burst from her lips and she begged him for release, she felt his entire body go rigid over her. And as Claudia felt the final, and most powerful explosion of longing, she heard Gavin cry out her name. In all her life, no sound had ever touched her so profoundly.

SEVERAL HOURS LATER, Claudia awoke by degrees: first aware of the smell of Gavin, then the darkness, and finally the dead silence, even though she was certain it had been a sound that roused her from her deep slumber.

She turned her gaze toward the clock on the nightstand. Two-fifteen. Moonlight still filtered through the blinds, but now it stretched no further than the foot of the bed.

She was alone. She reached a hand to where Gavin had lain beside her, holding her in his arms as she'd found sleep. The sheets were barely warm.

From the open doorway of Gavin's office, light fell across the hardwood floor. A shadow passed over it. Claudia slipped from under the covers and pulled on Gavin's robe. Barefoot, she padded across the bedroom to the office door.

A warm flood of affection washed through her when she saw him. He stood at his desk, with his back to the door as he looked at something in his hands. He was barefoot, as well, wearing only a pair of loose-fitting pajama bottoms. Even so, Claudia could well imagine the tight form beneath the light cotton. She felt another tantalizing rush of longing flare inside her, and a smile tugged at the corners of her mouth as she stepped into the office.

He mustn't have heard her, because the second her hands brushed across his skin, she felt his body stiffen. She pressed her cheek against the hard angles of his back, but the tension didn't leave his stance.

He cleared his throat. "I thought you were sleeping."

"Not anymore," she murmured. "Why don't you come back to bed?"

"I'll be there in a minute," he said, turning to face her. But the smile on his lips was a lie.

Claudia knew instantly that he was hiding something, though she tried to give him the benefit of the doubt. She returned his smile, tightening the sash of the robe as suspicion took root.

"What's got you up at two in the morning? You working some big case, Detective?" Her attempt at a lighter tone was a feeble one.

"It's nothing, Claudia," he said, placing a brief kiss on her lips. "Go back to bed. I'll join you in a second." He tried to kiss her again, but she pulled away.

"No," she said. "No more secrets. What is it, Gavin?"

She didn't wait for him to offer to show her the paper. She snatched it from his grasp before he had a chance.

"Claudia, don't—"

But his warning went unheeded.

Instantly she recognized the logo at the top of the sheet—the Baltimore Police Department labs.

"What is this?"

He might have responded, but she didn't hear. Her focus was riveted on the report. Her eyes took in the date—December of last year—ten months old, and then moved to the various lab results. A numbness crept over her, paralyzing her.

Words like "preliminary findings" and "results," then Frank's name and "gunshot residue test-ing"…and finally, the most galvanizing word of all: *negative*.

CHAPTER FOURTEEN

SHOCK AND DISBELIEF darkened Claudia's face. Gavin watched her read the report, then read it again, obviously making certain she understood it correctly. He watched the paper begin to shake in her hand and saw how her breathing had become shallow as she attempted to process the gravity of the report's results.

He wanted nothing more than to take her into his arms and ease the conflict he saw on her face. But she would never have allowed him to. He knew that.

When she lifted her gaze, it was brief. But not too brief that he couldn't see the anger and hurt...the accusation, before she looked at the report again.

He should have told her. He'd tried to last night, several times. He should have tried harder. But he'd given in to his desire. Once she'd stood before him, as naked as her declared feelings for him, Gavin had been lost. There had been no way to tell her he'd been the agent investigating Frank.

Should he have told her from the start? Would it have made any difference?

Definitely, Gavin decided. If he'd told Claudia from the beginning who he really was, he would not have been sharing his bed with her, he would not have been allowed to come so close to her, to love her and imagine a future with her. More than that, he certainly would not be feeling the emptiness he did now at losing the greatest happiness he'd ever experienced.

And there was no question about that. He didn't need to see the pain in Claudia's eyes to know she could never forgive him for this.

"What... Where did you get this, Gavin?" she demanded, anger furrowing her brow and causing her knuckles to go white as her grip on the report intensified.

"From the lab. It's the preliminary findings. They write down the results as they go. Only the final report is submitted to the Medical Examiner's office. The preliminaries aren't usually filed or kept very long."

"How?"

"After we talked to Doc Carver, I went to the lab and started digging through their old records. It took me a few days to find it. Ten months ago the lab wasn't suspect in the evidence tampering. They're still not. But neither was the ME's office nor Carver himself. No one bothered to question the results. If there had been any question, it would have been up to the ME's office to check back with the lab for inconsistencies in the preliminaries."

She shook her head and dropped her gaze to the report again, as if not believing the truth she held in her hands.

"Frank didn't..." Her voice was barely audible. "He was murdered. How long have you had this?"

she asked. "How long have you known Frank didn't fire his gun, that he didn't kill himself?"

"Claudia, I didn't manage to locate that copy until yesterday."

"You never told me."

"I wanted to. But how could I know...I...I didn't know how you'd react."

Her expression was darkening by the second. Last night, after she'd shown up on his doorstep, she'd stood in the middle of the living room and practically begged him not to make the same mistakes and assumptions, not to adopt the same ruthlessness as the man who'd investigated Frank. And now she knew the truth. She had to. He could see the realization take hold. She had to recognize the extremes it had taken him to dig through months of old lab preliminaries, and she had to guess that he wouldn't have gone to such lengths unless he had some personal stake in the results.

"Claudia, listen to me, last night I tried to tell you. I wanted you to know that I was the initial investigator. I—"

When she spoke at last, her voice held a coldness he hadn't thought her capable of.

"You *son of a bitch!* It was you...all along. God, how could I have been so stupid, so naive? You were the heartless son of a bitch who—"

"Claudia! Listen to me!"

Her eyes widened, and she took a step back from his instant rage.

"I did what I had to do!" There was no tempering his voice or his anger.

"I have to leave," she said flatly, the words sounding almost strangled in her throat. She thrust the report back at him and started to turn away.

But Gavin wouldn't let her. He snatched her arm with such a fierceness he was certain she would bruise. But he had to make her listen.

"You can storm out of here if you want, Claudia, and never speak to me again, but not until you've heard me out."

He watched the muscle along her delicate jaw flex several times as her mouth tightened into a thin line of hate.

"A year ago I was assigned to investigate the evidence tampering within the department. But I came in late in the game. IAD had already taken into consideration all the other obvious sources—everything from the individual districts to Evidence Control. And the resounding conclusion was that the corruption stemmed from the Homicide unit. By the time I was brought in, Frank was already IAD's target."

An invisible wall of anger separated them, but Gavin tried to take a shred of encouragement from the fact that at least Claudia was listening.

"Whether you believe me or not, from the very start I didn't agree with the way things were being rushed, and I voiced my objections loudly. It was IAD…my superiors, who targeted Frank. *Not* me. And they wanted the situation resolved immediately. I was getting pressure from everyone above me."

"So that's your excuse?"

"I'm not making excuses. I'm telling you that if it had been anyone else conducting that investigation, they might not have done as much as I did to try to prove Frank innocent despite his apparent guilt. I did everything I could to conduct a fair investigation.''

''Well, it wasn't enough, was it?''

It was hard not to take her caustic remark personally. ''No, it wasn't enough.'' He took a deep breath before going on. ''I stepped down from the case the day Frank was killed. I almost left IAD. Even considered leaving the force. But at the same time, it was the need to know the truth that made me stay, and eventually made me take up the investigation again when they asked me a few weeks ago. I've always thought Frank may have been wrongly accused and I hoped to right that wrong.''

''Why? Because you felt guilty?''

''Of course. How could I not feel guilty? But no matter how much guilt I felt, I knew I couldn't hold myself responsible, whether Frank had been murdered or whether he'd killed himself. I couldn't blame myself. The most I could do was find the truth and clear Frank's name. That night...when I heard about Frank's death, I swore that one way or another I'd find the real person behind the tampering, because I *knew* it had to be someone else, or at least someone who had inadvertently involved Frank.''

''Someone like me, right? You figured you could pin it on Frank's partner, is that it?''

''No. That's what my superiors want to do.''

''And I suppose you're going to tell me that sleeping with me had nothing to do with your investigation.''

''Of course it didn't. And if you believe otherwise,

then you're not only very wrong about me, but very wrong about yourself. I think I know you well enough to say that you wouldn't have come into my bed last night unless you were very sure.''

''Wrong. You don't know me well enough to make any assumptions. In fact, you don't know me at all.''

It was her anger speaking. He realized that. He was certain Claudia had very real feelings for him. If she didn't, he wouldn't be seeing the hurt in her eyes right now.

He paused, allowing himself a breath as he held her cold stare, and when he went on, he tried to inject calm into his voice...anything to keep her there until he could convince her.

''I'm not going to lie to you, Claudia. Of course I suspected you at first, but not to the same degree as my superiors. I wanted evidence first.''

''Well, you've found that, haven't you?''

''And the .44 is sitting down there on my coffee table, isn't it? If I didn't believe you were innocent, why would I still have it? It's a murder weapon, and I can't turn it in because the only person it incriminates is *you!* And do you want to know something else? Before you arrived last night, I sat on my couch and debated whether or not to get rid of that gun. I actually contemplated tampering with evidence myself! And why? Because I believe in you, Claudia. Because I know you're innocent. Just like Frank was.''

The muscle along her jaw continued to twitch.

''No matter what you think of me right now, Clau-

dia, I can promise you that at the end of all this, I'm
going to prove that Frank was innocent," he told her.
"And I'm going to do the same for you. I'm going
to clear your name, but I'm not going to do it by
getting rid of that gun downstairs. I'm going to get
to the bottom of this case. And I'll do it right."

He watched her shake her head, uncertain of what
she was feeling—defeat, anger, resentment, or a
combination of all three. The glow of the desk lamp
warmed the sudden harshness of her features. It required no stretch of the imagination to remember the
passion they'd shared only a few hours ago.

But it was over. No question about it. He'd lost
her.

"I don't know what else to tell you," he said
eventually. "I hope you'll trust me enough to know
that I'll do the right thing. More importantly, I hope
you'll believe me when I tell you that I do love you,
Claudia. Everything I said last night is true."

She shook her head one last time, taking a step
back as though no space could be far enough.

"Claudia—" When he whispered her name, he
heard defeat in his own voice.

Silently she lifted a hand to stop him. She was
finished listening. In fact, she'd probably heard more
than she wanted to. Gavin could do nothing as she
turned at last and walked out. He stood, too numb to
move, knowing by the sounds in the bedroom that
she was getting dressed. Even after he heard the front
door, and moments later the rev of her car engine,
he couldn't move.

He'd said what he had to. There were no more

secrets. His conscience was clear. But his heart was as empty as the silence that wrapped itself around him.

CLAUDIA KNELT to the cold earth and lowered a single rose onto the dried grass at the base of the gleaming marble headstone. Overhead, the wind rattled dryly through what few leaves clung to the poplars lining the west side of the Parkwood Cemetery.

She brought the zipper of her jacket further up her throat, shivering against the afternoon's damp chill. With one hand she traced the sharp edges of the letters carved into the stone.

"I'm sorry, Frank," she said under her breath, although there was no one to hear the admission.

Ever since meeting with Doc Carver over a week ago, she'd felt guilty—guilty for the months of allowing herself to believe that Frank had taken his own life. Ten months ago, she'd caved to others' opinions, to the evidence and reports, instead of relying on her own feelings.

And now that she'd seen the proof that Frank had been murdered, there seemed no way to ease the guilt that had steadily consumed her. That's why she was at Frank's graveside.

She'd come to apologize.

But she'd also come to say goodbye.

Because, no matter what became of her and Gavin, Claudia knew one thing: Faith was right—until she said goodbye, no man could come close to what Frank represented in her mind or what he'd come to mean in her heart. She needed to close the past to

get on with the future, even if that future might not
include Gavin.

Across the expanse of grass and the neat rows of
headstones that swept down the gentle slope, Claudia's attention was drawn to a dark-clad figure. The
man stood over a freshly covered grave, a young
child clinging to his side. Claudia watched the wind
tug at the man's black coat and whip the girl's shim-
mering blond hair around her face.

It must have been the man's stance as he stood
over the grave—the slump in his shoulders and his
bowed head so clearly displaying his grief—that reminded Claudia of her very first homicide case. It
was during that case that she'd learned of the unpar-
alleled defeat a person suffers when death claimed a
loved one. A young woman had been shot and killed
in the course of a robbery. A senseless killing, not
that many of them ever made sense. But seeing the
grief of both the victim's mother and her fiancé had
stayed with Claudia. For days and weeks, she'd wondered how the young man could ever go on. He had
been absolutely devastated by the loss of his fiancée.
She could still remember watching his shock gradually fade to realization, and then, finally his sobs,
sounding as though they'd been wrenched from his
very soul, as she'd held his hand in one of the interview rooms at headquarters.

Most of all, Claudia remembered Frank's words
after the incident.

In the front seat of their unmarked car, parked
along the harbor, he'd told her that he'd learned, after
seeing too many deaths and too many grieving sur-

vivors, that those who were left behind had a choice to make—to either keep on living or to die along with their loved one. However, it had been an easier philosophy to adopt when it involved other people.

Standing now, Claudia cast her gaze back to Frank's headstone. She'd let herself die along with him, drowning herself in her work, letting her cases be the reason she went on each day.

He wouldn't have respected her for that. Not Frank. He would have wanted her to choose life.

And she'd come so close to doing that.

In Gavin's arms, after the many, many dark months, she thought she'd found light. She thought she'd found life again.

And last night, in Gavin's bed, she'd believed she had finally *chosen* life.

A blast of damp wind lashed at her hair and chilled her skin. Claudia lifted the collar of her jacket and glanced up. Low storm clouds raced across a bruise-colored sky, as another shower of yellow poplar leaves fell to the ground around her.

"Goodbye, Frank," she murmured, her hand settling onto the top of the cold stone for a moment. When she turned to walk to where she'd parked her car, Claudia didn't look back. Even once she had closed the door and slid the key into the ignition, she didn't so much as glance at the grave site as she had during her visits in the past.

Her thoughts were on Gavin. There was no denying that his words had affected her. "I don't just think I'm falling in love with you, Claudia, I'm *sure* of it," he'd said. From no one had she ever received

such heartfelt sincerity. Never had she felt such passion and love as she'd found in Gavin's arms. Could
she simply turn her back on that?

Steering the Volvo down the graveled driveway to
the gates, Claudia decided to call him. He'd already
left two messages on her answering machine, and as
his partner, she'd have to speak with him eventually.
After all, there was still the issue of James Silver's
murder. And Frank's.

But more than anything Claudia needed to speak
with Gavin for herself, because no matter how hurt,
she couldn't simply walk away.

THE FORECASTED STORM LOOMED heavy over the Inner Harbor. Turning on his bar stool, Gavin looked
beyond the dingy windows of The Portside bar. Dark,
low clouds rolled in from the east, over the Domino
Sugar Plant's monolithic neon sign, and swallowed
the last of the day's light.

"So you're telling me you've got nothing new?"
Lieutenant Randolph had long since warmed his own
stool and managed to peel away most of the label
from his third beer.

"That's what I'm saying." Gavin took a second
swig from the Natty Bo he'd ordered, but the taste
of the local brew did little to ease the tension he'd
begun to feel when he'd received his lieutenant's
page a half hour ago. It had mounted steadily after
their telephone argument during which Gavin had demanded they meet anywhere but in the IAD offices.

There were no more secrets between him and

Claudia, but that didn't mean he could risk exposure. His investigation was far from complete.

"You've got to give me something here, Monaghan. I can't just hand the chief an empty progress report."

"You can hand the chief whatever you like, but I don't have anything new. I told you from the beginning that I wasn't going to rush this investigation. And I'm certainly not going to do it just to please the captain. If there's nothing new, there's nothing new. Tell him I'm working on it."

Gavin held Randolph's bleary stare, until his superior gave in and diverted his gaze. Frustration drew the man's heavy brows together and he picked more determinedly at his bottle's label.

Gavin took another swig of his own beer and scanned the near-empty bar. He hadn't told Randolph about the .44 Magnum Claudia had found under her bed. No question it had been planted, but he'd be unable to convince his lieutenant of that. Not until he could find the person responsible.

Nor had he dared to mention the preliminary GSR report that proved Owens hadn't taken his own life. As he had too many times already, the lieutenant would claim Gavin continued to be obsessed with Frank Owens's death and couldn't be objective enough to proceed with the investigation.

"All right, Monaghan. I'll do what I can to hold off the captain for another few days. But I'm serious, we're going to need something to give the brass sooner or later."

"Right." Gavin took a final swallow of beer and left his bar stool. Fatigue rippled through his body.

"Listen, Lieu," he said, about to head to the door, "I just thought I'd tell you, once I'm through with this case, I'm leaving."

Disbelief deepened the creases in Randolph's face as he looked up from his beer. "What the hell are you talking about?"

"After this investigation, I'm finished with IAD. I've had it."

"You can't be serious. You'd give this up? You're the best we got."

Gavin shoved his stool under the scarred mahogany bar, its legs scraping noisily against the old floorboards. "Maybe I'm tired of being the best rat in the house."

There was an unintended bitterness in his voice, Gavin realized, and it didn't surprise him to see Randolph's offense at the comment.

He softened his tone. "Honestly, Lieutenant, I would've left sooner if it weren't for this case. You know I wanted to leave the day Owens killed himself. The only reason I stuck around was...well, I thought maybe I'd have a chance to get to the bottom of this mess. I'm going to finish the job I started a year ago. After that, I'm gone. You can expect my request for transfer along with my final report."

He left Randolph then. Only when he reached the door did he hear Randolph's voice again.

"Aren't you even going to finish your beer?"

Gavin didn't look back. "I don't have the stomach

for it,'' he said as he opened the door and left the bar behind him.

Out on the sidewalk, Gavin hunched his shoulders against the sharp wind and headed to his car as the first cold drops of rain spat down.

What was he going to do after five years with IAD? He certainly wasn't ready to quit the force, and going back to patrol was not an option he'd consider. The appeal of joining Homicide had played in his mind more times than he could count over the past few days. He'd thought about going to Sergeant Gunning, asking him if he'd consider taking him onto his squad. They were still short one detective, and Gunning had seemed to warm to him from the very first night they'd talked.

Of course, there was the issue of having been IAD. Once he completed this investigation, it wasn't likely anyone in that entire unit would be willing to work with him, especially Claudia.

No, Homicide wasn't a realistic option anymore. Ironically, he'd probably be much better off driving the commissioner's car, he thought, unlocking his car and getting in behind the wheel. He brought a hand up to his shoulder in an attempt to loosen the knot that had settled there early that morning.

Try as he might, he couldn't stop thinking of Claudia, couldn't wash from his mind the image of her standing before him, defeated and hurt.

There was no question of his feelings for her. Or that those feelings had not biased his investigation. Claudia was a good detective, and he knew her well enough to know she wasn't capable of tampering

with evidence. Hell, she hadn't even been able to
bring herself to get rid of the .44 she'd found planted
under her bed.

He loved her for that. He loved her for many
things.

And now it was all gone.

Closing his eyes, he could remember holding her
last night in his bed, how he'd pulled her close to
his body and felt her mold against him. And he remembered thinking even then that it could be their
last time together. He'd lain awake for a long time,
listening to the comforting sound of her breathing
and her quiet whimpers as she dreamed. He had
thought about what he had tried to tell her, thought
about how he possibly could have…and when. No
matter when, it would have been too late.

He'd also thought about Owens. When she'd first
confessed her relationship with her former partner,
Gavin had wondered if she would ever be able to let
go of the love she so obviously had for the man. But
last night, Gavin had known that Claudia had been
with *him*. With him totally. In the way she'd made
love to him last night, the way she'd looked at him,
the way she'd held him, he'd been certain she too
had hoped for a future together. And he was certain
she had, finally, said goodbye to her past.

He wanted to see Claudia once more. In his head
he'd rehearsed the words he needed to say to her,
things he hoped would convince her that he'd done
his best during his initial investigation.

But he doubted Claudia would ever hear a single
word he had to say. His deception had cut close to

the heart. The most he could do now was get to the bottom of this mess as quickly as possible. Only then could they get on with their lives…even if they were to be separate lives.

And it would start tonight, Gavin thought. He *would* get to the bottom of things. He'd had a hunch for a couple of days now, and it was time to act on it. Turning over the car's engine he checked his watch—six-forty. If he didn't leave now, he'd be late for his meeting.

CHAPTER FIFTEEN

TAKING THE STAIRS to her apartment, Claudia wedged the grocery bag against her hip as she dug her keys from her pocket. She made her way up the stairwell by feel mostly, unable to manage the light switch at the front door with her arms full.

Even before she'd reached the second landing, exhaustion swept through her. She hadn't slept after leaving Gavin's house that morning. She couldn't recall much of the drive home, nor the passing of time once she'd stepped into her apartment. She remembered only the cold numbness that had gripped her, and then the morning light breaking behind her blinds as she'd sat on the couch.

And the day hadn't been much better. She'd risked going into the office because she knew Gavin was off. She'd put in a few hours going over prosecution notes and typing up her office reports, before deciding to go to the cemetery.

During the drive back, and then while pushing a cart down the aisles of the grocery store, Claudia had gone over and over in her head what she could possibly say to Gavin if…no, *when* she called him. Even now she wasn't quite certain what could be said.

Claudia stopped. She'd heard something. She was positive. A throat being cleared?

Standing at the bottom of the final flight, her eyes already adjusting to the dimness, she caught the movement on the landing outside her apartment. For one crazy moment, she thought it was Gavin, that he must have come to see her.

But the shadows were deceiving. Her heart sank when she recognized the figure as a woman's.

"Hi, Claudia."

She knew that voice. "Lori?"

"I'm sorry for coming over without calling." She cleared her throat again, and sniffed. "I just…"

"What's wrong?" Claudia asked, making her way up the last of the stairs. When Lori sniffed again, she was certain the woman had been crying.

"I just needed to talk to someone. I'm really sorry for showing up this way." She reached out and took the groceries from Claudia. "Did you…do you have plans? Because if you do, I can go. In fact, I probably should. This is stupid. Why don't I—"

"No. It's all right. Really." Claudia unlocked her door. "Why don't you come in?"

In the light of the front hall, Claudia could see the puffiness under Lori's eyes. She *had* been crying, and from the looks of it, quite severely.

"Lori, what's going on?"

She took the grocery bag from Lori, setting it on the kitchen bar, before ushering her to the couch.

The crime-scene technician was distressed. Her hands trembled as she wiped her eyes and tucked her dark hair behind her ears. She attempted an embarrassed smile.

"I'm sorry, Claudia. I didn't mean to—"

"Why don't you stop apologizing and just tell me what's got you so upset?"

The sound of a car backfiring sent a spark of fear across Lori's face. Instantly she stiffened, her body going rigid as she perched on the edge of the couch.

It was then that Claudia noticed the red welt along her right cheek. She caught Lori's chin in her hand and turned her to examine the mark.

"Who hit you?" she demanded.

But Lori only shook her head. She dropped her gaze to her lap, then closed her eyes.

Leaving the couch, Claudia went to the fridge. She took out an ice pack, but when she returned, Lori was already standing and shouldering her purse.

"I should go," she told her. "This wasn't a good idea. I really—"

"You're not going anywhere, Lori. Not until you tell me what's going on. Here—" She offered her the ice pack and waited for her to sit down again before joining her.

There was a silent pain in Lori's brown eyes as she gently put the ice pack against her cheek. The quiver of her lips told Claudia Lori was about to start crying all over again.

"Talk to me, Lori."

"I…I'm not really sure where to start. So much has gone on."

"Well, maybe you can start by telling me who the hell hit you."

Lori closed her eyes and shook her head one more time. "I can't…I shouldn't be dragging you into this."

"Into what?"

She bit her bottom lip, seemingly incapable of response.

"Who hit you?" It was no longer a question but a flat-out demand, and Lori seemed to recognize that.

"Tony."

A wave of disbelief washed over Claudia. She must have heard wrong.

"Tony? You don't mean Tony Santoro?"

Lori offered a feeble nod.

It wasn't possible. Not the Tony she knew. Not the man she'd worked next to for the past three years.

Still not believing, Claudia's memory stumbled over the number of times she'd been on a case with Tony. She'd seen his sensitivity toward the families of victims; she'd witnessed his ability to comfort and console. In her wildest imaginings, she couldn't visualize Tony raising a hand to anyone, much less the frightened, apparently shattered woman before her.

"We've been seeing each other…for about a year now. Off and on."

"That doesn't explain why he hit you."

Lori rose again, clearly planning to leave, but Claudia grasped her wrist before she could step away. She didn't let go, even once Lori settled back onto the couch.

"Lori, listen to me. You can trust me. Tell me. Why did Tony hit you? Does he…has he done this before?"

"No. No, this was the first."

"Then why?"

"Because...I guess he was upset."

"That's no reason."

"And...maybe he sort of wanted to scare me."

"Well, he's done a damned good job of that." Claudia jumped to her feet, anger propelling her as she started across the living room.

"What are you doing?" Lori asked, a sob in her throat.

"I'm going to call that bastard and get him—"

"No! You can't! Claudia, he said he'd kill me if I talked to anyone."

"What?"

"He warned me that if I told anyone—"

"Told anyone what?"

But sobs began to rack Lori's body, and she buried her face in her hands. "I can't...oh, God, I can't..." she muttered between gasps for breath.

Claudia wrapped her arm around Lori's hunched shoulders and took her hand into her own.

"Lori, I promise, I won't let anything happen to you."

GAVIN LIFTED THE COLLAR of his jacket, feeling a chill move through him. But it was from more than the damp cold working its way through the open window of the Lumina. A growing uneasiness gripped him as he surveyed the entrance of The White Horse pub on the corner where Holly Street met Lexington, a quarter block up from where he was parked.

He checked his watch. Seven-twenty.

Tony was late.

Gavin watched as a late-model sedan turned off Lexington. He squinted against the glare of headlights and lowered himself a little further behind the wheel. The car didn't stop. It wasn't Tony.

He checked his watch again, in case he'd read it wrong the first time. Then he checked his pager and cell phone. Both were on. Perhaps something had come up, but there was no reason Tony couldn't have made contact. No reason he wouldn't have unless he suspected there was more than a friendly beer behind Gavin's invitation.

His uneasiness deepened. Unconsciously he unsnapped the safety strap of his holster and sat a little straighter.

When he'd driven up Lexington, he'd slowed his car as he passed The White Horse. There had been no sign of Tony. He'd circled a few times, checking the side streets, but it was clear Tony's maroon-colored LeSabre was nowhere in the immediate vicinity.

He'd seen Tony in the shiny new Buick only two days ago in the parking garage. In fact, it was because of the incident that Gavin was here tonight.

It had been early morning, and Gavin had just arrived at headquarters. He'd been sitting in his own car, about to get out, when Tony had pulled in. The detective obviously hadn't realized anyone was watching as he leaned over to give his passenger a quick kiss. And when both car doors opened, Gavin had been mildly surprised to see Lori Tobin step out. He'd seen her flash Tony a smile, then give his hand a parting squeeze before they went their separate ways.

There had been volumes in that single smile, something in the look she and Tony had shared. Gavin had already begun to wonder about Tony—the man's avoidance of him around the office, the forced brevity of their few exchanges. Gavin had figured Tony's sudden reservedness had to do with Claudia. No doubt she'd told Santoro the truth about Gavin's identity. Certainly Tony had good reason to give Gavin the cold shoulder.

But the look Lori Tobin had given Tony that morning aroused even more suspicions. Knowing that Tony had a very personal connection to Evidence Control made Gavin uncomfortable. And that's why he'd called Tony this afternoon, asking the other detective to meet him for a beer. If Tony didn't show, and if he had no good excuse, Gavin would definitely have to investigate the man further.

He'd give Tony another fifteen minutes, then call it a night. He thought about heading over to Claudia's. Her apartment was only a few blocks west of here.

Not that he had any idea what he could possibly say to her. But maybe, if he kept the conversation on the case, on the investigation into Frank's murder and on his hunch about Tony Santoro…maybe she'd listen. Although, he wouldn't blame her if she didn't even answer the door.

CLAUDIA HANDED LORI a glass of water and resumed her position next to her. The crime-scene technician was even more shaken than before, the thought of Claudia calling Tony obviously more than she could handle.

She seemed to calm somewhat, sipping from the glass that trembled in her grasp.

Claudia gave her time. And when Lori's wide-eyed gaze lifted to meet hers once again, there appeared to be a hint of reason struggling behind the fear.

"Can you guarantee my safety, Claudia?"

"There's no way I can do that personally. We'd have to go into headquarters and—"

"No! I won't go in. Not until you can promise I'll be safe if I turn State's evidence."

"State's evidence? Against Tony, you mean?"

Lori nodded.

"Turn State's evidence on what exactly?" Claudia already suspected the answer before she'd finished asking the question.

Lori returned her stare in silence. It was obvious she would say nothing more until Claudia made some assurances.

"It's not just protection from Tony you want, is it?" she asked, not at all surprised by the woman's nodded response. "Are you asking for immunity?"

"Yes."

"I'm not the one who makes those deals. You know that. All I can do is set up a meeting with the State's Attorney Office. I can voice my support, but that's the extent of my authority. Ultimately it's up to the attorney assigned to the case."

"Well, what are my chances then?"

"Until I know what this is about, I can't even hazard a guess."

Lori took another long drink from the glass, obviously considering her options.

"It's about the evidence tampering, isn't it?" Claudia prompted when Lori appeared to search for a place to begin. "It's Tony who's behind it, right?"

When Lori looked at her again, Claudia was certain she saw a flash of relief as she nodded.

"He's the one taking payoffs and making evidence disappear," Claudia continued. "And you've been helping him, haven't you?"

"I swear, I didn't know what was going on at first. Honestly. He'd asked me for evidence, and since he was with the squad I didn't think anything of it. Then there were a couple of times he asked me to let him into Evidence Control so he could check on a few things. We were swamped. I didn't have time to help him, so he offered to take care of it himself. It wasn't the first time we've let you guys into the back."

"This was before you were seeing each other?"

Lori nodded. "That didn't start until August of last year. And it wasn't until then that I started to put the pieces together. Internal Affairs had sent down a couple of queries, asking for more detailed information on the processing of specific pieces of evidence. That was when I found out some evidence had gone missing."

"And was it evidence Tony had looked at personally?"

"I wouldn't be able to prove it. The few times I

let him into the back, there was no telling for sure which cases he was looking at.''

''Did you question him about it?''

''Of course I did. And he denied it. Then we broke up. He couldn't stand the fact that I'd doubted him. I didn't see him for almost a month. Then he came to Evidence Control again. Like before, we were busy, so I let him in. Only that time I managed to see which case he was looking into. Sure enough, IAD questioned it a few weeks later.''

''But you didn't tell anyone, did you, Lori?'' Claudia tried to temper the accusation she heard simmering in her tone.

''I couldn't. Tony and I...we were seeing each other again. And this time he admitted what he'd done.''

''And you still didn't come forward?''

''No. It was just little stuff, you know? I mean, I know that sounds lame, but I was in love with Tony. I *had* to overlook it. And besides, he...he promised he'd stop if I kept quiet.'' She bit her lower lip and looked past Claudia to the far wall.

''What other promises did he make?''

''He promised he wouldn't involve me. And...he promised things wouldn't get out of hand.''

''But they did, didn't they, Lori? Things got way out of hand.''

There was a look of defeat in Lori's brown eyes now.

''Maybe you should tell me about James Silver,'' Claudia prompted delicately, needing to know yet realizing the risks of pushing the already distraught woman.

Lori shook her head. She closed her eyes, as if thinking she could block out the truth. But, of course, she couldn't.

"God, it was never supposed to go this far. He promised me, Claudia. He *promised.* No one was supposed to get killed."

"So you knew what Tony had done?"

"Not right away. It was only later that I started to suspect, after Tony mentioned something about Silver being Frank's former partner. But on the Silver scene, when I was processing the evidence, I honestly had *no* idea it was Tony who..." She was unsuccessful in her attempt to swallow her sob then. *"I had no idea, Claudia."*

She wouldn't get much further with Lori unless she calmed her, Claudia realized. But she didn't want to comfort her; she wanted to shake Lori by the shoulders and make her confess that Tony had killed Frank, as well.

She reached over to take Lori's hand in hers and managed to squeeze it reassuringly.

"When did you know for certain?" she prompted gently.

"Only the other day. I swear. It wasn't until you and Gavin came by my apartment. Tony was with me. We were..."

She didn't need to fill in the rest. Claudia remembered Lori standing in her doorway, tugging nervously at the edges of her bathrobe.

"Tony overheard our conversation and when you

left, he got dressed. He was angry. I thought he was going to hit me then, but he didn't. He just stormed out.''

The car, Claudia thought. Tony must have been worried they were getting close, so he'd followed them. There was no other explanation for the car that had followed them all the way to Fells Point that night, taking off only when Gavin attempted to pursue it.

''He came back a couple hours later,'' Lori said. ''He'd been drinking. And he had even more at my apartment. That's when he told me about Silver, when he admitted he'd killed him. He didn't go over to Silver's office that night to do it. I swear, Claudia, he never meant to kill him.''

But Claudia knew he had. There was no question, given the evidence. Whoever had come through Silver's office door that night had done so with his gun ready.

''Tony told me that James Silver was threatening to expose him. He said Silver had something on him and was going to take it higher up, so Tony went over to talk. That's all. But Silver pulled a gun on him.''

All lies. Claudia remembered Silver's gun, still in the top drawer of his desk.

''And what about Frank, Lori? What has Tony admitted to you about Frank?''

Claudia didn't even bother to soften the harshness in her voice this time. Anger won out. The color bled from Lori's face and fear came into her eyes. The tears started to flow at last, but Claudia didn't reach for her. She couldn't.

Claudia's hands balled into fists in her lap as she tried desperately to control her emotions. "What about Frank?"

"That's why Tony hit me," she sobbed. "This afternoon...I tried to...I tried to convince him to turn himself in, Claudia. Really, I did. I suggested that he speak with Sergeant Gunning, that he'd know how to handle it. After all, he'd shot Silver in self-defense. But Tony wouldn't listen to me. He just got crazy. Shouting and breaking things. I thought...I worried he might try to kill himself...or worse. And that's when he confessed. He told me he couldn't turn himself in because of Frank. Because he'd shot him, and then...then he'd staged the scene to look like a suicide."

Lori's sobs were wrenching now, close to hysterical. "I'm sorry, Claudia, I'm sorry..." she repeated in between breathless gasps. "I should have put the pieces together sooner. I should have come to you. But I was afraid. I was so afraid. Still, I should have...you were Frank's partner. I'm sorry..."

She buried her face in her hands, her entire body shaking as she rocked back and forth at the edge of the couch. "I don't know what to do. I don't know what Tony will do. He's so desperate. I know he thinks it's all over. I'm so afraid for him...so afraid he'll hurt himself."

"Listen to me, Lori. You can't worry about Tony. You have to look out for yourself. I have to take you in to headquarters. We need to get you talking to a state's attorney. But I need some help.'' She got up, about to reach for the phone when Lori stopped her.

''Who are you going to call?''

''Gavin.''

''Gavin? No, you can't.''

''Lori, I'm not going to take you in on my own. It's not safe for either of us. I need help.''

''But…Gavin is with Tony.''

In that split second, Claudia thought the world had dropped out from under her feet. ''What the hell are you talking about?'' she whispered.

''Tony went to see Gavin. That's the only reason I'm here right now, the only way I knew that Tony wouldn't follow me. He stormed out of my apartment, said something about meeting Gavin for a drink.''

''Where, Lori? *Where?*'' She stopped herself from shaking the other woman. But she may as well have. Lori's eyes were wide with fear.

''I don't remember. I—''

''You'd better remember, Lori. Where are they meeting?''

''I…I'm not sure, Claudia. I don't think… Maybe…I think maybe The White Horse up on Lexington. I think that's what Tony said.''

Claudia was already across the room, punching out the number of Gavin's cell phone. And with each number she prayed she wasn't too late.

GAVIN NEEDED NO INSTRUCTION. Through the open window, the cold, smooth muzzle of Santoro's Glock nestled against his temple. He dropped the cell phone into his lap and placed both hands on the steering wheel.

He didn't have to look to know it was Tony. He'd felt it as surely as he felt the adrenaline that kicked through him. *If only he'd felt it sooner,* Gavin thought. But he'd been too busy answering the call at the same moment as Tony had made his appearance.

The detective said nothing until he fished Gavin's cell phone from his lap and ended the call.

"Get out." His voice was a cruel whisper, but it was the unconcealed agitation in his tone that worried Gavin. "Slowly," he added, swinging open the door.

Gavin eased from behind the wheel, stepping onto the dark sidewalk. The cell phone warbled to life a second time, and Tony tossed it through the open window with the kind of disgust he might have afforded a dead rat.

It had to be Claudia calling again. Gavin was sure it had been her voice he'd heard so briefly before the gun had been pointed at his head.

"Give me your gun, Monaghan."

Gavin cautiously pushed back the edge of his jacket, allowing Tony to slide the 9mm from its holster. He watched him jam the gun into the deep pocket of his black leather jacket. There was a coldness on Santoro's face, a determination that bordered on ruthlessness, and Gavin knew he had to play this with great care.

He didn't challenge Tony when he nodded toward the mouth of an alley twenty feet down the street.

With his hands held palms out and his arms raised away from his body, Gavin started down the sidewalk. The staccato beat of Tony's shoes echoed along the empty street behind them.

"In here," he demanded once they reached the alley.

Stepping over broken trash bags and their spilled contents, and avoiding oil-slicked puddles, they moved farther into the alley. Gavin assessed the surroundings in a quick glance. There were no windows in the filth-blackened brick walls that lined either side. No possible witnesses. At the end of the alley, past the hulking outlines of rusted Dumpsters and rain-soaked cardboard boxes, were the lights of Borden Street. But their glow barely touched the darkness of the alley.

"This is good. Right here," Tony said. "Turn around."

Gavin did so, his hands still out at his sides as he watched Tony raise the police-issue Glock. When a clang of tin against concrete cut the silence, Tony flinched, and Gavin saw his hand tighten around the grip of the gun.

It had been a startled cat. Maybe a stray dog. Nothing more. But Tony was wound up tighter than Gavin had initially thought, though the other man tried his best to appear unflustered, in control.

"So what's the plan, Tony?" Gavin asked at last.

Again Tony's fingers flexed around the Glock, and a thin line of light shivered across the black metal.

"The plan is that you get shot, Monaghan."

"And you expect to pull this off how exactly?"

In the sallow light, Gavin watched Tony's smirk widen. He thought he recognized a glint of pride in the expression, as well. "It's all in the line of duty, of course. I figure I owe you that at least. See, it's just a case of two fellow detectives meeting for a friendly beer. We get out of our cars, start heading to the bar and hear a scuffle in the alley. Maybe someone shouting. Even off duty, we can hardly ignore a cry for help, can we?"

Gavin watched for any sign that Tony might let down his guard, but the other man's concentration remained steady.

"We move in to investigate. You head into the alley first, so I really can't see what's going on. A shot is fired, and I manage to get off a couple of rounds, but you're shot by some backstreet thug they'll never find."

"And the murder weapon?" Gavin asked.

He'd expected it, almost didn't need to ask.

With his free hand, Tony lifted the hem of his jacket to reveal the polished wood grip of a revolver tucked into the waist of his black jeans. "They'll find it in one of the Dumpsters. Clean of prints, of course."

"Where's it from, Tony? Did you force Lori to help you sneak it out of Evidence Control, as well?"

A flash of surprise rippled across his sharp features. If Gavin had blinked he would have missed it, because it was promptly replaced with a calculating resolve as Tony withdrew the revolver.

CLAUDIA PARKED SOMEWHERE east of Lexington after the short but frantic drive from her apartment. She had no idea what to expect, she only knew she had to reach Gavin before Tony did. Hearing the connection break when she'd reached Gavin on his cell phone had only heightened her fears.

From her car it was only a quarter block jog down to The White Horse, but dread made her breathless by the time she burst through the front door. Her entrance garnered curious stares as she tugged her jacket over her sidearm and took a quick scan of the dingy bar. There was no sign of Gavin or Tony.

She turned from the bar, the door swinging shut behind her. Pausing outside under a flickering flamingo-pink neon sign, she scanned the streets. And then she spotted the unmarked Lumina parked along Holly Street.

Gavin. It had to be, she thought, starting down the ill-lit street.

She'd find him sitting in the driver's seat, waiting. They'd take Lori to headquarters together, talk to Sarge and put out a warrant for Tony. And then it would be over.

In the shelter of the side street, the noises of the city were muffled. There was the sound of her low heels against the asphalt, and then the coursing of her blood as her heart hammered against her rib cage.

Gavin would be in the driver's seat. He *had* to be.

And if he wasn't? No, she couldn't think that. She'd never be able to forgive herself if she was too late. *She* was the one who had alerted Tony about Gavin. *She* was the person who'd told him Gavin was

IAD. If not for her, Gavin would not be in danger now.

The Lumina was empty.

A fresh wave of panic swept through her when she neared the unmarked police car. As she stopped at the driver's side, she could just make out the cell phone on the shadowed floor.

Instinctively she reached for her holster. Brushing aside her jacket, she unclipped the safety strap and looked up and down the dark street.

Nothing. Only a few parked cars lined the curb. A newspaper rustled across the pavement, skittering along the street until it wrapped itself around a signpost.

"Where are you, Gavin?" she whispered anxiously under her breath.

And then, as if her prayers had been answered, Claudia heard voices. She didn't breathe, listening, and then she heard it again. A male voice. Hope flared.

She worked her way silently to the mouth of an alley to her right. She couldn't make out the words, but the tone of the voice was clear—agitation, anger, hostility.

Pressing herself against the rough brick wall, she drew her Glock from its holster. Two deep breaths to steady herself, and she dared to snatch a glimpse around the corner. The alley was as dark as the street. The only light was from the next block at the end of the alleyway. It was barely enough illumination to silhouette the two figures. She allowed herself no more than a split-second look, but it was enough.

Gavin and Tony stood to one side of the garbage-cluttered alley, less than forty feet away. And Tony held a gun.

This was her fault. She'd trusted Tony with knowledge she should never have divulged. Gavin had asked to meet him for a beer, probably intending to question him, but if she'd kept her mouth shut, Tony would never have taken the offensive, and he certainly wouldn't be holding a gun on Gavin in the middle of a dark alley.

Claudia inched closer to the edge of the wall. She scanned the ground, mindful of anything that might alert Tony of her presence. Her grip tightened around her own gun, its muzzle aimed down, as she took another breath. She held it and slipped around the corner. A Dumpster provided her with cover.

"Tony, I really think you need to take a minute and consider things." Gavin sounded calm. "If you shoot me, you're only adding to your chances of getting caught. You know that. No murder is perfect. What is it they say? In every murder, there are at least a dozen mistakes made, and half of those you don't even realize. You've already made mistakes, Tony, otherwise I wouldn't be standing here with you now, would I?"

"You're only here because of a hunch, Monaghan. You don't have anything concrete. If you did, you would have brought backup. You'd have a warrant."

"Don't you think it would be in your favor if you turned yourself in, even before I draw up an arrest warrant?"

Claudia dared to peer around the corner of the

Dumpster, the steel cold against her cheek. Gavin's arms were at his side, held out slightly in a display of submission, while Tony's stance was firm—his feet planted and his gun raised. She could almost make out the sneer in the detective's face as she heard his caustic laugh.

"Oh, right. Turn myself in. You gotta think I'm pretty damned stupid. *Turn myself in*," he repeated, a hint of fear apparent just beneath his bravado. "As if they're really going to go easy on a cop."

"Why not? I can talk to IAD. Probably convince them to give you a deal."

"Man! You really do think I'm stupid, don't you? The only deal IAD's going to give me is a private cell so that I don't have to bunk with some toad I was responsible for locking up. That's about the best deal I can hope for, so don't you go giving me some bullshit about them cutting me a deal, okay?" Desperation punctuated each word.

Claudia shifted her gun to her left hand and wiped her right palm down her hip, drying the sweat against her jeans before taking the gun firmly in her grasp.

She couldn't waste another second. Time was precious.

With her heart pounding in her ears, Claudia stepped from her hiding place. Instinct propelled her. Her Glock came up, its sight trained on Tony even before he spun around.

He might have cursed, but it was lost in the scuffle. In an instant, Tony was at Gavin's side. He was smaller than Gavin, but that hardly mattered since he had the gun. In one hand he grasped the collar of

Gavin's jacket, while with the other he jammed the muzzle under Gavin's jaw.

But it was the crazed look she saw in Tony's eyes that caused the wave of dread to coil through Claudia. She hadn't expected this, despite what Lori had said.

Panic threatened to immobilize her. The thought of Gavin being hurt... She'd die before she let anything happen to Gavin. She needed him. She loved him. And she sure as hell wasn't going to lose him.

Her grip tightened on her weapon, and she lowered her finger to the trigger, caressing the checkered curve with her fingertip.

"Come on, Tony," she said, wishing she could adopt the same calm she'd heard in Gavin's voice only seconds ago. "Just take it easy here. Let's talk."

She attempted a few steps forward, but froze when she saw Gavin wince against the gun's muzzle that Tony drove even deeper into his throat.

"Damn it, Claudia. I really wish you hadn't gotten involved in all this."

"You killed my partner, Tony. *You* involved me."

He shook his head, letting out what sounded like a defeated grunt.

"It's over, Tony. You know it. Even if Gavin didn't have evidence against you, I do. Lori does."

He seemed to wither at the mention of Lori's name.

"She told me everything. She's going to be talking to the State's Attorney Office tonight and they'll issue a warrant. There's no getting out of this unless you turn yourself in. Now.''

She'd hoped for, but she certainly hadn't expected, his next move. Tony released Gavin, shoving him away and taking two steps back. In the same instant, he trained his gun on Claudia.

"Tony, no." Gavin started to move forward, but Tony held up his hand in warning. "We can work something out. There's still time—"

"No, there isn't," Tony told him, his eyes locked onto Claudia. "You just stay put, Monaghan. No deals."

Claudia's pulse surged. Every nerve and muscle in her body seemed alive, quivering with readiness to squeeze the gentle curve of the trigger.

And then, at long last, there were sirens. Distant. Piercing. Steadily coming closer.

"I had Lori call for backup," she explained quietly as relief spread through her. She'd almost given up hope, imagining Lori back at the apartment, too afraid to call headquarters.

All three of them listened to the sirens. It sounded like a thousand cars screaming across the city, but one or a dozen, it didn't matter if they didn't get here in time.

And then something flickered in Tony's expression, a look of final and complete resignation.

In a split, heart-stopping second, Tony raised his gun and turned it on himself. He held it unflinchingly against his temple, and time slowed, shuddering to a near standstill. She watched Tony, but in her mind's eye she saw Frank—dead on the floor of his apartment.

Somewhere to her left, she heard Gavin shout, but it sounded as muted and distant as the rest of the world that spun around her. She could see Tony's grip tighten on the gun and then watched his eyes close. In that instant, Claudia ceased to think. She only reacted.

She lowered her own Glock and squeezed the trigger. She felt the kick of the gun and saw the flare from its barrel as the shot echoed through the alley.

Past the wavering muzzle of her gun and through the brief plume of smoke that hung in the cold air, she watched Tony collapse to the ground. It was his cry that brought her world back up to speed.

Tony's gun slipped from his hand and skittered across the asphalt to rest in a puddle. Gavin scooped it up and was at Tony's side before she was.

Between a clenched jaw, Tony let out a nonstop string of expletives as he clutched his leg. Gavin snatched his hand away from the injury in order to inspect it. But he didn't offer Tony much sympathy. He took a second gun from the man and cuffed him, oblivious to his moans of pain.

The bullet appeared to have gone clean through his thigh, and blood flowed freely from the ragged hole. It wasn't arterial, but Claudia didn't take any chances. Kneeling on the filthy ground, she placed her hands over the wound, applying pressure as Tony continued to curse her. The feel of his blood, hot and thick, pulsing against her palm threatened to make her sick. She fought back the urge, knowing that it wasn't the blood itself, but the fact that *she* was responsible. In all her years on the force, she'd never been forced to fire her weapon before, never shot anyone.

Vaguely she was aware of the sirens coming closer. Then there was the shriek of tires, and the flash of the red and blue lights. Gavin must have run out to alert them. She heard his voice over others: "We need some medics here. We've got an officer down."

And finally, there was light. Several uniformed officers hurried down the alley, flashlights in hand. At last she could see Tony's pain-stricken face.

"Why, Tony?" she whispered, her voice almost lost amid the clamor around them, and she started to wonder if he'd even heard. But he had. His eyes met hers—vacant, hollow.

"You killed Frank." A coldness settled over her as she thought about her friendship with Tony over the years, and then the camaraderie and the closeness that had deepened over the past few months, countless personal conversations. All this time she'd been confiding in Frank's killer.

There was no holding back the shudder of contempt that moved through her.

It was Gavin who stopped her from saying or doing something she might have later regretted. Placing both hands on her shoulders, he pulled her to her feet, away from Tony, as one of the medics took her position.

Wordlessly Gavin handed her a small towel he must have retrieved from his car, and she worked it over her hands, wiping away the blood. He said nothing as he guided her back to the street. There, he turned her to face him. She watched the blue light of the radio cars flicker across his features, as he studied her for a long moment.

"Are you all right?" he asked softly.

All she could do was nod.

"You're shaking."

"I...I just shot someone."

"You saved my life, Claudia. And Tony's."

"I know. But...why? He killed Frank and then made it look like..." She wiped harder at the blood on her hands. "You know, when I was standing there...with my gun trained...for one second...maybe longer, I *wanted* him dead."

"You did right. Don't think about it. Don't beat yourself up."

But it wasn't that easy. She'd never be able to forget the sensation of squeezing that trigger, the sound of the shot, the kick of the gun. And she'd *never* forget the icy darkness that had come over her when she'd wished Tony dead.

Gavin held her then. "It's over," he murmured several times. "It's over."

He stroked her hair as she clung to him, and she fought back tears.

"You're going to be all right, Claudia. It's over."

EPILOGUE

THREE WEEKS AFTER HIS ARREST, Tony was indicted on two counts of first-degree murder, assault with a deadly weapon, conspiracy, and several other charges. Claudia had undergone the required session with a police psychologist, but had declined the woman's suggestion that she pay Tony a visit to better cope with the shooting. She hadn't seen him since the medics carried him out of the alley that unforgettable night.

And she hadn't seen Gavin, either.

They'd gone from the scene to headquarters in separate cars. Her gun had been taken from her for ballistics tests, while she gave her statement. It wasn't until hours later that Internal Affairs and her fellow Homicide detectives had finished with her. Gavin's work, however, was far from over.

He'd stayed on, although he'd taken the time to walk her to her car. One of the officers had parked it behind headquarters, and Claudia remembered the rush of crisp, cold air filling her lungs and the sounds of the city as it started to stir. They had washed over her numbness, granting her a brief moment of lucidity.

Gavin pulled her into his embrace once more after

she'd unlocked her car. She'd expected him to kiss her good-night, but he hadn't. Instead, he'd held her, as though needing to assure himself that she was all right. After some time, he placed a tender kiss on her forehead, and then suggested they not see each other for a while.

Claudia had started to protest, but Gavin wouldn't hear it.

He'd said she needed time. She'd argued that she needed him.

He'd said she had to recover. She'd argued there was nothing for her to recover from.

He'd pressed a finger to her lips, then brushed them ever so briefly with his own before leaving. She'd watched him walk down Baltimore Street, his long, slow strides taking him back to headquarters, and she couldn't help wondering if maybe it was Gavin who needed the time.

Well, if time was what he'd wanted, he'd certainly gotten it. Almost three weeks' worth of time, Claudia thought as she opened her desk drawer and put away several files. She leaned back in her chair and surveyed the near-empty offices. The shift change had already come and gone, as had the rest of her squad. She should have left with them. She'd been trying to lessen the amount of overtime she worked, spending more time at home or seeing Faith and the friends she thought she'd lost over the past year.

More time for herself, Claudia had vowed.

But it hadn't been easy. When she *was* by herself, her thoughts invariably turned to Gavin. She'd find herself questioning her sanity at thinking they could still have a future together, and yet, the thought of not seeing him again was almost unbearable.

How many times had she picked up the phone, ready to call him? How often had she gotten into her car, certain she would drive to his house? Too many to count.

Even now, as she reached for her briefcase, Claudia eyed the phone on the corner of her desk. From there her gaze traveled to the empty desk abutting hers.

Silently berating herself for the nostalgia, Claudia shoved a couple of files into her briefcase. She'd work at home tonight. Not because there was anything urgent in the files, but because she knew that only work would keep her mind from straying to thoughts of the impossible…thoughts of Gavin.

"Hey, stranger."

She didn't need to look to know it was him. His voice sent a familiar flutter through her that intensified the second she *did* look up.

He stood in the doorway, leaning one broad shoulder against the jamb as he buried his hands in the pockets of his leather jacket. He wore a white cotton shirt tucked into faded jeans—nothing particularly dashing, and yet Claudia couldn't imagine anyone looking better than he did just then.

His smile was slow, as if he was uncertain of his reception. It widened slightly, the faint cleft in his chin deepening as small lines bracketed his mouth when she smiled back.

"You heading out?" he asked.

She nodded, wondering how it was that the ability

to talk could have escaped her when she'd spent so many sleepless nights rehearsing the things she wanted to say to him.

He gestured to the elevators down the hall behind him. "Can I walk you down?"

"Sure." She took her gun from her bottom drawer and holstered it, before standing to put on her jacket. Shouldering her briefcase, she followed him to the elevators.

The ride down was brief but unnervingly silent. She wanted to ask why he hadn't called. She wanted to know where he'd been. More than that, she wanted to know what had brought him to her now.

"I'm parked on the street," she told him as they stepped through the elevator doors.

He only nodded, keeping pace with her brisk stride. The last orange tinges of sunset touched the otherwise gray sky, and there was a chill to the air that should have offered her some clarity.

It was only once she stopped at her car, unlocking it and turning to face him, that Gavin cleared his throat.

"You look good, Claudia."

She leaned back against the car, watching his gaze take an appreciative sweep, and managing to get in another one of her own. "So do you."

She wasn't surprised when he reached over to take her hand in his. What did surprise her was the raw desire that swept through her, and then the overwhelming urge to hold him, to feel his arms around her and to fall into the comforting familiarity of his embrace.

"I've missed you, Claudia." He squeezed her hand, caressing the back of it with his thumb. "I can't even begin to tell you how much."

"You could have called."

His gaze dropped for a moment, and when he looked back up, she recognized the regret in his eyes. "I know. I figured you needed time. But then...well, I realized that I had a couple things to sort out myself."

"What kinds of things?"

"Feelings mostly."

She didn't see him move, but suddenly Gavin had closed the narrow gap between them. She was aware of his leg against her thigh, his hip brushing against hers, and finally his hands settling on her waist.

"And did you come to any conclusions?" she asked.

"Yes. I did. I've come to the conclusion that I definitely cannot live without you, Detective Parrish."

She couldn't stop the smile that curved her lips, or the ache of longing that flared deep within her. But it was bittersweet.

"There are still issues, Gavin." She struggled with the words. "You agreed before that no matter what the outcome of your investigation, even once you proved me innocent, we couldn't have a relationship. There are going to be questions. Regarding your conduct, regarding your findings."

"That was before I knew we could ever be so lucky as to get a full confession."

"A confession? You mean Tony—"

Gavin nodded.

"But he pleaded 'not guilty' at the arraignment." She shook her head in disbelief. "When did he—"

"A couple of hours ago. Let's just say I had a chat with him. He came to his senses."

"But how?"

"After I outlined everything I had on him, including Lori's testimony, I offered him a deal. If he pleaded guilty to the murder one and conspiracy charges, *and* exonerated you of any involvement or knowledge regarding the evidence tampering, the State's Attorney Office would guarantee him his very own cell in a federal prison. He not only cleared your name, but he admitted to planting the .44 in your apartment."

Gavin lifted a hand to tuck a stray curl behind her ear.

"Claudia, no one has any doubts about your innocence. In fact, Lieutenant Randolph has recommended that you receive a commendation. There aren't going to be any questions regarding my conduct during the investigation.

"To add to that," Gavin continued, "the truth about Frank's death has been officially recognized. He was killed in the line of duty, and there's going to be a memorial service in two weeks. He'll be granted the full police honors he didn't receive before. I told you, Claudia, I'd get to the bottom of this case."

She took a moment to process everything Gavin was telling her, and when he finally kissed her, she didn't care who saw them. She wouldn't have traded that kiss for anything.

"So, what other things did you have to sort out?" she asked, coming up for breath even though the kiss had hardly begun to make up for the time they had lost. "You said you'd needed to sort out a couple of things."

"Well, for one, I had to clear out my desk over at IAD."

"You transferred?"

Gavin nodded. "The only reason I stayed as long as I did was to see this case through. I filed my request for transfer along with my final reports this morning."

"So what now? Chauffeuring the commissioner?"

His smile of amusement sent a warm tingle through her. She couldn't imagine ever tiring of seeing that smile.

"Not exactly," he said. "I thought I'd aim a little higher than that. In fact, I had a meeting with Gunning the other day."

"You're coming to Homicide?"

"What other choice do I have? I won't be on your squad, so we won't be working side by side, but if I didn't transfer to Homicide I might never get to see you, what with the shifts and the hours."

"Ah." This time it was Claudia's turn to smile. "So you do plan on seeing me then, Detective?"

"Very much so."

His response to her kiss was more passionate than anything Claudia could have imagined. And for a moment she forgot where they were. It was the sound of a passing car that caused them both to draw back, but their gaze never broke.

"I plan on seeing you every spare second I get...and then some," Gavin added. "And if the truth be told, I have even greater plans than that. I plan on spending the rest of my life with you. That is, if you'll have me."

Claudia was already moving to kiss him again. "Oh, I'll have you, all right," she murmured.

There was no damming their passion now. If another car passed, Claudia was unaware of it. For her, there was only Gavin and the love she felt in his embrace. And in their kiss, she saw their future—a future together, a future strong, loving and bright. A future everlasting.

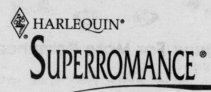

Welcome to cowboy country!

MONTANA LEGACY by **Roxanne Rustand**
(Superromance #895)

Minneapolis cop Kate Rawlins has her own reasons
for wanting to sell her inheritance—half of the
Lone Tree Ranch, Montana. Then she meets
co-owner Seth Hayward and suddenly splitting the property
doesn't seem like a good idea....

On sale February 2000

COWBOY COME HOME by **Eve Gaddy**
(Superromance #903)

After years on the saddle circuit, champion bronco
rider Jake Rollins returns home—determined to find
out whether his ex-lover's daughter is *his* child.

On sale March 2000

Available at your favorite retail outlet.

Visit us at www.romance.net   HSRRANCH

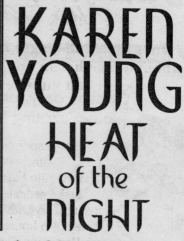

Come escape with Harlequin's new

Series Sampler

Four great full-length Harlequin novels bound together in one fabulous volume and at an unbelievable price.

Be transported back in time with a Harlequin Historical® novel, get caught up in a mystery with Intrigue®, be tempted by a hot, sizzling romance with Harlequin Temptation®, or just enjoy a down-home all-American read with American Romance®.

You won't be able to put this collection down!

On sale February 2000 at your favorite retail outlet.

HEART OF THE WEST

Every Man Has His Price!

Lost Springs Ranch was
famous for turning young
mavericks into good men.
So word that the ranch was
in financial trouble sent
a herd of loyal bachelors
stampeding back to
Wyoming to put themselves
on the auction block!

July 1999	*Husband for Hire* Susan Wiggs	January 2000	*The Rancher and the Rich Girl* Heather MacAllister
August	*Courting Callie* Lynn Erickson	February	*Shane's Last Stand* Ruth Jean Dale
September	*Bachelor Father* Vicki Lewis Thompson	March	*A Baby by Chance* Cathy Gillen Thacker
October	*His Bodyguard* Muriel Jensen	April	*The Perfect Solution* Day Leclaire
November	*It Takes a Cowboy* Gina Wilkins	May	*Rent-a-Dad* Judy Christenberry
December	*Hitched by Christmas* Jule McBride	June	*Best Man in Wyoming* Margot Dalton

HARLEQUIN®
Makes any time special ™

Visit us at www.romance.net

PHHOWGEN

3 Stories of Holiday Romance from three bestselling Harlequin® authors

Valentine Babies

by

ANNE STUART

TARA TAYLOR QUINN

JULE McBRIDE

Goddess in Waiting by Anne Stuart
Edward walks into Marika's funky maternity shop to pick up some things for his sister. He doesn't expect to assist in the delivery of a baby and fall for outrageous Marika.

Gabe's Special Delivery by Tara Taylor Quinn
On February 14, Gabe Stone finds a living, breathing valentine on his doorstep—his daughter. Her mother has given Gabe four hours to adjust to fatherhood, resolve custody and win back his ex-wife?

My Man Valentine by Jule McBride
Everyone knows Eloise Hunter and C. D. Valentine are in love. Except Eloise and C. D. Then, one of Eloise's baby-sitting clients leaves her with a baby to mind, and C. D. swings into protector mode.

VALENTINE BABIES

On sale January 2000 at your favorite retail outlet.

HARLEQUIN®
Makes any time special ™

Visit us at www.romance.net

PHVALB